"We can't keep ru other..."

Cal threaded his finge   at the
nape of Ashley's neck and tilted her face to his.
"We have to figure out a way to make this
marriage of ours work."

Fear mixed with her desire. "And what if it
doesn't?" The whispered words were out before
Ashley could stop them.

Cal's expression hardened. He took his hand away
from her hair. "We'll never know until we try."

True.

"All right." Ashley moved away from him. She
twisted the glossy length of her hair into an
austere knot and caught it in a butterfly clip.

"But if we do this and we do it on your timetable,
then we do it on my terms."

Cal lifted a brow. "Which are?"

"If I come back to North Carolina with you,
then we can't make love."

Cal tried his best to keep his jaw from dropping.

Dear Reader,

I'm one of the lucky ones. The love of my life is also my very best friend. Marrying him was the easiest decision I ever made. Learning how to *be* married was a little tougher. (i.e., Should the toothpaste cap be left on or off? Is taking out the garbage a gender-oriented chore or an equal-opportunity event? Just how much information is too much? Or too little?) And though in the early days of our marriage our life together sometimes resembled a Hepburn-Tracy comedy, we eventually achieved a very nice balance and a healthy respect for each other's wants and needs.

This is not, however, yet the case for Cal and Ashley Hart. College sweethearts, pursuing dual careers in medicine, they both expected everything to be just perfect when they finally tied the knot. It wasn't. And neither could figure out why.

The problem? A failure to communicate.

And now Cal and Ashley are on the precipice. Do they cut their losses and prevent further hurt? Or roll up their sleeves, renew their commitment and get to work on the challenging task of making their marriage work in a very fundamental and satisfying way?

I hope you enjoy this story as much as I enjoyed creating it. For more information on this and other books, visit my Web site at www.cathygillenthacker.com.

Best wishes,

Cathy Gillen Thacker

Cathy Gillen Thacker

HER
SECRET
VALENTINE

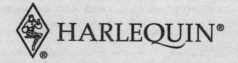
HARLEQUIN®

TORONTO • NEW YORK • LONDON
AMSTERDAM • PARIS • SYDNEY • HAMBURG
STOCKHOLM • ATHENS • TOKYO • MILAN • MADRID
PRAGUE • WARSAW • BUDAPEST • AUCKLAND

ISBN 0-373-75058-7

HER SECRET VALENTINE

Copyright © 2005 by Cathy Gillen Thacker.

This edition published by arrangement with Harlequin Books S.A.

® and TM are trademarks of the publisher. Trademarks indicated with ® are registered in the United States Patent and Trademark Office, the Canadian Trade Marks Office and in other countries.

www.eHarlequin.com

Printed in U.S.A.

This book is dedicated to Charlie, with all my love.

Chapter One

"How long is this situation between you and Ashley going to go on?" Mac Hart asked.

Cal tensed. He'd thought he had been invited over to his brother Mac's house to watch playoff football with the rest of the men in the family. Now, suddenly, it was looking more like an intervention. He leaned forward to help himself to some of the nachos on the coffee table in front of the sofa. "I don't know what you mean."

"Then let us spell it out for you," Cal's brother-in-law, Thad Lantz, said with his usual coach-like efficiency.

Joe continued, "She missed Janey's wedding to Thad in August, as well as Fletcher's marriage to Lily in October, and Dylan and Hannah's wedding in November."

Cal bristled. They all knew Ashley was busy completing her Ob/Gyn fellowship in Honolulu. "She wanted to be here, but since the flight from Honolulu to Raleigh is at minimum twelve hours, it's too far to go for a weekend trip. Not that she has many full weekends off in any case." Nor did he. Hence, their habit of rendezvousing in San Francisco, since it was a six- or seven-hour flight for each of them.

More skeptical looks. "She didn't make it back to Carolina for Thanksgiving or Christmas or New Year's this year, either," Dylan observed.

Cal shrugged and centered his attention on the TV, where a lot of pre-game nonsense was currently going on. "She had to work all three holidays." He wished the game would hurry up and start. The sooner it did, the sooner this conversation would be over.

"Had to or volunteered to?" Fletcher muttered with a questioning lift of his dark brow.

Uneasiness settled around Cal. He'd had many of the same questions himself. Still, Ashley was his wife, and he felt honor-bound to defend her. "I saw her in November in San Francisco. We celebrated all our holidays then." In one passion-filled weekend that had oddly enough left him feeling lonelier and more uncertain of their union than ever.

Concerned looks were exchanged all the way around. Cal knew the guys in the family all felt sorry for him, which just made the situation worse.

Dylan dipped a tortilla chip into the chili-cheese sauce. "So when is Ashley coming home?" he asked curiously.

That was just it—Cal didn't know. Ashley didn't want to talk about it. "Soon," he fibbed.

Thad paused, his expression thoughtful. "I thought her fellowship was up in December."

Cal sipped his beer, the mellow golden brew settling like acid in his gut. "She took her oral exam then and turned in her thesis."

Fletcher helped himself to a buffalo wing. "Her written exam was last July, wasn't it?"

Cal nodded. "But her last day at the hospital isn't until January 15," he cautioned. In a couple of days from now.

"And then she's coming back home, right?"

That had been the plan, when Ashley had left two and a half years ago to complete her medical education in Hawaii. Now he wasn't so sure that was the case. But not wanting to tell his brothers any of that, he simply said, "She's looking for a job now."

"Here, in North Carolina."

Cal certainly hoped so, since he was committed to his job at the Holly Springs Medical Center for another eighteen months, minimum.

"If she were my wife..." Mac began.

"Funny," Cal interrupted, the last of his legendary patience waning swiftly. "You don't have a wife."

"If it were me," Mac continued, ignoring Cal's glare as he added a piping-hot pizza to the spread, "I'd get on a plane to Honolulu, put her over my shoulder and carry her home if necessary." His take-charge attitude served him well as the sheriff of Holly Springs, but his romantic track record hardly made him an expert on dishing out relationship advice.

"That John Wayne stuff doesn't work with Ashley." Never had. Never would.

"Well, you better do something," Joe warned.

All eyes turned to him. Cal waited expectantly, knowing from the silence that fell there was more. Finally, Joe cleared his throat. "The women in the family are all upset. You've been married nearly three years now, and most of that time you and Ashley have been living apart."

"So?" Cal prodded.

"So, they're tired of seeing you so unhappy." Dylan took over where Cal left off. "They're giving you and Ashley till Valentine's Day—"

Cal and Ashley's wedding anniversary.

"—to make thing right."

"And if that doesn't happen?" Cal demanded.

Fletcher scowled. "Then the women in the family are stepping in."

"IF YOU KEEP this up, people are going to start calling you the Artful Dodger."

The low sexy voice with the hint of Southern drawl echoed through the Honolulu General staff lounge. Her heart leaping with a mixture of pleasure and surprise, Ashley turned to see her husband of almost three years standing in the doorway. Joy swept through her as she hungrily surveyed him.

Cal was wearing a loose-fitting tropical print silk shirt that made the most of his hard-muscled chest and broad shoulders. Pleated trousers nicely outlined his trim waistline and long sturdy legs. His short, traditionally cut ash-blond hair was brushed away from his face, and his smooth golden skin glowed with good health. The hint of a traveler's beard clung to his strong—and exceedingly stubborn—Hart jaw. Taken alone, his features weren't particularly outstanding. His nose bore the scars of a childhood athletic injury. His brows and thick, short eyelashes were so light in hue that you could hardly see them, and his upper lip was a little on the thin side. And yet, together, those penetrating pewter-gray eyes and not-so-perfect features combined to make a drop-everything, he-is-so-arresting man. Not to mention, she thought wistfully, how stealthily he moved—as if all that male power were just waiting to be unleashed. Or how intimately he looked at her, which suggested he couldn't wait to get her back into his arms and into his bed.

"Cal." Ashley stared at him in shock.

"Well that's something anyway." He grinned at her lazily. "At least you recall my name."

Beneath the teasing tone was a hint of hurt that was baffling, since Cal rarely revealed the inner workings of his heart and mind to her or anyone else. Ashley swallowed around the sudden lump in her throat, sensing that was about to change.

He had four inches on her, so at five foot ten, she still had to tilt her head back to clearly see into his face.

"What are you doing here?" she demanded, wondering if his sturdy masculine presence and six-foot-two frame would ever stop making her feel tiny. "I thought—"

Cal arched his blond brow. "That I was going to wait until you gave me the signal it was okay to come and get you?"

Aware he was now standing close enough for her to inhale the sea-and-sun fragrance of his cologne, Ashley shoved aside the familiar anxiety bubbling up inside her, ducked beneath a Congratulations, Ashley! banner and went back to pulling things out of her locker and dropping them in a cardboard box. "Who said anything about you coming to get me?" She had wanted to be prepared for this no doubt difficult tête-à-tête. She had wanted to know precisely what to say.

Cal stepped closer. "Exactly. There were no plans made. And yet," he observed, his voice dropping a seductive notch, "your last shift at the hospital was today."

Ashley drew a deep breath and turned to face him. "What's gotten into you?" Feeling the need for some protection from the emotions shimmering between them, she held her rain jacket in front of her like a shield.

Cal took it from her and dropped it into the box of belongings. "What do you mean?"

Her pulse pounding, Ashley whirled back to get a few books. "You're normally so…easygoing and patient when it comes to stuff like this," she said as she dropped them on top of her jacket. Today he seemed anything but that.

Cal's eyes gleamed with a predatory light. He flattened his hand on the locker next to her and leaned in close. "Which is perhaps the problem, Ash. Maybe I'm too good at waiting and not nearly as good at going after what I want."

Oh, my. "Which is—?" Ashley countered.

Cal took her in his arms and swept her close, until they were touching intimately. "For starters, this," he told her as his lips came down on hers.

Their first kiss after a long separation always radiated lots of feeling and passion. And this one, Ashley noted as Cal's lips and tongue laid claim to hers, was no exception. He tasted like the spearmint gum he carried in his pocket. And, as his arms wrapped tightly around her, she felt that she had finally come home. Not that this was any surprise.

Ashley had loved Cal practically from the first moment she had set eyes on him, during her freshman year of college at Wake Forest. Maybe it was because he was four years older than she was—already a first-year med student when they met—but he had always overwhelmed her with his confidence and sexy Southern charm. She felt safe when she was with him. Desired. Every inch a woman.

It was only when they were miles apart, out of each other's arms, that the doubts crept in about their love lasting forever. But when he was kissing her like this, his lips moving surely over hers, all she could think was how right he felt pressed up against her.

They could have gone on forever like that, wrapped in each other's arms, kissing madly, if it hadn't been for the sound of a door opening behind them. Followed by a discreet cough and laughter.

"No need to ask what you two are doing," the maternity-ward nurse said.

Cal lifted his head reluctantly. "Celebrating!" he said, looking more than ready to do it all over again.

Ashley relaxed in Cal's arms, laying her head on his chest, as the nurse beamed. She looked at Ashley. "You must have told him about the job offer in Maui! Isn't that fabulous?" The nurse turned back to Cal. "Do you know how many of us would give up our vacations to work there?"

Silence fell as the impact of her words sank in. Cal's expression turned troubled, as did Ashley's and then the nurse's. Ashley held up a hand before an apology could be made.

The nurse took another look at their expressions, then smiled again and quite wisely made for the door. "I'll, uh, see you two aren't disturbed," she stated delicately on her way out.

Cal just stood there, looking as if he felt as shut out of Ashley's life as she often did of his. Guilt flooded her. As usual, it seemed she was going to be damned if she did and damned if she didn't. If she declined this job, her parents and Dr. Connelly, her mentor here, and everyone else she worked with was going to be disappointed in her. And Cal wouldn't be pleased with her no matter *what* she did. He expected her to be as successful in her career as he was in his, yet he didn't want any work-related demands interfering with their time together. Given the fact she was an obstetrician and he a surgeon—both of them prone to be called out at any moment on patient emergencies—that was one tough bill to fill. Aware he was still waiting for an explanation, she said finally, "I was going to tell you."

Cal studied her, his gray eyes distant. "I take it this means you haven't turned the position down yet," he replied.

Ashley shrugged, wishing she were clad in something other than blue cotton scrubs and tennis shoes. Maybe if she were dressed like Cal—in sophisticated street clothes—she'd feel more confident. Feeling errant strands escaping down the back of her neck and brushing the sides of her face, Ashley released the butterfly clip that held her hair. She straightened the strands with her fingers, twisted them into a loop and put her hair back up. "I just found out about it last week."

"Your coworkers know about it."

Ashley knew he expected first dibs on news like that. And she would have told him, if she'd had any other job offers to go along with it. But she hadn't because she'd been so busy finishing up her fellowship that she hadn't even had time to really start looking for a permanent position. This one had just fallen into her lap. When she had talked to Cal, she had wanted to have more options to present. So he wouldn't be as disappointed in her as her parents were likely to be to find her lax in her search for employment after all those years of expensive education and training. Cal had had about six job offers waiting his decision when he finished his residency. But then he had devoted the entire first five months of their marriage to making sure that was the case. Whereas she had reserved her precious few days off to spend with Cal, instead of searching for a position.

"Some of the staff just happened to be here when I got the phone call from Maui about the offer," Ashley explained.

A mixture of anger and disappointment flashed briefly in his eyes. "Phones work on the mainland, too," he muttered.

His displeasure cut right through her worse than anyone else's ever had. "I thought it was something we should discuss in person," she said, her voice trembling with emotion.

He regarded her with mounting dismay. "You can't seriously be considering taking it."

"Actually," Ashley hesitated, "I don't know what I'm going to do yet."

Cal nodded and said nothing else.

Realizing he didn't want to have this conversation in a communal staff lounge any more than she did, Ashley continued getting ready to leave.

After Cal helped her gather up the rest of the things, she said her goodbyes to the staff, and they drove back to her apartment.

Located in a high rise that overlooked Waikiki beach, the furnished efficiency was as sparely decorated as it had been the day Ashley had moved in two-and-a-half years ago.

Cal had only been at her apartment a handful of times, and Ashley had been there mainly to shower and sleep. The majority of her time had been spent at the teaching hospital and various clinics served by it around the island.

There was a stack of collapsed moving boxes for her clothes and books shoved along one wall. A pile of mail on the coffee table. The large square room and bath normally felt cold and empty to Ashley. Tonight, with Cal here, it felt suffocating. Almost too small for comfort.

"Aren't you going to ask me anything else about the job I've been offered?" Ashley said, wishing Cal would open up to her more instead of always keeping everything inside. Except, of course, when it came to his desire for her. He was very open about expressing that. As was she, she admitted reluctantly to herself.

"Actually—" Cal set down his small duffel bag "—first, I'd like to go for a swim. We can get into all that over dinner?"

Ashley swallowed. If they were going to fight, she just wanted to do it already. "But—"

He cut her off with a derisive look. "If there's bad news coming, I think I'd rather wait until later to hear it, if you don't mind."

The decision made—as far as he was concerned anyway—Cal methodically emptied his pockets. No sooner had he unclipped the cell phone from his belt than it began to ring. He glanced at the caller ID and tossed the phone to Ashley. "See what Mac wants, would you?"

Cal grabbed his swim trunks from his overnight bag and disappeared into the bathroom. Ashley was left holding the still-buzzing phone. By the time she figured out how to use the unfamiliar keypad, the call went over to message. She waited for it to finish and then retrieved it, using Cal's password.

"Well?" Cal said. Emerging from the bathroom, he tossed his shirt and slacks onto the back of the sofa. "What did Mac want?"

Despite her quickly mounting irritation from the message she'd listened to, Ashley couldn't resist admiring his tanned, muscular physique. "Actually, the message was from all four of your brothers and your brother-in-law." Defiantly, she kept her gaze from wandering below the waist of his loose-fitting tropic-print swim trunks.

Cal tensed, but his expression did not change. Hence, Ashley couldn't tell if he had been expecting this "fun-filled call" from his brothers or not.

"Go on," Cal demanded.

With pleasure, Ashley thought, as she caught her husband's gaze and held on for all she was worth. "Mac reminded you that 'a woman appreciates strength in a man.'

"Fletcher said, 'There's nothing more seductive than making someone laugh.'" *Hah! As if Cal had ever needed help getting her into his arms and his bed!*

"Dylan said, 'When it comes to women, patience is a virtue that is highly overrated.'" Since when had Cal waited for anything he wanted from her? It was more his style to conquer first and ask questions later.

"Joe suggested you think 'offense' this time around." *Offense for what?* Ashley wondered. *Their marriage? That made it sound like a game!*

"And Thad suggested that 'you not forget to listen.'" Which was, Ashley considered, actually something Cal needed to do more of.

Her diatribe over, Ashley tossed the phone back to Cal. "So," she fumed. "Do you want to tell me what that is all about? Or should I just guess?"

Chapter Two

"They're just clowning around," Cal said lamely, as he opened the sliding-glass doors to her balcony and stepped through them.

"And that's it?" Ashley prodded warily, joining him on the lanai.

Here was his chance to tell her his whole family was worried about them. Ready to step in and help, if need be. But sensing she would not take this news well—Ashley had never really gotten how close the Harts were, or how much they depended on each other for moral and emotional support—Cal simply said, "The consensus is we've spent so much time apart in the three years since we said our 'I do's,' that we're still newlyweds."

"And in other ways," Ashley sighed, turning her glance to the blue ocean and shimmering white sand dotted with palm trees, "sometimes it seems like we're hardly married at all."

Precisely the problem, in Cal's estimation. "That will all change once we're living in the same house in the same city again," Cal told Ashley confidently. He studied her carefully as the warm tropical breeze fanned across them. "That is still the plan, isn't it?"

Ashley hesitated, much to Cal's dismay.

Resentment roiled in his gut. "You can't seriously be thinking about taking the position!"

To his increasing disappointment, Ashley made a palms-up gesture that reflected her uncertainty. "It's a dream job, Cal. Something I would feel lucky to be offered even ten years down the road. To get the opportunity now is a real coup. One that would make my parents proud. And you, too, I would think." Her voice trembled, despite her strong resolve. "After all, didn't I support you when you landed a position that would allow you to treat members of the Carolina Storm professional hockey team and a lot of the premiere college athletes in the area?"

Cal turned his glare to the beautiful blue horizon. "I never said you didn't support my dreams to be the best sports medicine specialist and orthopedic surgeon around."

"Good." Ashley waited until he turned back to her, then tossed her head. His breath caught at the image of her dark hair falling like silk around her shoulders. "Because I have, Cal."

"But what about us?" Cal demanded, hating the need radiating in his low voice. He tried so hard not to be selfish.

Hope shone in her china-blue eyes. "You could move here in eighteen months, when your contract with the medical center in Holly Springs is up. There are plenty of athletes in Hawaii, and on the West Coast, who would be lucky to have a physician of your expertise."

Cal knew she was avoiding the point. "Your coming to Hawaii was supposed to be a temporary measure," he reminded her coolly. A move made more out of necessity than choice.

Abruptly, Ashley stilled. She looked wary—as if she were afraid to commit herself too fully to him and their marriage again. As if she wanted them to continue the long-distance charade of a marriage. "Things change, Cal," she told him softly.

And not always for the better, Cal thought.

He had never understood why Ashley had withdrawn emotionally from him in the first six months of their marriage. True, it had been a hellishly bad spring and summer. The fellowship program Ashley had been enrolled in had abruptly lost its director and its funding. She'd had to scramble to find a place that could take her as a second-year fellowship student, while he was studying for the medical boards that he had to pass in order to practice orthopedic and sports medicine. A physician in training herself, Ashley should have understood the kind of pressure he was under. She'd certainly said she did. But that whole summer, she'd been on an emotional roller coaster—crying one minute, too quiet the next. First overeating to the point she had gained weight, then barely eating at all.

He'd known she was in a crisis brought on by the potential interruption of her education. But overwhelmed by his own mountain of studying, he realized in retrospect that he hadn't been there for her or helped her as much as he should have. By the time he had completed his testing, she had already secured another fellowship and left for Hawaii.

Cal had tried to make up for his earlier lack of understanding and support by being as enthusiastic as possible about the stellar opportunity Ashley had secured for herself. But, by then, the damage had already been done. At least emotionally. They had continued to make love, as if nothing were wrong. In fact, a lot of their interludes were even more physically passionate than ever before. But when it came time for them to bare their souls... Well, that just didn't happen. It had been as if a wall were between them—and it had gotten wider with every month that passed. A wall that was impenetrable even now.

"There was no way I could have anticipated being offered

the position of Director of the Maui Birthing Center." Ashley sat down in one of the striped vinyl chairs on the lanai and propped her feet up on the rail.

Cal dropped down into the chair next to hers. "How long do you have to decide?" he asked, wishing he could be more charitable. But he couldn't. His patience with this long-distance marriage of theirs was at an end.

"A month."

Ashley fanned her hand in front of her face, as if that would dispel the heat of the late-afternoon sun that pinkened her cheeks and added perspiration to her forehead. "Of course they'd like my answer sooner."

Cal watched her pull the fabric of her cotton top away from her breasts. "Of course." *Why couldn't you just say no?* Cal wondered. *Why are you even considering this?* Unless his gut fear was right, and she really did not want to be married to him after all.

"Look, I know how little time off you have," Ashley said sympathetically.

Figuring he wasn't going to like this either, Cal tensed. "So?"

Ashley swallowed and brought her feet down off the pastel green metal railing and stood. "We need to be practical here. There's no reason for you to stay while I'm job-hunting and getting ready to move out of this apartment."

Cal bet she wanted him out of the way. But his time for being the understanding husband, with no demands of his own, was over. He grimaced, knowing he hadn't needed his brother's advice to react in a take-no-excuses manner now. He'd had it up to here with the separations and it was time his wife knew it! "I'm not leaving, Ashley."

She blinked. "Excuse me?"

He stood and faced her, legs planted apart, hands braced

on his waist. "I'm not going back home without you. Not this time. Nor do I plan to let you make a decision about your professional future without considering the impact that decision will have on our marriage."

"What has gotten into you?" Ashley demanded.

Two and a half years ago, Cal had pushed her to be all she could be. Insisting—just as her parents had—that Ashley take the fellowship slot in Honolulu, rather than face a one-year interruption in her medical education. It hadn't seemed to matter to any of them that she hadn't really wanted to go all the way to Hawaii or be apart from her husband of just five months. The opportunity in Hawaii was worth the sacrifice, or so everyone had told her.

She'd let herself be convinced of that, because she had truly needed time apart from Cal to deal with her own mistakes. Mistakes that Cal and her parents still knew nothing about. And she hoped guiltily, they never would.

Oblivious to her own inner angst, Cal impatiently answered her question. "Let's just say I've finally come to my senses. Living apart for two-and-a-half years is much too long. I'm your husband. You're my wife. Enough of the long-distance marriage, Ash. We need to be together."

If only he had said this to her back then, Ashley thought sadly. She wasn't sure she could trust his sudden devotion to her now. She didn't want to start counting on something that would, in the end, only be snatched away from her by circumstances yet again. Right now they had a commuter marriage that was working, despite the occasional glitch. At least to the point that he still wanted her when they were together. That wouldn't necessarily be the case if they were together day in and day out and she ended up letting him down.

Ashley was afraid that if she returned to Holly Springs, it could be the end of her marriage. After all, what if the members of the Hart clan passed judgment on their less-than-per-fect union and it pushed Cal even further away? Right now, she would rather have "half a marriage" than none at all.

"And if I go to Maui tomorrow?" She posed the question to him casually, as if her entire well-being weren't riding on his reply.

Cal gestured, as if the answer to that were a no-brainer. "Then I guess I'll go to Maui with you."

Now he *definitely* was not making sense. Nor was she sure she quite believed him. "What about your family and your pa-tients back in North Carolina?" Ashley asked bluntly.

For the first time, there was a hint of conflict on Cal's face, reminding Ashley how tied he was to his hometown.

Cal shrugged, still refusing to back down. He walked through the sliding-glass doors and into the apartment. "I guess they'll all have to get along without me," he drawled.

Right on cue, her deeply ingrained sense of responsibility reared its ugly head. She couldn't be responsible for Cal shirking his duty, and he knew that. Ashley followed him, then folded her arms in front of her and glared at him. For once she wished she weren't so inherently responsible. "This isn't funny, Cal." She pushed the words through her teeth.

Still clad in nothing but swim trunks, he sank down on the mattress and made himself comfortable on the pillows of her bed, folding his arms behind his head, as if he slept there with her every night. He narrowed his eyes at her and replied, "It isn't supposed to be."

Ashley glided closer, being careful to stay out of easy reach. "You can't just stop working in Holly Springs on a whim!" She planted both her hands on her hips.

Cal's inherently sexy smile widened. "Want to bet?" he tossed right back.

Heat flooded Ashley's face as her glance moved over his

sinewy chest, broad shoulders and long, muscled limbs. With difficulty, she forced her attention back to the matter at hand. "You'll get fired from the medical center or sued for breach of contract by the state if you pull a stunt like that," she warned. He wasn't serious. He couldn't be. And yet...he looked as if he was fully ready to do just that!

"Change into your swimsuit and we'll go for a swim, Ash."

She stared at him. Their discussion had apparently come to an end as far as he was concerned.

He patted the mattress. "Okay, if you don't want to take a swim, then come to bed with me."

Ignoring the sexy command, she looked right back at him. "In your dreams," she retorted.

NOW IT WAS Cal's turn to be stunned. No matter how rocky their relationship got at times, Ashley had never refused to make love. "All right." He got up lazily, closing the distance between them. He was determined to feel close to her in whatever way he could. "I'll come to you, then."

"This isn't going to work, Cal," Ashley murmured as he took her into his arms and kissed her neck. Ashley splayed her hands across his chest and pushed him away. "Every time we find ourselves alone we end up doing this!"

Cal drank in the intoxicating fragrance of her hair and skin, then drew back to savor the sight of her. With her heart-shaped face, long-lashed china-blue eyes, high sculpted cheekbones and slender nose, she was just as beautiful now as she had been the day they had met, nearly ten years ago. Her thick, glossy dark-brown hair was still shoulder-length, although she now wore it in a sexy, layered style, and her skin had retained its radiant golden glow. The only change, it seemed, was her weight. There was a new voluptuousness to her breasts, a slight thickening of her waist and hips, that hadn't been there the last time he had been with her. He was glad to see she had put a little weight on her tall, willowy body. Last fall and summer she had been almost too thin.

"We *are* married," Cal reminded her, stepping back enough to take in her long curvaceous legs.

Ashley reached for a brush on her bureau and ran it through her hair. "We make love so much when we do see each other it feels like we're having an affair!" She rummaged through her bureau and brought out a turquoise tankini.

Cal leaned against the wall and folded his arms against his chest. "I can think of worse things than trysting with my wife."

Ashley disappeared into the bathroom with her swimsuit. "Making love right now won't solve anything," she called through the door.

"Neither will you not coming home where you belong." Cal waited until she emerged in the demure swimsuit. The sight of her breasts pushing against the confines of the top confirmed his observation that she had gained weight.

With effort, he turned his glance away from the swelling curves. He paused as their glances met in a firestorm of emotion once again. "You want to work things out with me, don't you?"

"Of course I do," she said hotly. She didn't know why her husband even had to ask that! The problem was she was scared that if they tried Cal would discover what she already knew in her heart—that this marriage of theirs was a sham.

"Then," Cal continued, moving away from the wall. He sauntered toward her, all insouciant charm. "I expect you to do the practical thing and take the next month to figure out what you want and where you want to live. And do it while spending time with me."

As he neared her, Ashley felt as if she was being backed

into a corner and she hated that as much as she hated being instructed what to do or feel or think. "How do you know I haven't already made up my mind?" she challenged.

The corners of his lips turned up smugly. "Have you?"

"Well, no, I haven't had time."

A mixture of affection and promise gleamed in his gray eyes as he took her in his arms once again. "Come home with me and you'll have all the time in the world."

Ashley didn't like feeling trapped. When Cal behaved this way, he reminded her of her youth, of growing up with parents who had everything all plotted out for her, there had been no time for discussion or dissension. All the decisions regarding Ashley's life had already been made for her. Telling her parents that what they wanted was not necessarily what *she* wanted had been futile. They had argued and pushed and prodded until it had been easier just to give in and go along. Her cooperation had made them happy. But it had made her miserable.

Cal didn't seem to realize it, but his relentless expectations had often left her feeling just as hemmed in. The only difference was Cal had not pushed to rule every situation they encountered in their marriage. He had allowed her to do what she wanted, when she wanted. But that freedom had not come without a price. She had seen the disappointment in his eyes when she failed to live up to his dreams of what his wife and lover—and the potential mother of his children—should be. She had felt his hurt, and known she was responsible. And that had been worse to her in many ways than the distress she had caused her parents when she had thwarted their expectations of her.

So Ashley had done the only thing she could to preserve her marriage—she'd put enough distance between them to prevent such clashes on a daily basis. Her hope had been that "absence" would make their hearts grow fonder…and strengthen their relationship.

Only it hadn't worked out that way; they'd become even more emotionally distant than before.

Cal pulled her closer. "We can't keep running from each other," Cal said quietly as the warmth of his tall strong body penetrated hers. He threaded his fingers through the hair at the nape of her neck and tilted her face up to his. "We have to figure out a way to make this marriage of ours work on an everyday basis."

Fear mixed with desire. "And what if it doesn't?" The whispered words were out before Ashley could stop them.

Cal's expression hardened. He took his hand away from her hair, let it fall back to her waist. "We'll never know until we try."

She couldn't deny the truth of his words.

"It's time we stepped up and confronted the problems that have been dogging us since the moment we said our vows."

"All right." Ashley moved away from Cal. "But we do it on my terms."

He lifted a brow. "Which are?"

"No sex." Ashley bartered the condition she had been thinking about for quite a while.

He blinked in surprise. "Excuse me?"

Ashley held up a cautioning palm. "I mean it, Cal. Sex between the two of us is great, but it never fails to derail us when we are trying to work out a problem. We end up making love and not talking about whatever it is that needs to be dealt with in the first place. So, if I come back with you to North Carolina while I job hunt, then we can't make love."

As Ashley had expected, her husband had to think about that. Hard. Which confirmed all of Ashley's worst fears—that without the sex they really had nothing to hold them together.

Nothing that would keep their marriage going for the next fifty years.

A wealth of emotions flickered in Cal's eyes. Finally, to Ashley's relief, he assented. "But I have a few conditions of my own," Cal said firmly as Ashley found her beach sandals and sat down on the sofa to slip them on.

"One, you live with me under the same roof the entire time you are in Holly Springs. And two, you stay until our third wedding anniversary on Valentine's Day and celebrate the occasion with me. You can have your own bedroom—either the master suite or the guest room," he offered expansively. "Your choice."

Ashley stared up at him, her hands braced on either side of her. "That's a whole month, Cal."

Nodding, he held out his palm and helped her to her feet. "Which ought to be long enough to figure out where we go from here."

Chapter Three

"You've really done a lot to the place," Ashley remarked late the following morning. Despite her wool coat, she shivered a little from the brisk winter air. They had taken the red-eye back to Carolina. And now, some twelve hours later, they were back at the farmhouse he had purchased during the first year she had been in Honolulu. "It was in pretty rough shape the last time I saw it."

"That's right," Cal recalled. "You've only seen the place once." He set their suitcases down in the front hall and went to adjust the downstairs thermostat that had been lowered in his absence.

Ashley felt the chill seep from her bones. "You've obviously worked hard on it. I'm impressed."

The two-story farmhouse had been painted a sunny yellow on the outside. The pine-green shutters and door coordinated nicely with the new slate-gray roof. Inside, the hardwood floors had all been redone. The walls were painted a creamy sand that went well with the white crown moldings and trim. She couldn't help noticing, however, that the parlor and formal dining room at the very front of the house were empty and the walls bare.

"I thought you might like to help me decorate these

rooms," Cal told her casually. "So I haven't done anything with them." Looking happy to have her there again at long last, he took her hand and led her back toward the rear of the house.

He continued to show her around proudly. The country kitchen had all new glass-front maple cabinets and marble counters and was painted a soothing shade of taupe that blended well with both. The color continued into the laundry room at the rear of the house, as well as into the tastefully decorated family room that overlooked the fruit orchards edging the backyard. A big stone fireplace was the focal point of the room. The mantel was lined with photos of Ashley and Cal. Formal engagement and wedding day portraits, as well as casual snapshots of them with family and friends from happier times. Before things got so complicated, Ashley thought wistfully.

Cal moved to the entertainment cabinet and showed her where the remotes for the wide-screen TV, stereo and DVD player were kept. "There's no cable out here—so we've got satellite. I'll show you how to use it whenever you want."

"Later would be fine," Ashley said, wondering at the formality that had risen up between them now that they were physically together again. When had things become so awkward between them they didn't even know how to be in the same house together? she fretted miserably. A house they co-owned as husband and wife.

"Want to see the upstairs?" Cal asked, continuing to play the perfect host.

"Sure." Ashley nodded agreeably. "And then I'm really going to have to crash." She was so fatigued from the flight back, she was nearly light-headed. She turned and looked at the dark circles beneath his eyes that hadn't been there sixteen hours previously. "You must be beat, too." He had flown to Hawaii, and then hours later, turned right around and flown back to North Carolina.

"I am," Cal admitted, stifling a yawn. Logging nearly twenty-four hours travel time in a thirty-two-hour period was finally catching up with him.

He led her past the hall bathroom, which looked as if it had been outfitted for guests and was rarely used, and two empty bedrooms. A guest room was next. It had the cozy brass bed they had used the first five months of their marriage and an antique bureau with a mirror that conjured up a lot of memories for Ashley that she wasn't sure she was ready to remember yet.

Next was the master bedroom. A brand new king-size sleigh bed with matching cherry nightstands and antique brass lamps took up most of the space. Two separate walk-in closets had been built. And where the fifth bedroom and bath had been was a brand-new master bathroom.

Ashley gaped at the changes. There were dual pedestal sinks, a sit-down vanity, a separate water closet for the commode, and a whirlpool tub beneath a bay window of privacy glass. But it was the shower that commanded her attention. Pale-green marble covered the floor, walls and ceiling of the six-by-eight-foot space. A high window at one end let in plenty of sunlight, and a long green marble bench was situated beneath it. There were two showerheads—a handheld and an overhead—and the glass shower door stretched all the way to the ceiling.

"This doubles as a sauna," Cal boasted, showing her where the controls for that were.

"Wow," Ashley said. She had never seen anything quite so luxurious.

Cal's gaze drifted over her appreciatively. "The sauna can feel pretty good after a long day or night at the hospital."

As would their lovemaking, the implication seemed to be. Ashley swallowed, pushing away the flutter of desire deep inside her. She had promised herself she would not let passionate sex distract them from the work they needed to do on their relationship. She would keep that vow.

Cal frowned, apparently registering the sudden drop in temperature between them. "Anyway, I know I promised you separate accommodations," he said gallantly ushering her back out into the hall.

And it was good they'd made that agreement, Ashley thought. Otherwise she would have been tempted just to say the heck with caution and fall into bed with her husband once again.

He gave her a hot, assessing look. "So unless you've changed your mind…"

"I haven't," Ashley said, pretending her thoughts weren't traveling down the same ardent path as his.

To Cal's credit, if he was disappointed by her careful outward demeanor, he did not show it. He paused to turn the upstairs thermostat higher. "I'll take the guest room then," he said mildly.

"You don't have to do that," Ashley said, knowing that she'd be more comfortable in the bed she had used before than in anything that had been exclusively his.

He looked at her a long moment, the faint hint of disappointment radiating in his pewter-gray eyes. "I'll carry your suitcase up then," he said quietly. And that was that.

THE PHONE RANG AT 6:00 P.M. Cal reached for it with a groan, and dutifully talked to his mother on the other end of the line. By the time he hung up two minutes later, he found Ashley standing in the doorway of the master bedroom. Tousled and adorable, she looked as disoriented as he felt after only a couple of hours sleep.

"Everything okay?" she murmured.

Damn, she looked sexy in a thigh-length cotton nightshirt and bare legs, Cal thought as he struggled to shake off his jet lag and sit all the way up against the headboard. Since she had obviously gone right from the shower into bed, her dark hair had dried in thick unruly waves.

"Who was that?" Ashley stifled a yawn with the back of her hand as she padded closer.

Knowing they would both adjust to the change in time zone if they stayed up the rest of the evening and went to bed at the normal time, Cal rubbed the sleep from his eyes. "My mother wants us to come for dinner. I told her I wasn't sure you'd feel up to it. She said, if not, she'd send something over."

"Is the whole family going to be there?" Ashley asked, with the hesitation she always evidenced when confronted with all five of his siblings. And now, thanks to a recent round of satisfying romances, four of them had spouses, too.

Cal shrugged. He didn't want to make things any more awkward than they already were between him and Ashley. "We can always see everyone later," he told her.

Looking as sleepy and out of it as he felt, Ashley perched on the end of the bed and tucked one hand around the sleigh-shaped footboard. "I know everyone wants to see me."

An understatement if there ever was one, Cal thought. Particularly since his whole family had decided to help "fix" his marriage, unless he managed to do it first.

"So we might as well go this evening," Ashley continued practically. "If you feel up to it."

Cal figured it had to be better than staying here alone with Ashley, wanting to make love to her when he had promised to abstain. At least for the time being. He was still hoping she would change her mind about that and realize making love to each other always brought them closer. And now, more than ever, with so many important things ahead of them to decide, they needed to be closer. "We can make it a quick visit," he said. He didn't want to stay long lest his brothers decided to get into the advice-giving business again.

Ashley nodded her assent. "Just give me a few minutes to get dressed."

Forty minutes later, Cal was still waiting for Ashley. When she finally came downstairs she was wearing a jewel-necked, long-sleeved black knit dress that she usually reserved for cocktail parties.

"I thought you were wearing slacks," he said with a frown, wondering if he should go upstairs and change out of his jeans and corduroy shirt into something more formal, too.

"I was. Or I tried."

He looked at her, not understanding.

"I guess I've gained a little weight over the holidays," she said, her cheeks flushing bright pink. "I didn't think I'd had that many Christmas cookies, but...suddenly none of the pants I brought with me want to zip. So it's either this or another dress or the sweats I wore on the plane—and those need a run through the washer first." Cheeks flushing all the more, she swept past him. "I'm sorry I kept you waiting."

"I'm not. You look great." The black knit fabric clung to her newly voluptuous curves, and the swirling skirt and high heels made the most of her sexy legs. She'd left her hair down, and it looked as wild and untamed as he knew her to be in her most unguarded moments.

Cal paused to remove her winter coat from the hall closet. "Would it make you feel less self-conscious if I went up and changed?" He knew everyone in his family would probably be wearing jeans, too, but he could put on a sport coat and tie.

"No. It's fine, really." Ashley waved off his concern. She slipped on the long black wool coat and looped a cashmere scarf around her neck. "I'm just going to have to get back to exercising on a regular basis again."

Cal held the door for Ashley. "Well don't lose any weight on my account," he said. He let his eyes travel over her appreciatively. "I think you look amazing. I mean it, Ashley," he continued when she scoffed. "Any extra ounces you have put on are definitely in all the right places."

"And those would be…?" Ashley prodded dryly as he unlocked the passenger door on his SUV and helped her inside.

In answer, Cal grinned and let his gaze touch her breasts, waist and hips.

She blushed again.

"You're perfect," Cal repeated. Wishing—just once—she would believe it. "And I like the glow on your face, too," he added softly. He touched her cheek with the back of his hand.

Ashley wrinkled her nose, and shook her head. "I'm going to pretend I agree with you…just so we don't have to talk about my embarrassing predicament anymore. It's probably what I get for living in scrubs and lab coats, anyway. All those loose-fitting tops and elastic waistbands…I'll be more careful in the future. Just do me a favor and don't mention my wardrobe crisis to your sibs? I'm embarrassed enough already."

"DON'T YOU LOOK WONDERFUL!" Helen Hart told Ashley when she and Cal walked in to her home behind the Wedding Inn, the palatial three-story white brick inn Cal's mother had turned into the premiere wedding facility in North Carolina. As always, Ashley noted admiringly, Helen's short red hair was perfectly coiffed, her amber eyes as warm as they were astute. Ashley's mother-in-law favored clothes that were classic, not trendy. Tonight she was clad in a cream wool turtleneck sweater and gray slacks perfect for an evening with family.

"You think we look good now, wait until we get some more sleep!" Cal winked at his mom as he helped Ashley off with her coat and went to hang it up.

Ashley returned Helen's hug warmly. Although her husband's siblings could sometimes leave her feeling overwhelmed, she adored Cal's mom. Maybe because the openly loving, family-oriented woman was everything her own mother wasn't. Helen Hart loved and accepted her kids, no matter what. She did not demand they succeed at all cost. She simply wanted them to be good, kind, loving people. Which wasn't to say Helen was a pushover. If the fifty-six-year-old Helen saw one of her brood making a mistake that could hurt someone else, she was always quick to intervene and make sure that the situation was corrected. But she also gave them plenty of room to live their own lives. And as a result of that, her six adult children were a very tight-knit group. The death of Cal's father twenty years ago had made them even more so. They understood the value of family. And they loved each other dearly. So dearly that even after ten years of being Cal's one and only, Ashley sometimes still felt like an outsider looking in.

Oblivious to Ashley's anxiety over the evening ahead, Helen linked arms with Ashley and led her toward the Great Room at the rear of the house, where everyone gathered. "If we'd had more notice, I would've invited your parents to be with us this evening, too," Helen noted cheerfully. "They must be very anxious to see you, too!"

Were they? Ashley wondered.

"When are you and Cal going to visit them?" Helen paused in the kitchen to check the big pot of spaghetti sauce simmering on the stove.

"I'm not sure," Ashley hedged, watching Helen put water on to boil.

"But they do know you're back in Carolina?" Helen ascertained, concern lighting her eyes.

Ashley nodded. "I e-mailed them my plans before I left Honolulu." And hadn't yet checked to see if there had been a response, largely because she hadn't felt ready to face the constant pressure to achieve that her parents were likely to exert on her when they did see her.

Aware this was a touchy subject with Ashley, Cal motioned them all to the family room, where the rest of Hart clan was gathered around the television, watching two NHL teams do battle on the ice in Montreal. Had the Carolina Storm professional hockey team been playing that evening, three of the men in the family would have been absent. Janey's husband, Thad, because he was the coach. Dylan, because he was a game announcer, and Joe, because he was one of the hockey players. But since the team had the day off, and the next game was at home, they were all there. As was Janey's twelve-year-old son Christopher—who was petting Lily and Fletcher's recently adopted yellow Labrador retriever, Spartacus. Mac and the newest members of the Hart clan—Joe's wife, Emma, Dylan's wife, Hannah, and Fletcher's wife, Lily—were gathered around, too.

A happier bunch couldn't have been found, Ashley noted, accepting hugs and warm hellos from one and all. And it was then the trouble she'd been anticipating began.

"SOMETHING WRONG?" Janey asked two hours later as the two of them carried the containers holding leftovers out to the spare refrigerator in Helen's garage.

Besides the fact that everyone there seemed to be keeping a careful eye on everything she and Cal did and said? Ashley wondered.

Ashley figured if anyone understood the five Hart brothers it was their only sister, Janey. "What do you know about the advice the guys have been giving Cal about me?" Ashley asked, opening the fridge. She was willing to bet whatever had prompted the phone message Cal had received in Hawaii was still going on among the men. Sly looks, approving nods, the occasional slap on the shoulder, one brother to another, had been going on all night.

Abruptly, Janey looked like a kid who'd been caught with knowledge she had no business having.

Ashley held up a palm. "I heard it all, Janey. I just want to know what prompted the onslaught of friendly guidance in the first place." Cal was the most private of the Hart brothers. Definitely the least likely to seek advice regarding his marriage.

Janey slid her containers into the spare fridge, then knelt to make room for Ashley's. "They were just worried about you two." Janey kept her head down. "We all were." Even more quietly she said, "Cal's been so lonely while you were away."

This was news. Ashley's heartbeat picked up and anxiety ran through her anew. "Was he complaining to the rest of you?" If so, she wasn't sure how that made her feel! Not good, certainly.

"No, of course not." Finished, Janey straightened. "Cal never complains. You know that." Janey paused to look at Ashley seriously. "But even though he shrugged it off, we all knew he was pretty miserable whenever he wasn't busy working."

Then why hadn't Cal said something? Ashley wondered, hurt and dismayed, instead of acting as if the weeks and months apart were just something to be endured.

"HEY, YOU'RE NOT still upset about the clothes-not-fitting thing, are you?" Cal asked as they turned into the driveway of the farmhouse. He stopped in front of the two-car garage and hit the automatic door button.

"That's the least of my worries," Ashley muttered as she watched the door lift.

Cal steered his SUV into the garage. He frowned as he cut the motor and depressed the remote control. "Did someone say something to you tonight?"

Ashley got out of the Jeep, aware the jet lag she had felt earlier had vanished in the face of her anger and disappointment. She watched his face as she waited for him to join her at the door to the softly lit interior of the house, wishing he weren't so darned handsome and appealing. It would make it so much easier to stay angry with him. "Did you expect them to?"

Cal unlocked the door and held it open for her, turning sideways to let her pass. Their bodies brushed lightly, igniting her senses even more. "I know my family can be a bit overwhelming, all at once."

Ashley put her purse on the kitchen counter and pivoted to face him. She had to tilt her head back to see into his penetrating gray eyes. "Tell me something, Cal. Whose idea was it for you to come to Hawaii early and surprise me?"

The guilt she had hoped desperately not to see flashed across his face. His fingers tightened on the keys in his hand. "You heard about the Hart posse coming to see me," he surmised grimly.

She had now. Wondering just how deep his family's interference in their marriage went, Ashley folded her arms in front of her. "I'd like to hear it from you," she retorted, just as quietly.

Cal shrugged as if the incident were so insignificant it had barely registered on his radar screen. "It was suggested to me that I might want to do a better job of taking charge of our… situation…and bring you home."

Her spirits deflated even more. "So that's the only reason," Ashley presumed, the knowledge blindsiding her.

Cal clamped his hands on her shoulders, preventing her from running away. "No," he corrected with exaggerated patience. "I flew to Hawaii because you're my wife, and I'm your husband. And I thought you could use some help packing up your belongings, shutting off utilities and turning over your apartment."

How...romantic. Ashley struggled to contain her zigzagging emotions, even as she wondered when the last time Cal had said he loved her had been. Six months ago? A year? Longer? With effort, she kept the too-casual smile on her face. "Be honest with me, Cal. Would you have come and gotten me if your family hadn't intervened?" she demanded.

Cal released her as suddenly as if she had burned him. He leaned against the opposite counter and watched her in that strong, silent, aloof way of his. "Originally, I was planning to let you come home on your own timetable," he said eventually.

"And then you changed your mind," Ashley ascertained, aware neither of them had yet taken off their winter coats, and yet she still felt chilled to the bone in the cozy warmth of the farmhouse.

Cal gestured off-handedly, not about to apologize for what he had or had not said or done. "Look, I didn't ask for their interference, but what they were intimating made sense."

Feeling the sting of tears behind her eyes, Ashley turned away from him. She didn't know what it was about her lately—maybe it was the wealth of life-determining decisions ahead of her, or her continuing emotional distance from Cal—but she was so much moodier than usual!

"Where are you going?" Cal demanded in a low, gruff voice when she headed for the hall that ran the length of the house.

Ashley shrugged as she removed her black wool coat. "Does it matter?"

"Hell yes, it matters." In three long steps, Cal had overtaken her. He shackled her wrist, stopping her flight. She whirled toward him and they stared at each other in silence. "You don't believe I had our best interests at heart, do you?" he said quietly.

Achingly aware of the warmth of his fingers lightly encircling her wrist, Ashley drew a deep breath. "I think your family wants us to be together—here in Holly Springs—and you want to please your family." *Just like I want to please mine.* She swallowed around the rising lump in her throat. "So it's only natural—"

Cal's lips thinned. He shook his head at her disparagingly and tightened his grasp on her wrist. Swearing passionately beneath his breath, he steered her through the house to the door leading to the backyard. "Enough of this baloney!"

Ashley trembled as he struggled with the deadbolt on the door and yanked it open. "What are you doing?"

"Exactly what it looks like!" Cal said as he switched on the backyard lights. He took her out onto the deck, down the steps and onto the lawn. "I'm taking *you* to the barn!"

Chapter Four

"I don't know what has gotten into you," Ashley fumed as Cal charged through the floodlit darkness of the backyard to the barn a hundred yards away.

He gave her a wickedly teasing look. "A little John Wayne perhaps? And for the record," he wrapped an arm about her waist, tucking her into his side, "it's long overdue."

"It is not!" she told him with a determined toss of her head. She dug in her heels, flung off his arm and turned to face him. "And you can *not* do this!"

He lowered his face until they were nose to nose. "Want to bet?"

Ashley's heart pounded in her chest. She stabbed a finger at his chest, trying not to notice what a beautifully sculpted body he had. From his broad shoulders and well-muscled chest to his narrow waist and long legs, there wasn't an inch of him that wasn't fit and toned to the max. "I mean it, Cal."

He inclined his head at her, just as stubbornly. "So do I," he told her in a voice that brooked no dissent. "I don't care if you like it or not, Mrs. Hart." He drew in a slow breath and stayed just exactly where he was. "You're coming with me and you're coming right now."

The next thing she knew, he was swinging her up into his arms and striding across the lawn.

"The last time you did this was on our wedding night!" Ashley said breathlessly.

He grinned with customary self-assurance. "You planning to give me one of those?"

Ashley tried not to notice how the skirt of her dress was riding up her thighs, or how his powerful arm felt clamped beneath her hips. "Not tonight I'm not!" She wiggled in an attempt to get free. "Not after this!"

Oblivious to her machinations, he regarded her with a mysterious glint in his eye. "We'll just see how romantic you're feeling in a minute," he murmured huskily. He set her down in front of the double barn doors and opened the latch.

Once used to store farm equipment and fruit from the orchards, the big, red-sided building had been empty the only other time Ashley had been to the farm. She discovered it wasn't empty now as Cal hit the switch that brought on the overhead lights hanging from the rafters. A lawn tractor, hand mower and edger occupied one corner. But it was what was in the center of the cement-floored space that left her speechless.

"Oh, my…" Ashley stared at the big red heart on the windshield of a red '64 Mustang convertible in letter-perfect shape, from the pristine retractable white top and fancy silver wheel covers, to the candy-apple-red vinyl interior. It looked like the borrowed vehicle they'd had their very first date in.

Still watching her carefully, he took her gently by the hand, and led her toward the car. "Happy early Valentine's Day," he said when they neared. Wrapping both hands around her waist, he brought her close enough to kiss her temple affectionately. "This is for you."

She stared at him in amazement.

"You bought this for me?"

"For us. Yes."

"But we've never done anything this extravagant for each other for Valentine's Day!" Ashley protested. Usually, they exchanged cards, and went out to dinner, and that was about it.

"I know."

"Then why now?" She gazed at him. Was this part of his family's influence, too? Or all Cal's idea?

"Because we used to be closer," Cal told her in a low, sincere voice. Abruptly, all the love he had ever felt for her was in his eyes. "And I know we could be that connected to each other again if we just let ourselves go back to the beginning and start over. And where better to do that than in the car where our courtship began, eleven-and-a-half years ago?"

Ashley had to admit, the Mustang had already generated a lot of good memories in just a few scant minutes.

He regarded her with distinctly male satisfaction. "Want to test drive your new Mustang?"

Her hopes rising about them being able to fix the problems in their marriage after all, she took the keys he handed her. "Absolutely—if you'll come with me."

He winked at her cheerfully, suddenly looking like the carefree, charming med student she had fallen in love with years ago. "Wouldn't miss it for the world."

Cal opened the door for her, and Ashley slid behind the steering wheel. Circling around to the other side, Cal dropped into the passenger seat. Electricity sizzled between them as Ashley recalled how they used to do a little "parking" in this car, too.

"As much as I'd like you to try it with the top down…" Cal said.

Ashley shivered, just thinking about the wintry air blowing over them. "Yeah. I think it's too cold for that tonight, too."

"But when warmer weather comes," Cal predicted, fastening his old-fashioned lap belt, "we'll have a lot of fun with it."

It certainly sounded as though he was in this for the long haul, Ashley thought, as she fastened her belt, too. She shook her head, marveling at how accurately Cal had targeted her feelings.

To her delight, the motor started easily and ran with a gentle purr. "I can't get over how much this looks like the Mustang we started dating in," Ashley commented as she took it out on the country road and drove it through the moonlit countryside.

Cal draped an arm across the back of the seat. "It doesn't just look like it, Ashley." He leaned over and kissed her shoulder. "This is *the Car*."

A quick glance his way showed her he wasn't kidding. Ashley turned onto a road that would take them back in the direction of the farm. Enjoying the quick responsiveness of the motor, and the tight command of the wheel, Ashley asked, "How did you manage that?"

"I talked to Marty—the friend we used to borrow it from— and got the serial number and worked backwards from there," Cal told her as she slowed the car and turned into the long, narrow driveway.

"Unfortunately, the guy who owned it last summer didn't want to sell it to anyone because it's such a collector's item now," Cal continued affably. "So Hannah had to help me convince him to part with it. And then she spent the fall putting on a new coat of paint and making sure it ran like a dream."

Ashley guided the car back into the barn and cut the motor. "You were working on this all the way back then?" she asked in amazement. He'd never said a thing!

Shrugging, he released the catch on his safety belt. "I wanted you to have a spectacular coming-home present."

Spectacular was the word for it, all right. Ashley couldn't think of a better, more meaningful gift he could have given her. Except the gift he had unknowingly given her and she'd lost, before. The gift he still knew nothing about.

Ashley paused, aware yet again how much she loved Cal. More than anything, she wanted to be close to him again.

Maybe it was time she stopped guarding her heart. Instead, she could concentrate on tearing down the walls between them and building a better foundation for their marriage. Heaven knew this was a remarkable start. Just knowing he, too, wanted things to be better between them made all the difference. For the first time in months, she was optimistic about their future together. Optimistic that it wouldn't be just great sex and their love of medicine holding them together…

She wreathed her arms about his neck and leaned over to kiss him. "This is without a doubt the sweetest thing you've ever done for me."

His lips moved warmly on hers. To her relief…and disappointment, he didn't try to take the caress further. "I'm glad you like it," he whispered, holding her close as she snuggled against him.

"I more than like it, Cal. I love it." Ashley splayed her hands across the solidness of his chest. As she looked at him, her heart felt lighter than it had in ages. "But you know what this means, don't you?"

Cal shook his head, still holding her eyes with all the tenderness she had ever wanted to see.

"I still owe you a Valentine's Day present. And it's going to have to be a whopper to live up to the gift you've given me."

"Ah, Ashley, don't you understand?" Cal chided her gently, pulling her close yet again for another long, soulful kiss that ended much too soon. He threaded a hand through her hair. "Just coming home with me and spending the month with me in Carolina is present enough."

THE NEXT MORNING, Cal woke at his usual time of 6:00 a.m. Congratulating himself for going against his baser instincts to seduce Ashley back into his bed the night before, he rose and headed downstairs to put on the coffee. And then waited. And waited. And waited.

When Ashley still hadn't stirred five and a half hours later, he went up to check on her. She was curled up on her side, sleeping soundly, one hand tucked beneath her pillow. Knowing she'd never get on Eastern Standard Time unless she made an effort to adapt to the five-hour time difference, he opened the drapes and let the January sunshine pour across the guest bed. "Rise and shine!"

Ashley moaned and burrowed deeper in the covers. "What time is it?" she asked without opening her eyes.

"Almost noon," Cal leaned against the brass railing at the end of the double bed. She appeared to be going back to sleep. He nudged her foot. "Want to go for a run with me?"

Ashley opened one eye. "Mmm." She made a soft, sexy sound low in her throat. "Maybe later?"

Cal was about to coax her further when he heard a car in the drive. He crossed to the window and saw Ashley's father's Mercedes coming up the lane. This was…unexpected. "Ashley, I think your dad's here," Cal said.

Ashley scoffed and put one of the pillows over her head. "Get real," she mumbled.

Cal plucked the pillow away from her ear. "I mean it, Ash. I'm not kidding. Your dad just drove up to the house."

Ashley started, and ran a hand through her "bed-head" hair.

As usual, she looked more apprehensive than pleased when confronted with a meeting with her parents. "I'll keep him company while you get dressed," Cal promised, aware he wasn't much more comfortable with his father-in-law than Ashley seemed to be.

By the time Cal made it downstairs, Harold Porter was standing on the front porch of the farmhouse. Cal hadn't seen Harold for nearly a year but he looked the same as always. His impeccably cut silver hair was brushed away from his forehead in a suave, sophisticated style that didn't move even in the stiffest breeze. His skin bore the perennial suntan of a man who played golf, sailed and skied. Not that those activities were pleasure-oriented. Cal knew that everything Harold Porter did revolved around his work. And sometimes the only place a business meeting could be worked in was on the slope, the deck of a boat or a superbly manicured green. Hal Porter did whatever was necessary to get the job done, which was how he had risen through sales and marketing departments to become CEO of a prominent pharmaceutical company that was headquartered in the Research Triangle Park.

"Sir." Cal shook his father-in-law's hand and escorted him inside. Despite the fact it was a Saturday morning, Harold Porter was decked out in an expensive suit and tie.

"I can't stay." Harold shrugged out of his cashmere overcoat and handed it to Cal. "I've got a flight to Chicago later this afternoon, but I wanted to drop in and see you and Ashley before I headed to the airport."

Cal wasn't surprised. Harold traveled at least five or six days every week. Many weekends, he didn't make it back to North Carolina at all.

Cal hung up Harold's coat. "Ashley will be down in a minute. She's just waking up."

Harold frowned and glanced at his Rolex in obvious disapproval.

"She's still on Hawaii time," Cal explained, wishing Ashley's father wasn't so hard on her. "Can I get you some coffee or juice?"

Harold waved off the offer and regarded Cal soberly. "Actually, I'd like a word with you privately, if I may."

Aware this couldn't possibly be good, Cal led the way past the unfurnished rooms at the front of the house, to the family room at the rear. After Harold sat on the leather sofa, Cal took an easy chair and waited. The curt admonition wasn't long in coming. "I thought I had explained this to you when you asked her mother and me for her hand in marriage," Harold began sternly.

Cal was beginning to think of that conversation as the Devil's Bargain. One he never should have made in order to get their blessing for the union.

"Ashley is very much like her mother and me," Harold continued matter-of-factly. "She will never be happy unless she is free to be all she can be professionally. I know, because for the first six months after Ashley was born Margaret tried to give up her career goals and aspirations and be a full-time mother because she thought that would please me. She was never more miserable, nor was I."

Which meant Ashley couldn't have been happy, either. Cal knew that to have a happy baby—and a happy family—you had to have happy parents.

"I would hate to see you and Ashley walk down that same path, even for a short while."

Resenting the implication that he had behaved less than honorably in any instance, Cal held up a silencing palm. "Sir, with all due respect," he said angrily, "I resent what you are implying here. I assure you I have never done anything to hold

Ashley back professionally." Even when that meant biting his tongue when it came to her leaving him for a good two-and-a-half years. "In fact, I've done everything possible to help and encourage Ashley to follow her dreams." *At considerable cost to our marriage.* Cal was sure the time apart had contributed to the emotional distance between them.

Harold lifted a skeptical brow. "Then I don't understand what she's doing here for a month, lazing around and sleeping 'til noon, when she doesn't have a job yet."

Thinking of the emotionally and physically exhausted woman upstairs, Cal's patience waned. "She's earned some time off."

Harold frowned and cast a glance at the doorway, as if he didn't want them to be overheard. "She can take that once she's secured a position worthy of her education and training."

"Thanks for the advice, Dad." Ashley stood in the doorway. The expression on her face indicated she had caught the last of what Harold had said, but no more. And that was good, Cal thought, because he never wanted Ashley to know about the stipulations her parents had put on their blessing for Cal and Ashley's marriage. It was enough that he knew that their concern had not been that he love her with all his heart and soul, but rather that he wouldn't interfere with the stellar career achievements they expected of their only daughter.

Still moving tiredly, Ashley came farther into the room.

She was wearing a pink plaid flannel robe over her nightshirt, and slouchy pink sweat socks covered her feet. Her face was still bare of makeup, but she had brushed her hair and fastened it in a sleek chignon at the nape of her neck. She looked vulnerable and repressed—not at all like the carefree young bride who had been driving a Mustang convertible around country roads at midnight. Cal's heart went out to her once again.

Ashley had no trouble being her own woman when she was away from her parents. But when she was in their presence, she always seemed to shrink a little and fade into some stressed-out realm where Cal could not always reach her.

"Ashley." Harold stood, embracing her in a warm, paternal hug.

Cal noted with some relief that Harold looked genuinely glad to see his daughter. Ashley looked happy to see her father, too. But she was also wary. Nervous. On edge. Which was how she always acted around both her parents, no matter what the situation.

"I take it you haven't accepted the job in Maui," Harold said.

"No," Ashley said simply. Her glance cut over to Cal briefly before she turned her gaze back to her father. "I haven't."

"Well, it's probably a good idea to scout around first," Harold said, his tone gentling amiably as they all took a seat once again. "So where else are you looking?" Harold pressed.

Ashley folded her hands primly in her lap and sat with her back perfectly straight. "I haven't gotten that far yet, Dad. It was enough to finish my fellowship."

Her father frowned, making absolutely no effort to hide his disapproval about that. "I gather you are planning to job-hunt from North Carolina, then."

Ashley hesitated and this time she didn't look at Cal at all. "Yes." He reached over across the sofa and squeezed her hand reassuringly.

"Makes sense." Harold nodded thoughtfully after a moment. "Travel arrangements would certainly be easier from the mainland." Harold chatted on for several minutes. He gave Ashley a list of potential contacts who might know of suitable positions. Then he rose. "Well, I'd better get going.

Don't want to miss my flight to Chicago. I've got a business dinner there this evening."

"Where's Mom?" Ashley asked, also standing.

"She's still in Boston. She won't be home for another seven to ten days. A new semester is a very busy time for the university. As chancellor, she can't afford to be away."

"Right," Ashley said.

If Ashley was disappointed her father had so little time to spend with her, she was not showing it. "Well, travel safely, Dad." Ashley rose on tiptoe and kissed his cheek. Harold hugged her again, even more warmly this time, shook Cal's hand and was off.

Ashley and Cal stood watching until Harold had driven away.

As soon as he was gone, Ashley let out a long breath. Her slender body seemed to deflate. "I'm sorry about that," she said, shaking her head. "He should have called first, let us know he was coming."

"He's family, Ashley," Cal corrected his wife gently. "Your father doesn't have to call for permission first. He's welcome here anytime. In fact, I wish he would come here more," Cal said sincerely. Perhaps if Ashley and her parents spent more time together their relationship wouldn't be so strained. He knew they loved each other. They just hadn't quite figured out how to show it. A lot more interaction, on a more casual basis, might help that.

Ashley looked full of resentment. "If my father'd been coming here on business, he would have called ahead out of courtesy."

"Maybe he thought you'd duck him if he gave you too much notice," Cal teased gently and waited for her reaction. As he expected, it wasn't long in coming.

Ashley turned to Cal, moisture brimming in her china-blue eyes. "I love him."

"I know." Cal wrapped an arm around her shoulders and brought her in close to his side.

"I love both my parents," she insisted thickly.

"I know that, too." He comforted her with a kiss on the top of her head.

Ashley leaned into his embrace, as if soaking in the comfort he was trying to give, then moved away. She threw up her hands in frustration as she paced back and forth. "They just drive me crazy."

Cal knew that, too. "You could just tell your father you don't want to talk about the job search."

"That wouldn't stop him from putting his two cents in," she complained.

Probably not, Cal thought and released a long, frustrated breath.

"Anyway," Ashley sighed. She started to run her hands through her hair, the way she always did when she was restless, then stopped when she encountered the sleekly arranged chignon and pins. Looking as if she no longer wanted to discuss this, she eyed him up and down, taking in his ancient sweats and running shoes. "Did you say something about going for a run with me?"

He had, but that was before she was standing in front of him, looking so…wrung out and pale. He didn't want to say so, but physically she didn't look up for a long walk never mind a run in forty-degree weather. "Yeah, but—" Cal paused as the beeper at his waist began to buzz. He looked at the numbers running across the front, grimaced. He glanced at Ashley in apology, aware this was something he'd forgotten to mention. "I'm on call this weekend."

He turned the beeper off and headed for the phone.

"That the hospital or a patient?" Ashley asked.

"Hospital." Which meant it wasn't likely a problem that

could be solved over the phone. He picked up the phone and dialed. Ashley was still waiting when he had finished talking. "I've got to go. A sixteen-year-old kid got hurt on an ATV. From the sound of it, I'm going to be a while."

He was already grabbing his keys and wallet. "I'll call you later," he said.

Ashley flashed him a wan smile.

Cal headed for the door then came back, hooked an arm about her waist and pulled her close. Aggravation boiling up inside him, he kissed her soundly. He wished the demands of their profession weren't separating them again so soon. "Damn, I hate leaving you today," he said.

This time her smile was real. And sexy as all get out. "We've got time," she murmured reassuringly. Both hands on his chest, she shoved him in the direction he had to move. "Now, go."

LOOKING BACK, Ashley didn't know how she managed it. But she waited until Cal had driven off before she gave in to the nearly overwhelming nausea that had plagued her from the moment she had woken up. She rushed to the bathroom, where she promptly threw up.

Telling herself it was just nerves—and the pressure her parents were exerting on her to find a job "worthy" of her education and training—Ashley forced herself to shower and dress. And then she threw up again.

Wondering if she were coming down with something, she took her temperature, found it normal. Then she said to hell with it, and went back to bed.

By the time an hour had passed, and she had napped a little more, she felt remarkably better. At least as far as the steadiness of her stomach was concerned.

As far as the rest of her went...well, the more she thought

about it, the more questions she had. And there was only one way to get the answers she needed. So she got up, grabbed the keys to the Mustang, and went to see an old and dear friend.

Chapter Five

"Thanks for meeting me at the office on a Saturday afternoon," Ashley told Carlotta Ramirez, a petite beauty with dark hair and eyes and olive skin. Carlotta had been Ashley's "big sister" when she'd entered medical school—the fourth-year student assigned to help Ashley adjust. Now an obstetrician-gynecologist with a thriving private practice in Holly Springs, Carlotta was also married to another doctor, and the mother of three children: one born during her undergraduate years, the next while she was in medical school and the third during Carlotta's Ob/Gyn residency.

"No problem." Carlotta unlocked the door to her office suite, flipped on the overhead lights to dispel the wintry gloom and led the way inside. "I heard you and Cal were back this morning and I've been dying to see you. So how was Hawaii?" Carlotta continued as she shut the door behind them. "Beautiful?"

Ashley thought about the white-sand beaches, blue skies and even bluer ocean, the lush vegetation and a temperature that never varied much below seventy degrees or above eighty. "Very."

"I envy you the chance to do your fellowship there." Carlotta shook her head in awe. "Talk about paradise."

It had been, Ashley thought. But it would have been so much better if Cal had been there with her. Maybe then she wouldn't have felt such soul-deep loneliness the whole time she was there.

"So how long have you been feeling lousy?" Carlotta asked as they walked through the deserted inner office.

Ashley paused as Carlotta stopped at the linen closet and got out a soft pink cotton gown and a folded linen sheet, and handed both to Ashley.

"I just started throwing up this morning," Ashley said, telling herself that what she was worried about couldn't possibly be true.

"But—?" Carlotta prodded, experienced enough to know there was more.

Ashley confided reluctantly, "I've been tired and over-emotional and I suddenly can't fit into my pants."

"Any chance you might be pregnant?" Carlotta asked casually.

Yes, as a matter of fact, there was a slight chance—even though Ashley kept telling herself it couldn't possibly be true. "Cal and I were together in mid-November for a weekend in San Francisco," Ashley admitted with a rueful smile.

Carlotta grinned. "Sounds romantic," she teased.

Romance involved feelings, which Cal and Ashley had both been careful to keep tamped down. "It was certainly passionate, anyway," Ashley joked right back, aware her palms had begun to sweat as she faced finding out the absolute truth of her situation. A truth she wasn't sure she was ready to deal with.

Carlotta paused at another cabinet, and withdrew what she needed to do a screening test for iron-deficiency. "Did you two use protection?"

Ashley blushed as Carlotta tore open an antiseptic packet.

An Ob/Gyn, too, she knew these were the kind of questions she should be asking others, not answering herself. "I've been taking oral contraceptives."

"And that's it?" Carlotta asked.

Ashley cleared her throat, embarrassed to find herself in this position. "Right. Which was foolish, I know, since nothing is absolutely foolproof in and of itself." How many times had Ashley counseled her own patients in the women's clinic to use two methods of contraception simultaneously, and not just one, if they wanted to make absolutely sure they did not conceive?

Looking back, she couldn't believe she hadn't followed her own oft-given advice. But she had missed Cal so desperately, and making hot, wild love with him had always been the one sure way the two of them could connect, even when every other method of communication failed abysmally. Not wanting anything between them, she'd told him to forget about condoms and had been a little reckless.

"Well, there's one way to find out." Carlotta swabbed the end of Ashley's third finger with the antiseptic wipe, then pricked her finger. "I can do an in-office urine pregnancy test for you right now and, if that's positive, of course, we're going to want to take some more blood to send to the lab for a complete prenatal work-up and screening."

"Sounds good." Ashley watched as a dot of blood appeared on her finger and waited for Carlotta to fill a small plastic cylinder with a sample of her blood for the iron-deficiency screen.

Finished, Carlotta swabbed Ashley's finger again, then gave her a small plastic cup.

By the time Ashley emerged from the bathroom with the cup full, her blood sample was already in the machine that would render the results. Carlotta completed the in-office lab tests while Ashley undressed in one of the exam rooms.

"Well, you're not anemic," Carlotta announced, breezing in. Her cheerful grin confirmed what Ashley already knew in her heart. "And it looks as though the stork is going to be paying you two a visit next August."

Ashley drew a deep breath as her old friend started the physical exam by taking her blood pressure and listening to her heart and lungs.

"You're sure?"

Carlotta nodded. "Even without the test, I would have known. I'm surprised you and Cal didn't pick up on the signs. Your breasts appear swollen and you've got blue and pink lines beneath the skin." Carlotta moved to the end of the exam table while Ashley slid her feet into the stirrups and slid down.

Carlotta donned gloves and continued the physical exam. "Your uterus is enlarged and soft. Yep, you're definitely pregnant, all right."

Finished, Carlotta gave Ashley a hand and helped her sit up.

Ashley sat there, completely stunned. "Why don't you get dressed and then we'll talk in my office?" Carlotta said gently.

A few minutes later, wearing the same comfortable pale-blue sweats she had worn on the plane back from Hawaii, Ashley entered Carlotta's office. "Well," she said, as she sank into a seat. "This certainly explains why I've gained over five pounds in two months and suddenly none of my pants with waistbands fit."

"I take it pregnancy wasn't in the plans you and Cal have been making?" Carlotta said delicately.

Ashley shook her head. "We haven't even discussed children since the first couple of months we were married." Then they had both thought about having a child, except it hadn't worked out, and shortly after that, the troubles in their marriage had begun.

Carlotta handed Ashley a month's supply of prenatal vitamin samples. "You think he doesn't want children?"

Ashley hesitated. She was bewildered to discover she no longer knew the answer to that. "It's just…"

"I understand. It's a life-altering event, no matter how it occurs. But for the record, I think Cal would be very happy." Carlotta paused. "I mean, you are planning to tell him, aren't you?"

Happiness bubbled up inside Ashley, followed quickly by fear, and a disturbing feeling of déjà vu. "Yes, of course I'm going to tell Cal, as soon as I hit the three-month mark and pass the danger of miscarriage."

Carlotta blinked. "You're sure you want to wait that long?"

Ashley knew from her own patients that most women couldn't wait to tell their husbands.

"Yes." For very good reason.

Carlotta did some quick calculations, and grinned as she jumped to the logical conclusion. "Valentine's Day, huh?" Carlotta teased.

Ashley smiled. Now—heaven willing—she knew exactly what she was going to give her husband for Valentine's Day. And it beat the heck out of any car, even a red '64 Mustang convertible. "Promise me." Ashley looked Carlotta in the eye and did her best to quell her nervousness. "Not a word to anyone, even your husband, until I give the okay."

Carlotta crossed her heart. "You have my word. Now, is there anything else you want to discuss?"

Ashley sobered. "As a matter of fact," she related unhappily as she prepared to fill her friend in on the most private parts of her medical history, "there is."

"YOU HAVEN'T HEARD a word I've said, have you?" Cal said in frustration several hours later.

Ashley flushed guiltily and looked across the kitchen table at him. They'd been having dinner for a good twenty minutes now, and although he had been talking nonstop about the case he'd seen earlier and the difficulties the surgery presented, she had heard only a smidgen of it. Which had been most unlike her. Usually, she loved hearing about Cal's cases, and vice versa. Medicine was the one thing they could always talk about.

"What's going on with you?" Cal asked, narrowing his eyes at her.

I'm having a baby—our baby—and my mind and emotions are in awhirl. Ashley swallowed, embarrassed. "What do you mean?"

"One minute you're smiling like you just won the lottery," Cal observed.

That's because I feel happier than I've ever felt in my life.

"And the next you're frowning like you have the weight of the world on your shoulders."

That's because I'm scared to death that what happened before is going to happen again. And none of this is going to work out the way I want and hope.

"What did you do today, anyway?" Cal continued as he stood and began to clear the table.

Noting how the gray in the cashmere sweater he was wearing brought out the pewter shade of his eyes, Ashley stood and began to clean up, too. She wished she could think about something besides kissing him whenever they were this close. Especially today…

"I went to see Carlotta," Ashley finally answered.

Cal smiled and held her eyes for a long, breath-stealing moment. "I'm glad you two were able to get caught up."

"Me, too," Ashley said. *Even if I can't tell you everything about that meeting just yet.*

Cal slid the dishes into the dishwasher with the ease of a man who'd done dishes many times growing up. "Then what did you do?"

Ashley edged away from the enticing sea-and-sun fragrance of his cologne. "I drove to the mall to find some clothes that fit and a few how-to books on decorating." *And while I was at it, I stopped and looked at baby things. Lots and lots of baby things.*

Cal wiped his hands on a dish towel, then set it aside. He stood facing her, his back to the counter, hands braced on either side of him. "Is that what's worrying you?" he asked as Ashley backed away from him self-consciously, feeling guilty as all get out once again.

What's worrying me is the fear that I will let you and our baby down—again—and you'll feel the kind of hurt no parent should ever have to feel.

"You worried about needing a bigger size in clothing?" Cal continued sympathetically, oblivious to the real reason behind Ashley's distress. He caught her hand and reeled her in to his side. "Because I have to tell you," he confided appreciatively as he wrapped an arm around her waist, "extra five pounds or no, I've never seen you looking more beautiful."

As Ashley looked into his eyes, she had never felt more beautiful than she did at that very moment. Or more secure in his love. And maybe it was selfish of her, but she wanted it to stay that way. She wanted to get through this next month, and one of the riskiest periods of her pregnancy, and then on Valentine's Day tell him he was going to be a daddy. And by the time she told him the happy news, she wanted all the problems in their relationship worked out.

"You were kind of pale when I left this morning, but tonight your face is just glowing," Cal continued.

That's because I am about to give you the most wonderful gift a woman can give the man she loves. Ashley ducked her head and let it rest against the warm solidness of his broad shoulder. "Well, thank you," she said, blushing.

He cupped a hand beneath her chin and lifted her face up to his. "So maybe you should stay this weight," he told her sincerely.

Ashley's lips curved as she imagined how happy Cal was going to be if everything went as she hoped. "I don't think that's going to be possible," she said dryly.

"And feel free to buy yourself a whole new wardrobe," Cal suggested, as compassionate and generous to her as ever.

She inclined her head ruefully and deliberately held his gaze. "If I didn't know better, I'd think you were trying to spoil me," she teased.

He wrapped both arms about her waist and pulled her in until all of her was pressed against all of him. "You deserve spoiling," he muttered huskily

Ashley had known Cal wanted to make a move on her—she had seen it in his eyes all evening. She just hadn't thought, given the agreement they had made to abstain from making love until their marriage was on solid footing, that he would. But now that he was kissing her again, his lips tenderly coaxing and recklessly taking, she realized something else. She needed this connection with him, needed the fierce sensuality of his mouth moving over hers, and, above all else, she needed to be loved by him.

She wreathed her arms around his neck, kissed him back every bit as passionately as he was kissing her and let all the joy she felt over their baby growing inside her wash over her. It didn't matter that she wasn't ready to tell him yet. The baby forged a powerful connection between them that would last their entire lives and she wanted that just as fiercely as she wanted to have his child.

Cal had never been able to read Ashley's heart as well as he wanted to, but he had always known intuitively when she needed him to take her in his arms. And, for whatever reason, she required his physical closeness tonight. He'd seen it in the dreamy, distracted way she had looked at him all through dinner, and he'd felt it in her kiss and in the way her body cuddled against his. Not that he minded holding her. Kissing her. Touching her. Even if their hot embrace was picking up his heart rate and sending blood rushing to his lower half. But when she moaned, soft and low, in the back of her throat, and he felt her nipples budding tightly as they brushed against his chest, he knew he had to stop—now—or break the promise he had made to her. So, reluctantly, he let their steamy kiss come to a halt and drew away from her.

He wasn't all that surprised to see disappointment mingled with pleasure and relief on her face as she trembled and looked up at him. She had to know, good intentions or not, that with them both living under the same roof again it was only a matter of time before their passion ignited.

"So," he said in a low, gravelly voice, determined to be more noble than selfish, at least for this evening, "you want to show me your new clothes?" Maybe that would distract him from the sensual shape of her damp lower lip.

Ashley stepped back a pace. Her hand shook as she shoved her hand through the mussed strands of her dark hair. "I just bought two pairs of slacks." Oddly enough, she looked as if she were keeping something from him. What, he couldn't imagine.

"One gray and one black," Ashley continued, appearing a little embarrassed.

Disappointment swept through him. He had been hoping for a sexy fashion show. The kind she used to give him when they were dating. He quirked a brow, wondering why she had been so frugal when she didn't have to be. She loved clothes! Loved shopping for them, too. "That's all?"

A flash of guilt appeared in her eyes and just as quickly disappeared. "I know my larger waist is only temporary," she stated reluctantly, embarrassed. "I plan to get back into my old clothes. It's just going to take time." She turned her eyes from his once again. "And some dedicated working-out on my part. Which I plan to do."

Cal knew Ashley felt better and had more stamina when she was physically fit—they both did. Maybe he could help her here. Help them both. He walked to the refrigerator and took out a bottle of chilled spring water for each of them. "As long as we're talking about how to decorate the rest of the house, what do you think about putting in a home gym?" he asked her casually.

Ashley appeared surprised and intrigued. "Where?"

"Upstairs." Cal took her by the hand and led her up the back staircase to the second floor. He enjoyed the soft, delicate feel of her fingers clasped in his. "I was thinking maybe we could use the bedroom right next to ours," he told her, unwilling to admit how many lonely nights he had spent dreaming about the things they could do with this place, if only she would join him.

He steered Ashley to the room he was talking about and waited hopefully for her reaction.

ASHLEY KNEW CAL WANTED her to support his idea whole-heartedly, but she couldn't quite do that. She knew this room next to the master bedroom suite should definitely be the nursery. Beginning to see just how hard it was going to be to keep this news from Cal until another four weeks had passed and she was sure everything was going to be all right, Ashley said instead, "What about the other empty bedroom?"

Cal shrugged. She could see he was a little hurt by her immediate dismissal of his idea. "It's smaller, and it doesn't have as many windows. So the light wouldn't be as good as it is in here."

"Maybe we don't want as much as light." Ashley linked arms with Cal and guided him down the hall to show him the other room.

Cal studied her. "You really think this room would be better?"

"Well. What are you planning to put in here?" Ashley looked at the ten-foot-by-twelve-foot room.

"An exercise bike. Treadmill. Maybe a stair machine or an elliptical trainer. What would you like?"

Ashley thought about the exercises she recommended for her pregnant patients. "A place for a yoga mat. Maybe a TV with a DVD player built into it mounted on the wall. So I can watch the tapes while I work out."

"Sounds good to me," Cal said as he turned to survey the room one more time. "So when do you want to get on this?"

Ashley smiled, glad they had something to occupy themselves with the rest of the weekend. "Right away."

"I HAVE TO GO BACK to the hospital," Cal said as soon as he got off the phone Sunday evening.

"Another emergency surgery?" Ashley asked.

Cal nodded as he clipped his beeper back on his belt.

He looked disappointed their evening together was going to be cut short. Ashley knew exactly how he felt. The weekend had gone too fast. But this was the life of a practicing physician. They both knew that, although they were usually a lot better at taking it in stride.

Determined to be the kind of supportive spouse he needed, Ashley touched his arm and smiled at him gratefully. "We had a great day." They'd slept late, gone to 11:00 a.m. services and had lunch with Cal's family, then spent the afternoon finding everything they needed for their home gym. Ashley still had to purchase her pregnancy workout tapes, but she'd have to do that when Cal wasn't with her.

"I just wish I had Monday off so I could spend it with you," he murmured.

Instead, he was scheduled to work from seven in the morning until dinner time. Which left Ashley wondering what she was going to do. She knew she should be looking for a job, but right now all she wanted to do was stay here and "play house" with Cal. And how weird was that? She couldn't be nesting, could she?

"Promise me you'll miss me desperately," Cal said, pulling Ashley closer for a long, slow kiss.

Ashley sighed and sank into his luxuriant embrace. "I already do," she murmured back playfully. And to prove it, she kissed him again, even more thoroughly.

Cal smiled and ruffled her hair. "Don't wait up," was the last thing he said as he went out the door.

Figuring the best thing she could do for her pregnancy was get as much sleep as possible in this first trimester, Ashley took one of the prenatal vitamins she had spirited away in her purse, drank a glass of milk, and went on up to bed. She had no trouble falling asleep and slept for six hours straight, not waking until she heard Cal's car in the drive shortly after 3:00 a.m. He came up the back stairs and headed straight for the master bedroom.

Ashley heard him go into the master bathroom, come out again and fall into bed.

From the absence of sound, Ashley figured he'd gone straight to sleep. She was not as lucky. No matter how hard she tried, she couldn't fall back into dreamland. Eventually, her stomach began to growl. She knew if she didn't put something in it soon, her nausea would likely come back.

Ashley pulled on her robe and tiptoed down to the kitchen, where she studied her options for satisfying her pregnant cravings.

Chapter Six

Cal swore he was so tired when his head hit the pillow he wanted nothing more than to sleep until his alarm went off at six-thirty. And perhaps he would have if the aroma of something spicy and delicious hadn't wafted up to tease his senses. He rolled over and glanced at the clock. Four in the morning! What the heck could Ashley be doing up at this hour? And what was that he smelled cooking? Whatever it was, it certainly wasn't breakfast food.

Curiosity overrode fatigue.

He strode downstairs, wearing just his boxers, and found Ashley standing at the kitchen stove. Glossy dark-brown tendrils were escaping her ponytail to frame her delicate heart-shaped face. She was clad in a pair of loose-fitting light-blue cotton pajamas that brought out the blue of her eyes and were the perfect foil for the soft golden glow of her skin and the pinkness of her cheeks. Her delicate bare feet peeked beneath the hem of her pajama pants, and there was something so sexy about those polished red toenails, it was all he could do to stay where he was. Oblivious to his presence, she was pouring a dark-red spice into the palm of her hand. Satisfied with the amount, she added it to the pot of browning beef and onions. As it hit the sizzling meat and the aroma escaped into the room, his eyes widened in surprise. "Are you making chili?"

Ashley glanced up, for a moment looking like a kid who'd been caught with her hand in the cookie jar. Then she shrugged as if it were the most natural occurrence in the world. "Had a hankering for it," she said, in her best Southern drawl. She went back to the stove, adding salt and fresh-ground pepper to the sizzling meat.

Cal leaned against the counter, watching as she opened a can of crushed tomatoes and poured them into the pan. The kitchen smelled even more delicious. He grinned. "You're not the only one." Now he wanted some, too. He reached over and brushed a lock of hair away from her cheek. "How long until it will be ready?"

She trembled at his touch—evidence that she was no less affected by his presence than he was by hers. Flushing self-consciously, she slipped by him, to the open pantry shelves and returned with a can of ranch-style pinto beans. "Ten, fifteen minutes." She added those, too, and gave it another stir while he appreciated the intimacy of being with her like this. He realized there had been far too few moments such as this since the two of them had been married. More often, they had been hopping into bed and back out again as one of them rushed off to the hospital. Their union had been more like a hot, passionate affair than a marriage.

Which was why it was so awkward now...why, suddenly, as she picked up the tall glass of milk next to the stove and drank deeply from it, that she was having trouble meeting his eyes. "Sorry if I woke you," she said quietly, picking up the notepad on the table. Tearing off the top sheet, which had some sort of list on it, she carried it over to the far counter and slipped it into her shoulder bag. "I was trying to be quiet."

And she had been. He was the one who couldn't stay away

from her. But that was hardly a surprise. After all, he'd never been able to stay away from her.

"You're up awfully early," he observed, and watched her cheeks grow ever pinker as an almost guilty look came into her eyes. Wondering what was going on with her, Cal padded closer.

"I went to bed really early." She aimed a trigger finger at his exposed belly-button, before turning her gaze slowly back to his face. "And speaking of bed, shouldn't *you* still be in yours?"

Cal would be—if she were there with him. As it was, he couldn't think of anywhere he would rather be.

Ashley had obviously turned up the thermostat when she had come downstairs, and the kitchen was warm enough not to require additional clothing. Though from the distracted way Ashley kept looking at his bare chest, Cal knew she would have preferred he go and get a robe to cover up. "I'll get back there eventually," he told her, enjoying the ardent look in her eyes as much as the free-flowing electricity between them.

She frowned and looked at him as if she wished it would be sooner rather than later. She went back to stir the pan of fragrant, bubbling chili. She opened the cupboard and leaned across the counter to reach the shelf containing the soup bowls. "Want some?"

"Absolutely." Cal couldn't help noticing the way the neckline of her pajama top fell open as she moved. Instead of a glimpse of her breasts, however, he got a look at a stretchy white cotton undershirt that came up halfway to her collarbone.

Not that this wasn't sexy, too—especially when he thought about taking both garments off her.

Reminding himself of his promise not to make love to her

again—at least not yet—Cal went to get the crackers. Coming back to the table he was surprised to see her take something out of the oven. French fries?

Ashley caught his glance and blushed again. "I had a hankering for them, too," she said.

Obviously, Cal thought. Were these hankerings the reason Ashley was suddenly having trouble with her weight? Not that he minded her new voluptuousness.

He thought she looked amazing. Especially now that she looked as if she were catching up on her rest. "Want some ketchup?" he asked as he opened the fridge.

Ashley shook her head. "Extra-sharp cheddar?"

Cal grabbed it out of the cheese drawer and the milk off the shelf, then shut the door with the back of his arm, and carried both to the table.

He nodded at the paper she had slipped into her purse. "What are you working on?"

"Your Valentine's Day present. And don't even think about peeking," she scolded as she went to retrieve it and tucked it into the pants pockets on her pajamas. "Because you're not finding out what it is until next month."

Cal grinned as they sat down at the breakfast table in front of the bay window. Her working on a present for him had to be a good sign, didn't it? "Since when do you eat fries and chili first thing in the morning?" he asked her curiously.

She shrugged as she grated some cheddar over top of her chili and then dipped another crispy golden fry into the steaming bowl. Abruptly, he had the feeling in his gut that she was once again withholding every bit as much as she was telling him. Not that this was a surprise. It had been a pattern that had developed in the early days of their marriage.

"Since right now," Ashley said, looking as if she were in heaven as the concoction melted on her tongue. She washed it down with another swallow of icy-cold milk. Suddenly, the teasing look was back in her blue eyes, the flirtatious note in her soft voice. "I take it from the astonished look you're giving me that you've never eaten them together?"

She seemed happy again. Really happy. Maybe happier than he had ever seen her.

"No," Cal said, struggling to keep his mind on the conversation. "And I wasn't aware you had, either." Ashley was usually a lean grilled chicken or fish and healthy fruit and vegetables kind of woman. The carbs she ate were healthy and whole grain. Whereas he…well, Cal always had appreciated potatoes—any kind—and spicy calorie-laden foods like chili. Was her making chili for him now an attempt to find her way back into his heart? To better mesh their lives? Whatever the case, he appreciated her going to all the trouble.

She rested her hand on her upturned chin and regarded him inscrutably. "I thought it might be a good combination."

Cal leaned toward her as she fed him a fry dipped in chili and sharp cheddar. The combination *was* delicious—spicy and rich.

"You like it, don't you?" she teased.

I like you. "Actually, I do," Cal said with surprise.

Her blue eyes gleamed with pleasure and pride. "Tell me about the surgery," Ashley said.

He filled her in while they finished eating. "Sounds like it was a challenging case," Ashley noted when he had finished.

Cal nodded. It had been.

"So, shouldn't you be sleeping?" Ashley continued in a soft, wifely tone.

Yeah, Cal thought as he stacked their dishes and cleared the table, he *should* be catching twenty winks right about now. But it was hard falling asleep and staying asleep when she was under the same roof in another bed. It would be so much easier if he at least had her to snuggle with under the covers. He always slept better with Ashley wrapped in his arms. And maybe so did she.

He took her hand and brought her gently to her feet. "You should be in bed, too."

Drawn slightly off balance, she bumped into him, then steadied herself by putting one hand against his chest. "I wasn't in surgery most of the night." She turned away from him and began putting the leftover chili away.

Funny, how his energy came surging back whenever he was around her. "I'm a doctor. I'm used to getting by on little sleep. And so are you." He pitched in to help her finish the dishes.

"True." Ashley wiped down the table, countertops and stove.

"But that still doesn't explain what you're doing up in the middle of the night," Cal continued.

Ashley hesitated, as if trying to think of a reasonable explanation for her insomnia. "Must be the time difference," Ashley speculated finally, looking pleased she had come up with something that sounded logical, when Cal's intuition was telling him her excuse didn't ring true. Something specific was keeping her from sleeping. She just didn't want to share it with him, he realized, stung.

"After all, Hawaii-time it's only 11:00 p.m. right now," Ashley continued matter-of-factly.

She had a point there, Cal had to concede.

"But you're still on Eastern Standard Time and, as you pointed out earlier this evening, you have to work tomorrow. So you really should go back to bed right now," Ashley said.

He regarded her, reluctant to comply, even when he knew she was right. He could use more rest.

She batted her eyelashes at him flirtatiously. "Come on, doc." She crooked a finger his way. "I'll tuck you in."

He grinned and began to relax as she clasped his hand lightly in hers. "Oh you will, will you?" he bantered back. As they moved up the stairs and paused in the doorway of the master bedroom, Cal murmured hopefully. "I don't suppose I can convince you to join me."

Something akin to the deep and abiding love she used to have for him—and he hoped *still* did—flickered in her pretty blue eyes. "Something tells me neither of us would get much sleep if I were to do that."

"Yeah," Cal agreed, aware all over again as she led him toward the big empty bed how much he liked spending time with her. "But think of the fun we'd have." *Think of how much closer we'd feel. Think about the possibility of me getting you to lower your guard once and for all.*

But, he noted sadly, it wasn't going to happen now. Tonight, she was still holding onto her secrets and private doubts, whatever they were. "How about a rain check?" she countered, easing him down into the sheets.

Cal tightened his grip on her fingers and looked deep into her eyes. The fear that he had somehow unknowingly contributed to the distance between them filled him with guilt. "I'm going to hold you to that," he warned her soberly, letting her know once and for all he intended to make her his again.

She leaned forward and brushed a light kiss to his temple that was as tender as it was playful. "Somehow, Cal, I knew you would."

DURING LUNCHTIME on Monday at the Wedding Inn, Cal caught sight of his mother and sister-in-law. "Just the two women I wanted to see," he said cheerfully. "Have you got time to have a top-secret meeting with me?"

Helen glanced at her watch. The owner of the premier wedding establishment in North Carolina, she was usually on the run from the time she showed up for work in the morning until the time she left. Joe's wife, Emma, was just as busy in her wedding-planning duties.

Looking as stylish and pulled-together as ever in a pastel-pink business suit, Helen ran a hand through her short red hair. "I've got fifteen minutes," Helen said.

"I can spare you ten," the petite and elegantly pretty Emma said.

The three of them went back to Helen's office. Helen closed the door, insuring their privacy. She slipped behind her desk, her eyes focusing on Cal with maternal concern. "What brings you over here in the middle of a work day?" she asked, perplexed.

"I want to know if you're booked for Valentine's Day."

Emma and Helen chuckled as if that was the funniest thing they had ever heard and shook their heads. "Honey, we're booked three years ahead for Valentine's Day," Helen said.

"How can people book three years ahead?" Cal asked. When he and Ashley had decided to get married, they had only waited six months. He couldn't imagine waiting three years—for anything!

Helen smiled. "Some people just know."

"And are willing to wait for the exact time they want," Emma added.

Cal was willing to wait for the exact woman. He wasn't giving up no matter how long it took to make his marriage to Ashley work the way it should to give them the happily-ever-after they had both always wanted. Which was, of course, why he was here. He had come up with an idea to help speed the process, now that the groundwork had been laid. Especially since he only had three-and-a-half more weeks to convince Ashley they needed a lot more face time with each other than they'd been having.

"I want to have a wedding here on Valentine's Day," Cal told both women.

Two sets of eyebrows raised. "Mind me asking whose?" Emma interjected, with her usual tranquility.

Cal sat down in one of the chairs in front of his mother's desk and stretched his long legs out in front of him. "Ashley's and mine. I want to renew our vows on our wedding anniversary—February fourteenth."

Emma smiled and sat on the edge of Helen's desk, facing both Cal and Helen. "That's very romantic," Emma said approvingly.

Helen's eyes narrowed as if to say not so fast. "What does Ashley think about this?" she asked curiously.

Leave it to his mother to hit the nail on the head, without even trying. "She doesn't know," Cal stated, pretending not to see his mother's obvious reservations about his plan. "I'm going to surprise her."

Helen splayed a hand over her heart. She looked as if she might faint. "You can't surprise a woman with a wedding!" Helen said, aghast.

Au contraire. Cal held his ground. "I can if I want to," he said stubbornly.

Emma looked at Helen. Although no words were spoken, much seemed to pass between them. "I think it's a very romantic idea, Cal," Emma said tactfully at last, while Helen nodded in agreement. "But there are so many details that would have to be decided. And usually brides want very much to decide those things."

Cal knew that was true—Ashley had possessed very definite opinions on just about everything the first time around. "Can't we just use the same flowers and stuff we used at our first wedding ceremony?" Cal asked.

"I suppose." Looking reluctant to snuff out such a romantic idea, Helen bit her lip.

"What about the dress?" Emma asked. Again, she and Helen exchanged telltale looks. "Without sounding indelicate…are you sure Ashley will fit into the dress she wore the last time? As I recall it was quite form-fitting."

Cal hadn't thought about that, either. It was a good point. The last thing he wanted to do was point out to everyone else she had recently gained five pounds as well as several inches in all the right places. "So we'll get her a new one," Cal said.

"How?" Helen leaned forward, determined to be practical now. "We don't even have her measurements."

Cal shrugged, not going to let something that inconsequential derail his plans to add even more romance to his flagging marriage. "You know her style. I'm sure between the two of you that you could pick something out that she'd like to wear."

Helen and Emma exchanged trepidation-filled looks, then turned back at Cal.

"I really want to do this, Mom," Cal said before they could argue further.

"And you're sure it needs to be a surprise?" Emma ascertained slowly.

Thinking about how commitment-shy Ashley had seemed lately, he nodded.

"What about the Mustang you bought for her?" Helen interjected curiously. "I thought that was for Valentine's Day."

Cal rubbed the tension gathering in the muscles in the back of his neck. "I already gave it to her. She needed something to drive now, and well…it's a long story," he said vaguely, not willing to go into specifics because of Ashley's pique over the Hart family's involvement in their marital difficulties.

His mother looked at him as if she just bet there was much more to tell.

Emma glanced at her watch again. "Oh, darn, I've got an appointment with Polly Pruett and Peter Sheridan to pick out their reception-table settings."

Cal understood their business was important. He stood, knowing he had to get back to the hospital, too. "Can I count on your help with this? Especially the dress and all that?" he asked Emma.

Emma nodded and patted Cal's arm reassuringly as she passed. "Just get me some undergarments and a dress or a skirt or pair of slacks that fit Ashley well and bring those in to me. We'll run them over to the dressmaker and take the measurements off of those. If you're discreet about it, Ashley will never suspect a thing."

Cal had known he could count on the women in the family to come through for him. "Thanks, Emma." He stood, hugging her briefly.

"You romantic devil, you." Emma stood on tiptoe, bussed his cheek, then slipped out the door.

Helen picked up the pen in front of her and looked at Cal. "Now. Suppose you tell me what's really going on," she said.

LEAVE IT TO HIS MOTHER to cut straight to the chase. "What do you mean?"

Helen got up to close the door to her office, ensuring them privacy once again. "Are you really this insecure about your marriage?" she said.

Too restless to sit, Cal leaned up against the wall and put his hands in the pockets of his slacks. He should have known his mother wouldn't pull any punches. Especially when it came to something this important. But if she thought he was backing out, just because there were logistical details to be worked out, she had another think coming. "I'm being romantic," he defended himself.

Helen sat on the edge of her desk and folded her arms in front of her. She regarded Cal sagely. "Romantic or desperate?"

Ouch again! Cal let his jaw slide forward pugnaciously. "I admit I want her to stay."

Exasperation mixed with the kindness in Helen's eyes. She looked at Cal as if she didn't know whether to hug him or scold him. "To the point you're trying to buy her love?"

Cal tensed. A muscle working in his jaw, he moved away from the wall and began to pace the small confines of his mother's elegantly outfitted office. "That's not what I'm doing." Cal moved to the floor-to-ceiling window and looked out at the elegantly landscaped grounds where many spring, summer and fall weddings were held.

Helen walked over to adjust the elegant red and gold velvet drapes that were so perfectly suited for the century-old inn. "The car alone was a pretty big gift. Now you're talking about throwing yourselves another wedding."

So Cal was generous when it came to his wife? He wasn't about to apologize for gifting Ashley as she deserved. Besides, he had done something like this before—the first year they were married, he'd given her the farm and the house for Christmas.

"Albeit on a much smaller scale," Cal cautioned, letting his mother know the rest of his plans. He surveyed her sternly. "This time around I'd like it to be just family and a few close friends." Not the splashy social occasion it had been the first time.

"Still," Helen shook her head disparagingly, "for someone who is still in the process of paying off his medical school debts, that's a pretty big deal."

Cal knew the gift was impractical. That wasn't the point. "I want her to know I love her," he said firmly.

Helen dropped the pen back onto the center of her desk. Abruptly, she looked as restless and unhappy as Cal felt. "And you think giving Ashley presents will accomplish that?" Helen said, as if it were the dumbest idea he'd ever had.

"Well, God knows nothing else has."

Cal hadn't meant to say the words out loud. But now that he had, they just hung there in the increasingly uncomfortable silence that followed.

Helen stepped nearer and compassion resounded in her low tone. "You really think Ashley questions your feelings for her?"

Cal knew his mother wished he would admit otherwise. But he wasn't going to lie, not now, when he was finally putting voice to some of his own deepest fears. He dropped back down into the chair, suddenly feeling as exhausted—and uncertain—as he had every right to be. Finished pretending, Cal looked up at his mother and reluctantly confessed, "I don't know, Mom. We've said we loved each other dozens of times over the ten years we've been a couple."

Just not recently.

"But?"

"I think she doubts something about us." Cal just didn't know quite what it was.

Helen's mood turned as contemplative as Cal's. "And why would she do that?" she asked gently.

And wasn't that just the million-dollar question? Cal spread his hands wide. "Maybe because we lived apart from each other for two-and-a-half years. And you don't have to remind me, I know you told me it was a dumb idea from the get-go to put our careers before our marriage." But they had done it anyway and now they had to live with the consequences.

Cal shrugged again, aware his mother was waiting to hear

the rest. He needed to tell someone close to him what was bothering him deep inside. "Because we stopped knowing how to open up to each other what was in our hearts and on our minds. Because there's this *distance* between us, Mom, that sometimes has us feeling more like strangers than husband and wife." Even if Ashley didn't come right out and say so, he knew by the way she looked at him she felt that way. Damn. Listen to him. He sounded like some whiny kid. Cal shoved his hands through his hair. "I'm hoping that if we renew our vows, if we start fresh, we can fix this." Because God knew he needed to make his marriage right.

Helen sighed, suddenly looking as deeply worried and discouraged as Cal. "Maybe you should consider counseling instead," she suggested quietly.

Cal thought about how that was likely to go over. Not well, to put it lightly. He shook his head. "No. I know Ashley, Mom. If she won't open up to me, she sure as heck won't open up to any counselor. This is the way it has to be."

Cal was sure he was doing the right thing. He and Ashley had to start communicating with each other before they would be able to believe in their future. Putting someone else in between them at this point would be as bad as putting miles between them. The way he saw it, if the car had worked to get her moving toward him, renewing their vows would be even better. "Now, are you going to help me?" Cal looked at his mother sternly. "Or should I be looking for a location other than the Wedding Inn this time around?" he asked impatiently.

Helen went back to her calendar. "Of course you can have the ceremony here, but it will have to be February thirteenth. There's a wedding here earlier that day, but it should be cleared out by, oh—5:00 p.m., or so—and we could set up for yours for the eve of your wedding anniversary, if not the actual anniversary."

Close enough, Cal decided. "That'd be fine."

"And Cal, there's one more thing—"

A knock sounded on Helen's door. "Come in," Helen said.

And much to Cal's amazement and chagrin, Ashley walked in.

ASHLEY WASN'T SURE what had been going on between Cal and his mother before she opened the door, but the tension in the room was so thick you could cut it with a knife.

"You wanted to see me, Helen?" Ashley asked cheerfully, deciding this once ignorance was just going to have to be bliss. Because she had enough troubles, trying to keep her pregnancy secret, finding a job, pleasing her parents, and mending her struggling marriage to Cal, without borrowing any more.

Not that this strain was any surprise. Cal had always been among the most private of Helen's offspring, and the fact he wouldn't confide what was on his mind had always made it hard for Helen to help him, as a kid and as an adult. And that was a shame, Ashley thought, because Helen Hart was one of the most understanding mothers Ashley had ever come in contact with. Given the chance...

Helen smiled warmly and gestured for Ashley to have a seat in the chair next to Cal's. "I asked you to come over because I have a favor to ask. You're planning to be here through February seventh, aren't you?"

"Sure." Ashley settled in her chair and crossed her legs at the knee. "Why?"

"Well, we have a wedding going on here that is just a disaster waiting to happen, I'm afraid," Helen confessed, her anxiety apparent. "The bride will be eight-and-a-half months pregnant on her wedding day."

Ashley did a double take as she contemplated that. "Whoa."

"Yes, I know." Helen shook her head, commiserating. "Both Emma and I tried to talk Polly Pruett out of getting married so close to her due date, but Polly was adamant about wanting a big wedding as close to Valentine's Day as possible. Turns out her fiancé, Peter Sheridan, was insistent they tie the knot before the baby was born. And her parents—who are paying for this huge affair—refused to let the wedding happen any closer to Polly's due date than that, so this was the best compromise we could come up with."

"Where do I come in?" Ashley asked, aware that beside her Cal seemed to be relaxing. Maybe because the attention was no longer on him or whatever it was he and his mother had been discussing when she interrupted?

Helen continued, "I was wondering if you would agree to be here on call for any emergency, during the ceremony and the reception. Emma and I would rest easier knowing there was an Ob/Gyn on the premises. You know how stressful weddings are. And how emotional brides can be, under ordinary circumstances."

"That I do," Ashley said, recalling the hoopla surrounding their own ceremony.

Out of the corner of her eye, Ashley could see Cal had a funny look on his face. Why, she couldn't imagine. Struggling to keep her mind on the conversation at hand, Ashley asked, "Who is her regular obstetrician, do you know?"

"Carlotta Ramirez. I would ask her to be here on standby but I know she is stretched pretty thin as it is with a husband and three kids and a solo medical practice."

Unlike me, who has way too much time on my hands at the moment, Ashley thought. "I'd be happy to do this for you."

"Thank you." Helen released her breath. Looking relieved, she hastened to add, "The Inn would pay you your hourly rate, of course."

Ashley lifted a hand. This was family. "You don't have to do that, Helen."

"I insist. If we take your time, we compensate you. Otherwise, I wouldn't feel right about it." Helen rose. "Polly and her fiancé are with Emma right now. Would you like to meet them?"

Ashley stood, too. "Absolutely."

Helen looked at Cal, wordlessly inquiring if he wanted to tag along. "I've got to get back to the hospital," he said, rolling slowly to his feet. As Helen and Cal's glances collided, something unspoken passed between them that left Ashley feeling out of the loop.

Her heart aching that the distance between them would rear its head again now, Ashley forced herself once again to pretend she had noticed nothing amiss.

Relaxing slightly, Cal turned to Ashley and bussed her cheek. "I'll meet you at home tonight, okay?" he said as he squeezed her shoulder.

Ashley nodded. She wondered, even as he was walking off down the hall, what he and his mother weren't telling her.

"SOMETHING SURE smells good," Cal said when he walked into the house shortly after seven o'clock.

Ashley looked up from the vegetables she was sautéing on the stove. Amazing how her heart could still leap when he entered a room. "Better than the chili and French fries, hmm?" she said, taking in his work appearance. She had gotten so used to seeing him in vacation attire or nothing at all, she had nearly forgotten how good he looked in a coordinating shirt and tie and dress slacks.

"Like you said." Cal wrapped his hands around her waist and brought her close for a long, thorough kiss the moment he had his brown leather jacket off. His face and lips bore the

cold of the winter air outside, and the combination of cool lips
and hot wet tongue sent a ribbon of desire spiraling through
her. His gray eyes glimmered with affection as he gazed raptly
down at her, and murmured seductively, "An interesting
choice for an interesting woman with a hankering." He bent
his head to kiss her again just as the phone rang.

Heart pounding, Ashley slipped from the warm cradle of
his arms. Much more of this and she'd forget why she had felt
it so important they spend their time talking and working out
their problems instead of making love. "Saved by the bell,"
she said breathlessly as Cal went to answer it.

He grinned in a way that let her know she wasn't off the
hook—yet. "Cal Hart," he spoke into the receiver. His smile
fading, he said with careful politeness, "Yes, she is. Just a moment, please."

He handed the phone to her. "It's Dr. Connelly from Hawaii."

Ashley's mentor in the fellowship program.

If ever they needed a reality check, this was it.

Aware her husband no longer looked as happy as he had
when he'd walked in the door and found her in the kitchen—
barefoot and, unbeknownst to him, pregnant!—Ashley took
the receiver from Cal. Already tensing, her spine ramrod
straight, she walked into the dining room to finish the conversation. When she returned, Cal was standing at the stove,
stirring the vegetables Ashley had forgotten about. He had a
stoic expression on his face that pretty much matched the ab-
rupt change in Ashley's mood. "So, what's up?" he said, looking at the stove, rather than Ashley.

Ashley moved to take over the cooking duties once again.
"Dr. Connelly wanted to know if I was going to take the Maui
clinic job."

"And...?" Cal's fingers brushed hers as he handed over the
spatula.

Ashley tried not to make too much of the implacable look in his eyes or his newly subdued mood. "I told her I hadn't made up my mind yet, but I was leaning against it."

Cal's expression didn't change. He regarded Ashley cautiously. "And her response was?"

"Unhappy," Ashley admitted, wishing she and Cal had just let the phone ring and kept right on kissing.

Cal's eyes narrowed. "Does that surprise you?"

Ashley shook her head, guilt flowing through her anew. "She pulled a lot of strings to get me nominated for the position." In her mentor's mind, in a lot of people's minds, Ashley was indebted to her for the opportunity, and she should take it and make everyone who had helped train her proud.

Cal loosened his tie and the first two buttons of his starched gray-and-white striped shirt. "What changed your mind?"

Ashley watched him pull out a beer and twist off the cap. "You. This." *The prospect of—if everything went all right this time—having your baby.* She swallowed hard around the growing ache in her throat. "I don't think I want to be so far away from you again."

Cal met her gaze, held it until the familiar mixture of sadness and resentment appeared. "I don't want that, either," he said, very softly.

The phone rang again. Cal sighed. "I wish I didn't have to answer that." But he did because it might be one of his patients or the hospital calling. He picked up the phone, listened and smiled broadly. "Hey, Carlotta. Sure you can talk to Ashley. She's right here." He handed the phone over.

While Cal sipped his beer and sorted through the mail, Ashley listened to Carlotta's dilemma. "Of course. I'd be glad to help. No, it's not a problem. I've got the morning free. The afternoon, too. Okay. I'll see you at seven." She hung up and turned to Cal. He was watching her, an expectant look on his ruggedly handsome face. "Carlotta and Mateo's nanny, Beatrice, had a family emergency. She's boarding a plane to Denver as we speak. They can't find anyone to stay with the kids tomorrow. So I said I'd help out."

"That was nice of you." Cal wrapped an arm around her shoulder and brought her back, so she was cuddled against his body.

"After all she did for me in med school, I owe her. Besides," Ashley shrugged, "how hard can it be?"

Chapter Seven

"I don't like broccoli. And neither do Lizbet or Lorenzo," ten-year-old Juan told Ashley at five o'clock the next evening.

It had never occurred to Ashley that the three Ramirez kids wouldn't like broccoli. She had always loved the nutrient-filled veggie.

Aware she was in way over her head, Ashley did her best to hide her frustration as she regarded them all gently. "Well, how about corn then? Or green beans? No? Brussel sprouts? Um...." Suppressing a beleaguered sigh, Ashley scanned the contents of the freezer section, then turned to the refrigerator. "Carrots? Celery sticks?"

She struck out on all counts.

Juan regarded her glumly. "When is Beatrice coming back?" he demanded.

"I don't know," Ashley said honestly. Like her three charges, she wished the Ramirez's nanny was there.

"I miss her!" Five-year-old Elizabetta burst into tears. Two-year-old Lorenzo joined in.

Ashley picked up Lorenzo and placed him on her hip, but her soothing had no effect.

Juan pinched his nostrils shut. "That—" he pointed to the

sweet-and-sour chicken simmering on the stove "—smells yucky, too!"

Elizabetta cried harder.

Ashley turned the controls on the burners to the off position and sat down at the kitchen table. She put the toddler on one leg, and helped his wailing sister climb onto the other. "There, there, now," she comforted both Lorenzo and Elizabetta as best she could, aware she had never failed so badly at anything in her entire life.

"I'll get it!" Juan shouted.

"Get what?" Ashley asked, unable to hear anything above the din of crying children.

"The door!" Juan shouted, already racing off.

"No, Juan, let me answer it!" Ashley said, struggling to get up.

As she moved, the kids cried even harder, and Elizabetta clung to Ashley, refusing to be put on the floor. By the time Ashley reached the foyer, Juan already had the front door wide open, and Cal was walking in, his strong male presence like a port in the storm, two big sacks from a popular fast-food restaurant in his arms. Juan looked as though he'd just been saved from a fate worst than death by the handsome surgeon. Ashley couldn't blame Juan; she felt the same way. She couldn't recall ever having a more miserable day. Not because she didn't like kids—she did. But because they seemed to sense they were in the hands of a rank amateur and were reacting accordingly. In their place, she would have wanted her parents and/or nanny, too.

Cal set the bags on the table. Pausing only long enough to brush a kiss across Ashley's brow, he reached for Elizabetta and cradled her in his big strong arms. He looked down at her tenderly and smiled. As their eyes met, Elizabetta's misery began to fade. "Do you know anybody who likes French fries?" Cal asked her gently.

Elizabetta stopped crying as abruptly as she had started. She remained still as Cal used a tissue to wipe away her tears. "Me," she sniffed. "And Lorenzo, too."

"And me, of course!" Juan hustled to get the ketchup from the refrigerator.

"I wasn't expecting you," Ashley told Cal as Elizabetta and Juan scrambled to take their seats at the kitchen table. But she was very glad he had come.

"Carlotta and Mateo are both going to be late tonight—Mateo's in surgery as we speak, and Carlotta's delivering a baby. So I told 'em I'd come over and give you a hand until one of them got home."

Cal settled Lorenzo in the high chair and gave him a potato wedge cut into toddler-size pieces to keep him busy. In short order, they had plates for all three kids with chicken nuggets, applesauce from the fridge and fries.

"It didn't occur to me you would already have started dinner," Cal said, eyeing what was on the stove with interest while Ashley poured the milk.

"The kids eat early." Or at least that was what Juan had told her. Ashley peered into the sack to see what else Cal had brought. "And for the record, it wasn't a very popular menu," she told him dryly. "So what would you like to eat? Grilled chicken salad or what's on the stove?"

"What's on the stove looks awfully good to me." Cal helped Elizabetta put more ketchup on her plate.

Ashley served them both and sat down across from Cal at the table.

It was amazing how calm the kids were in Cal's presence, and that tranquility continued throughout the evening. "You were wonderful with them," a relieved Ashley said, once all three children were in bed, asleep. She and Cal settled in front of the TV.

"So were you." He brought her into the curve of his arm and looked over at her as if she were the most beautiful woman in the world.

"Not before you got here," Ashley lamented, exhausted. Then, it had been nothing but chaos and disaster, despite her very best efforts. "Lorenzo never did take a nap." Every time she had tried to put him down, he had just sobbed until she wanted to cry, too.

Cal shrugged, experienced enough to be unconcerned. "Lorenzo was probably just upset because Beatrice wasn't here. Kids get used to their routines. And that's especially true for the little ones."

Ashley rested her palm on his thigh. His muscles felt warm and strong beneath the fine fabric of his dress pants. "How did you know what they would want to eat?"

Cal shrugged and covered her fingers with his own. "Everybody knows that…"

"Except me," Ashley sighed. Was she going to be this bad at mothering their baby? Was what had happened before somehow a harbinger of that?

Cal noted her distress. He paused and started over, this time a lot more carefully. "I baby-sat my siblings a lot when I was a kid. And I've taken care of my nephew Christopher, too, since Janey moved back here. From what I've been able to see, French fries, chicken nuggets and applesauce are always a hit with kids of any age. And if it's from a chain restaurant with a trademark clown, even better."

"So how come I didn't know that?" Was she always going to screw up when it came to family matters, whether it be marriage or children or in-laws or her parents? Was her only real success going to be in medicine?

He gave her a look that warned her not to indulge in self-pity. "You've been around kids."

"Sure, on my pediatrics rotation in med school. And—to a certain extent—in the delivery room. But I realized today I still don't know anything about caring for them in their normal environment."

"You didn't baby-sit as a kid?"

"My parents wouldn't let me. They said it wasn't a good use of my time. They wanted me home, studying. And of course I didn't have any sibs, or even any cousins, since I was the child of two only children, so…today was just…"

"What?"

Difficult, Ashley wanted to say. Very difficult. But couldn't. Not given the fact she was about to become a mother herself. Feeling jittery, Ashley got up and headed for the kitchen.

"Where are you going?" Cal said from the sofa.

"To clean up," Ashley called from the kitchen.

He followed. "There's nothing to clean up in here."

Ashley wiped down the table and counters again, anyway. Cal put his hands on her shoulders, forced her to look at him. "Are you okay?" he repeated, looking into her eyes.

No, I'm not okay. I'm pregnant and I'm scared to death I am somehow going to screw up again, Ashley was about to say. And that was when Carlotta and Mateo Ramirez both walked in.

CARLOTTA SMILED and cocked her head, listening. "It's blissfully quiet in here."

Mateo nodded. The accomplished surgeon looked as beat as his obstetrician wife. "Kids asleep?"

"Fed, bathed and down for the night," Cal said. As glad as he was to have the kids' parents home, he wished they hadn't chosen that particular moment to walk in the house. Cal had the feeling Ashley had been on the verge of telling him something important that might explain her jitteriness whenever the subject of kids came up.

Before they had married, she had been all for having a big family. That had changed the first summer of their marriage. Why exactly, he still didn't know.

"We owe you both tons," Carlotta continued as she hung up her coat.

Mateo nodded. "Carlotta and I didn't realize how much we relied on Beatrice until last night."

"How long is Beatrice going to be gone?" Cal asked, curious.

"Three weeks. So I was wondering…" Carlotta paused, drew a breath and looked Ashley straight in the eye. "I know you're supposed to be taking a much-needed rest before you begin job-hunting in earnest, but would it be possible for you to continue helping me out?"

Beside him, Cal felt Ashley tense. He did the same. He didn't want Ashley spending all her time over here. Not when they still had so much to work out, and relatively little time in which to do it.

"You mean baby-sit?" Ashley asked.

Cal applauded the lack of emotion in his wife's voice.

"No. I think we've got that part worked out," Carlotta smiled. "I've found a friend to take Lorenzo during the day for me, another to take Elizabetta after kindergarten. But I'm really going to have to be here in the late afternoon and evening to cook dinner, help with homework, and ride herd on baths and bedtime. But with a full patient load now, I can't just close the office at two-thirty or three every afternoon."

Cal began to see where this was going.

"You want me to help out at the office?" The tension left her body. Ashley grinned at the suggestion.

Carlotta nodded. "I'd love it if you could do the afternoon

office hours and take calls for me one night a week. I'll do the other two nights, and my call partners will do the rest. It would help me out enormously."

"Not to mention show me what it's like to work in a small private practice here in Holly Springs," Ashley said.

"Then you'll do it?" Carlotta asked hopefully.

Ashley nodded, smiled. "With pleasure."

CAL'S HOPES to pick up their conversation where they left off were dashed by a series of phone calls from the hospital and Ashley's fatigue. Tuesday evening all Ashley wanted to talk about was what she had done at work that day. Cal had been only too eager to listen. He loved Ashley in doctor mode and he wanted her to settle down in Holly Springs with him more than anything. On Wednesday they were supposed to have lunch before she began afternoon office hours for Carlotta, but he ended up in surgery instead. That night he was home, but she was on call, and spent most of the night at the hospital, delivering twins. Thursday afternoon was his scheduled time off, so he went home early, changed clothes and went for a run. He had just gotten back to the farmhouse when he heard a car pulling into the drive. Bottle of water in hand, Cal went to the front window and then stepped out onto the porch to greet their visitor.

"Hello, Margaret." At fifty, Ashley's mother was every bit as beautiful as her only daughter. They shared the same elegant bone structure and tall, willowy frame. Margaret's dark-brown hair was threaded lightly with gray and cut in a short, sophisticated, easy-care style now favored by many working women her age. Unlike Cal's own mother, who had a clear delineation between family time and work, Margaret had a crisp, businesslike demeanor that carried over into her personal life. *Warm and fuzzy* were not words he would have used to describe her, even under the most sentimental of occasions. And judging by the cool look in her eyes, this was not one of those.

"Cal." Margaret nodded at him, brow raising at the sweat dripping down his face.

Cal mopped the perspiration with the sleeve of his sweatshirt. "I just got back from a run."

"So I see."

Telling himself not to be offended by the lack of affection in his mother-in-law's eyes, Cal ushered her in and helped her off with her coat. "Ashley didn't tell me you were coming."

Margaret straightened the hem of her tailored jacket. "I wanted to surprise her."

Margaret was going to do that all right, Cal thought. She followed him back to the furnished areas of the downstairs. "Where is my daughter?"

Cal glanced at his watch, saw it was only four-thirty. "She's still in Holly Springs seeing a few patients for a colleague she's helping out." He expressed his regret. "She won't be home until six." Or later. That left them with a lot of time to kill.

"Is she doing this temporarily—I hope?" Margaret said.

Cal nodded stiffly, wishing that his mother-in-law would keep her opinions to herself. "So it would seem."

"May I be frank with you?"

Actually, I'd prefer you wouldn't. But since he couldn't very well tell his mother-in-law to back off, Cal simply waited.

"What in the world is going on here, Cal?" Margaret sat down on the family-room sofa and crossed her trouser-clad legs at the knee. "Is Ashley even looking for suitable employment?"

"Suitable" meaning anywhere else but here, Cal thought. "I think you should ask her that," Cal said carefully.

"I have." Margaret looked annoyed. "She's not responding to my e-mails on the subject and she hasn't returned my phone calls, either."

"I don't know what to tell you," Cal continued in the same polite tone.

"Then let me tell you something." Margaret clasped her hands around one knee and leaned forward urgently. "I am not happy with this situation. You should be encouraging Ashley either to take the job in Maui, at least for a year or two, for the experience. Or you should be pushing her to look for employment worthy of her training and education elsewhere, instead of spending a lot of time and energy on getting married all over again," she finished with a disapproving frown.

Cal went into the kitchen to put a pot of coffee on. "I take it you don't agree with that idea, either?" he asked from across the counter.

Margaret shrugged. "I admit I don't see the point. You and Ashley said your vows to each other once. What has changed in the three years since?"

Everything. Nothing. Cal only knew things still weren't right between them. He wanted the chance to start over fresh with Ashley, and this was the surest way to do it. He didn't care if her parents approved of his romantic gesture or not.

Finished, Cal strode back to the family room and sat down opposite Margaret. "First of all, Ashley doesn't know anything about my Valentine's Day present to her. And I am relying on you and Harold to keep the information to yourself. Second, I think it would mean a lot to Ashley if both you and Harold could attend."

"Her father and I are very busy right now. I don't know if it's going to be possible."

Well, then, so be it.

"We did expect better of you, since you gave us your word at the time we gave you our blessing that you would never hold Ashley back career-wise."

That again. Cal pushed the words through his teeth. "I've supported her to the best of my ability, Margaret."

"Oh, really." Margaret leaned forward angrily. "Then why is she here now, doing nearly nothing professionally? Why isn't she still pursuing the dream she's had since she was a small child?"

IT FELT GREAT to be practicing medicine again, Ashley thought, as she greeted her last patient of the day. Great to be busy for at least part of every day all week long…although she had missed seeing Cal; she'd been seeing so much of him recently.

"Hey, Dr. Hart." Polly Pruett smiled. The twenty-three-year-old pregnant bride-to-be was all round, blond softness. Her pixie face glowed with happiness as she patted her burgeoning belly. "The receptionist said you were taking all of Dr. Ramirez's patients this afternoon."

"Yes." The nurse helped Polly lie back on the table while Ashley finished reviewing Polly's chart. Then she began the exam. "Is that okay?"

"Sure." Polly relaxed on the table while Ashley palpated her abdomen.

"How have you been feeling?" Ashley asked, reaching for the gloves.

Polly grinned. "Well, my back hurts. I have to pee all the time so I can't sleep more than a few hours at a time. I'm hungry enough to eat a horse and then some. And I have the gracefulness of an elephant on a parade. But other than that, I'm doing just fine."

Ashley chuckled at the humorous description of life in the ninth month of pregnancy.

"It feels like the baby is dropping, too. Does that mean I'm about to go into labor?" Polly asked worriedly, obviously thinking about the wedding, just two weeks away now.

Ashley switched on the lamp and sat down on the stool, so she could begin the pelvic exam. "A first-time mother can drop four weeks before the due date, and even go two weeks or so after that before she delivers."

Polly frowned. "So it could be six weeks?"

"More like four, max, for you. But nothing looks imminent," Ashley decreed as she finished and ripped off her gloves.

Polly breathed a sigh of relief and pantomimed wiping the perspiration from her brow. "Whew. I'm glad you're going to be at the Wedding Inn when I get married, anyway. That will make me feel better."

Ashley and the nurse both lent a hand and helped Polly sit up. "Well, we aim to please, both at the Inn and here in the office."

Polly made a face. "Now if we can just hold off that snowstorm…"

Ashley looked up from the notations she was making on Polly's chart. "What snowstorm?"

Polly went back to rubbing her belly. "The one in the mountains of Tennessee that is headed our way."

Ashley loved snow—when she didn't have to go anywhere. It was a pain when the roads were bad and you still had to show up for work. "When is it supposed to hit?" she asked, aware she hadn't driven on the wet stuff in almost three years.

"Tomorrow night, or possibly the following morning, depending on how fast the front moves," the nurse said.

Polly nodded. "Didn't you see all the people running in and out of the grocery and hardware stores today?"

Ashley tilted her head to the side. "I noticed a lot of cars. But I didn't think much about it."

"Well, you should," Polly said seriously. "'Cause you could get snowed in for days if we get as much precipitation as they are predicting. So you better make sure you have all the necessities on hand…"

The only necessity for Ashley was Cal, whom she had seen precious little of the last four days. It seemed as if when he wasn't on call, she was. But tonight, they were both due to have dinner together. And she couldn't wait.

Several phone calls and a stop at the med-center maternity ward later—where Ashley diagnosed the patient in question with Braxton-Hicks contractions and sent her home—Ashley was finally en route back to the farm. Unfortunately, Cal's car wasn't the only one in the driveway. Parked next to his was a rental car.

DINNER WITH ASHLEY'S MOTHER was a cordial if somewhat tense affair. All three of them cooked and then cleaned up together. Then Cal went upstairs to make phone calls to check on his post-op patients while the two women settled down for some private time in front of the fire.

"Obviously, I came all the way out here for a reason," Margaret said in a crisp, businesslike tone.

"To see me?" Ashley quipped.

"I made some phone calls." Margaret reached into the leather carryall that went everywhere with her and pulled out a business card. "Shelley Denova is a headhunter who specializes in getting academic postings for physicians. There is a position coming open at Yale Medical School that hasn't even been advertised yet."

Ashley tensed as her mother applied a pressure to succeed that was all too familiar. The one thing Ashley hadn't missed in Hawaii were the face-to-face confrontations with her folks, and the inquisitions about why Ashley wasn't doing better. It had never seemed to matter what Ashley did. When she had been named salutatorian of her high-school class, they had been disappointed she was not the valedictorian. When she had selected Wake Forest—rather than Harvard—to attend at the undergrad level, they had been upset; they had always envisioned her as "Ivy League" and could not understand why Ashley refused even to apply to the prestigious university. And she didn't even want to think about their reaction when she had decided to go to medical school in Winston-Salem so she could be near Cal, who was doing his five-year surgical residency there. But they had finally gotten their way when they had pushed her to go to Hawaii to finish her fellowship. Obviously, both her parents expected her to continue to put her career ahead of her family. And Ashley wasn't sure she wanted to do that. Especially since doing that for the past two years had brought her nothing but heartache and a loneliness so deep she didn't think she was over it yet. "Yale is in Connecticut, Mother."

Margaret pooh-poohed Ashley's concerns with a wave of her hand. "It's a two-hour plane ride from here to there. You could work there during the week and see Cal every weekend."

Assuming she got the position; Ashley wasn't sure she would. Not that this was the point, in any case. Ashley regarded her mother in frustration. "That's not the same as living together, Mother."

Her mother couldn't have cared less about the impact such a separation would have on Ashley and Cal's marriage. She looked at Ashley sternly. "You will not be happy practicing medicine here."

Ashley got up to poke at the fire. "You don't know that. I'm not even sure I want to practice medicine full-time!"

Margaret laid a hand across her chest, as if she were about to have heart failure. Her face turned pale. "Don't even joke about that, Ashley!"

Who was joking? Ashley wondered, the hurt and resentment inside her building. If she was going to have a baby she wasn't sure she wanted to work full-time. At least not right away! Not that she could discuss this with anyone just yet, either.

"Now, I want you to pull together your résumé and list of references and call Shelley first thing tomorrow morning. I've written her cell and home numbers down on the back of her card. She's expecting to hear from you. And do not delay. These entry-level positions at prestigious institutions go quickly. You have no time to waste."

Ashley didn't care what her mother thought—this was not a done deal. "And suppose I don't want to apply?" Ashley said angrily, surprised to find her emotions overriding her common sense. Because she, better than anyone, knew you did not talk to Margaret Porter this way. Not unless you wanted a serious dose of blunt talk dished right back.

Margaret covered her eyes with her hand for a long moment. Finally, she drew a deep breath and looked up. "Are you trying to ruin your marriage?"

Ashley slammed the poker back in the fireplace stand so carelessly the whole thing fell over. Embarrassed, she knelt to pick up the wrought-iron fireplace tools. As she stuffed them back in, two more fell out and clattered to the stone surround. "I fail to see how—"

Margaret pointed a lecturing finger at her. "Cal Hart did not fall in love with a slacker, Ashley Porter Hart. You persist along these lines and he is not going to love you."

Bitterness rose in Ashley's throat, choking her. "Are we talking about Cal now?" Ashley countered miserably. "Or you and Daddy, Mother?"

Margaret continued as if Ashley hadn't even spoken. "In successful marriages, the partners grow together." She paused to give Ashley a long reproach-filled look. "In unions where one spouse flourishes and the other does not, boredom and resentment inevitably set in, and the marriage falls apart." Another pause, this one longer and weightier than the last. "Cal is succeeding admirably, Ashley. He's treating pro sports players and college athletes. And you need to stay on track with your career, too."

CAL WAS JUST getting off the phone with the medical center when he heard the front door open and close. Then a car started in the drive.

He headed downstairs, reaching the foyer just as a shivering Ashley came back inside. He had only to look at her face to know she was upset. "What happened?" he asked warily.

Ashley shook her head, her eyes moist. She pushed both her hands through her hair. "The usual. She pushed. And then pushed some more. Only this time I *didn't* just bend to her wishes."

Cal was glad to hear that. He had always felt Margaret and Harold put way too many demands on their only daughter. He wrapped an arm around her shoulders, comforting her as best he could. "I'm sorry. Is she coming back tomorrow?"

"No." Ashley stalked back to the family room. Her hands trembled as she picked up the coffee cups and dessert plates. "She has a nine o'clock meeting at the university tomorrow, so she is taking the six o'clock flight out of Raleigh in the morning."

Noting a fireplace tool had fallen over on its side, Cal righted it and placed it back in the stand. "She could have stayed here overnight."

Ashley did her best to avoid Cal's gaze as she rinsed the dishes and slid them into the dishwasher. "She preferred to be at the hotel at the airport. She felt that would be easier."

Cal saw the business card on the coffee table in the family room. He picked it up. His heart sank as he read the writing on the back of it. "Are you going to call this person?" he said, afraid to know, and more afraid not to.

Ashley shut her eyes and rubbed at her temples as if she had the beginning of a migraine. "I don't know."

Cal thought about the promise he had made, never to stand in the way of Ashley and her dreams. Though it choked him, he forced himself to do the right thing and live up to his word. He drew a deep breath, ensuring his voice was calm, before he replied, "Maybe you should."

Slowly, Ashley opened her eyes. She looked even angrier. More resentful. "Is that what you want?" Ashley asked sharply. "For me to hook up with some high-powered headhunter with connections all over the East Coast so I can get some extremely sought-after job?"

The way she was looking at him then, Cal knew he was damned if he did and damned if he didn't. So he told the truth. "I want you to be happy, Ashley. Right now you don't look happy. So—" he struggled against the selfish need welling up inside him as he closed the distance between them "—if that is what it takes…"

Ashley held up her hands, holding him off. She wheeled away from him and began to pace the length of the two rooms. "I'm just so confused! I'm thirty years old and I feel like half my life is gone and I don't know how to have fun or relax or do anything but work, work, work! And that used to be okay—probably because I was always too busy even to let myself think. But suddenly, it seems like it's not enough anymore, not enough to make me happy, anyway."

"And you should be happy," Cal agreed. He caught her wrist as she passed and anchored her implacably at his side.

Looking more distressed than ever, she flattened her hands against his chest. "But if I don't strive and push forward, harder than ever, I'm going to let everyone else down." Ashley scowled, her frustration with the situation apparent. "My mentor. My mother. My father. Even you." She stomped away from him, her temper igniting into hot flames of emotion that were glorious to behold.

"Hey—" Cal arrowed his thumb at his chest "—don't lump me in with the rest of those clowns. I'm delighted to see you so confused. It makes you as human as the rest of us."

Ashley narrowed her china-blue eyes at him and restlessly tapped one foot. "You'd love me no matter what?" she challenged with a withering look.

Cal nodded emphatically, ignoring the way she had her fists balled and planted on her hips. "I'd love you no matter what."

She tossed her mane of glossy dark hair and snorted in a most unladylike fashion. "Liar."

Cal blinked, sure he couldn't have heard right. "What?"

She stomped closer, her breasts rising and falling with every infuriated breath she took. "Liar," she repeated, not stopping until they were squared off toe-to-toe and nose-to-nose. She angled her chin up at him, her soft lips taking on a defiant curve. "You cannot possibly feel that way!" she told him stormily. She leveled an accusing finger at his chest. "You have to have some opinion of what you want me to do with my life right now, but you won't tell me what it is!"

Cal caught her hand and held it against his chest. "Maybe because which job you take isn't my decision to make!" he shot back, just as irritably.

She regarded him with a hauteur as cold as ice. "So you're just going to let me guess what's going to make you happy?"

Cal frowned, his exasperation beginning to get the better of him once again. Reluctantly, he let her go and watched her step back a pace. "I can't tell you what to do here, Ashley," he told her wearily. He ran a hand across his jaw and realized that although he had shaved that morning, he needed to shave again.

"Why not?" she demanded.

Cal struggled to remain calm as their glances held. "Because if I did, it would make everything bad and selfish that anyone's ever thought about me absolutely true."

Chapter Eight

ASHLEY STARED at Cal, barely able to believe what she was hearing. "Who thinks bad things about you? Cal, you are the most compassionate, wonderful, giving man I have ever met!"

A haunted look appeared in Cal's gray eyes. "Maybe that's who I am now," Cal acknowledged, with a derisive shrug of his broad shoulders. He rubbed a hand across the front of the cashmere sweater he had put on for dinner with her mother. "But it's hard to erase the past."

Ashley took a deep breath to steady herself. He was standing so close to her she could feel the heat emanating from his tall, strong body. "Where is this coming from?" she probed gently.

Cal remained silent, as if he could think of nothing to say that wouldn't make him look even worse in his wife's eyes. She gave him a look that reminded him this was why she was here with him now, why they'd declared a temporary moratorium on sex. So they could start sharing all the stuff they'd been deliberately withholding from each other and really get to know each other, flaws and all.

"It started after my dad died," Cal said finally. He walked over to examine a basil plant on the windowsill that looked to be suffering from lack of care. He plucked off a few brown leaves, added a small amount of water. "At least I think that's when it did."

Ashley watched him throw the leaves into the kitchen trash can. "Keep going."

"You have to understand." Noting the can was nearly full, Cal lifted out the bag and tied it shut. He carried it outside to the cans and put it in. Ashley followed. "It was a very rough time." Cal grabbed a couple of logs for the fireplace while they were out there. Ashley held the door for him as they walked back inside. "We were all so stunned by what had happened," Cal continued as he took the logs over and put them in the basket next to the mantel. "There was no warning." Cal rose, dusted off his hands. "One day my dad left on a business trip. The next day we got a phone call, saying the plane he was on had gone down in the mountains, and there were no survivors."

Ashley could only imagine how terrible that had been.

"My mom, who had always been so strong, was a complete wreck. She had six kids, ranging in age from six to sixteen. The love of her life had just died and she was devastated."

As had been her children, Ashley noted.

"We all went into survival mode." Cal walked back into the kitchen to wash his hands, Ashley at his side. "Mac became the head of the household because he was the oldest son. My mother focused on sorting out my father's affairs, which were a mess, because my dad died without a will." Cal shook his head, remembering. "It took months to get everything straightened out," he related sadly. "And during that time, my mother kept telling us everything was going to be fine, we just had to gather up our courage and go on. And that's when the trouble began."

"Why?"

The brooding look was back in his eyes, stronger than ever.

Cal sighed and rubbed at the tense muscles in the back of his neck. "Because while Mac struggled to help my mom with the financial details, I tried to follow my mother's example of keeping a stiff upper lip and make my four younger siblings toughen up enough to carry on, too." A mixture of regret and self-admonition filled his low tone. "There weren't going to be any tears when I was around," he mocked himself bitterly. "And oh, by the way, since our life was supposedly worry-free financially, I intended to go on the week-long eighth-grade spring break trip to Washington, D.C." Cal sighed, drew in a long, defeated breath. "My mother didn't want me to go. I thought it was because it involved a plane ride from Minneapolis to D.C. and, at that point, she didn't want any of us on planes. But I felt unfairly hemmed in and kept pushing and pushing to do what I wanted."

Ashley felt a soul-deep ache at the pain in Cal's voice. "Tell me more…" she said softly.

Cal shook his head, recalling, his mood as bleak as the overcast winter evening outside. "And all the while I was taking out my own hurt and fear and frustration on my younger sibs." His eyes collided with Ashley's once again. "Until one day, I barely recognized myself," he told her sorrowfully. "And neither did my family.

"And that was when my mother stepped in," Cal continued in a low voice, "I had made poor little six-year-old Joey cry and my mother was furious. She took me aside and demanded to know where my heart was! How had I gotten so selfish? And above all, *why* couldn't I please understand that we just didn't have the money to send me on the eighth-grade trip?"

Ashley's brow furrowed. "You knew that and you still asked?" This didn't sound like the Cal she knew at all. He was selfless to the bone.

Cal turned his glance heavenward, shook his head in mounting remorse. "That was the hell of it—I *didn't* know. In the wake of my dad's death, my mother hadn't bothered to reveal to any of us, save Mac, how severe our financial troubles were. And that made me even more furious—because if I had been given all the information, I would *never* have asked to go on that trip or been such a jerk about it."

Ashley's heart went out to him as she touched his wrist. She looked up at him and commiserated gently, "I can see where you would be hurt and angry, being excluded that way." She certainly would have been!

Cal, however, didn't look as if he felt his behavior was all that justified, despite his lingering frustration with the way his family situation had unraveled back then. "And I was especially mad at Mac," Cal continued ruefully. "I knew my mother had been trying to protect me, but he had no excuse."

So Helen got a pass, as far as Cal was concerned, Ashley realized.

Cal's mouth tightened into a grim line. "But Mac had to know that, at fourteen, I was man enough to handle that information." Resentment clouded his eyes. "Mac said he was bound by the promise he had made to my mother to shield us from worry. But I felt he owed me, too, that he should've done what was right by the family, taken me aside and told me the truth about our family's precarious financial situation."

Ashley saw his point. Deep down, she knew Cal could have handled the news—if he'd been given the opportunity.

"I had a hard time forgiving him for that, though I eventually did it. But I also told him never to cut me out of the loop again."

Only Mac hadn't kept his word, Ashley realized with dismay. Because Helen Hart's secret was not the only one Cal's brother had been forced to keep.

"Anyway," Cal continued soberly, unaware of Ashley's sinking feeling of dread, "the way I was that year made me realize that I could easily be the most selfish SOB around if I let myself. I decided not to let myself."

"I understand not liking who've you become or started to become," Ashley retorted carefully. "I've had my moments, too." She knew all about deeply held regrets—the guilt and second-guessing of events, for she had suffered the same. Not like Cal, in her childhood, but in their marriage.

"But I don't get what all that has to do with me," Ashley continued, after a moment.

"You asked me what I wanted you to do about your job," he reminded her heavily. "You want to know the truth?"

Did she? Reassuring herself that she could handle whatever it was he was about to say, Ashley swallowed around the sudden parched feeling in her throat. "Yes."

He drummed his fingers on the gleaming stainless-steel stovetop. "I'll tell you," he offered in a way that made her heart skip first one beat, then another. "But you're not going to like it."

Ashley flushed under the heat of his regard. She backed up against the counter on rubbery legs, her hands braced on either side of her. She tilted her head at him in silent challenge. "How do you know?"

Cal compressed his lips together ruefully. "Because it's practically Neanderthal it's so damn selfish," he said, eyeing her with a depth of male speculation she found very disturbing. He jammed his hands on his hips and narrowed his eyes. "I don't want you working anywhere that we can't live together in the same house and sleep together every night. I don't want to be second fiddle to your career. And I don't want you being secondary to mine, either." He paused, looking her up and down, from the top of her casually upswept hair to her toes. "I want us—our marriage, our family—to come first. Now and always, even if that means that we both sacrifice some future career success for the sake of our family!"

Doing her best to keep a level head, Ashley folded her arms in front of her. She could feel the blood rushing to her cheeks even as she struggled to get hold of her soaring emotions. "Have you always felt this way—or is it just recently?" she demanded, not sure if she felt aggravated or relieved by his matter-of-fact confession.

Cal leveled his assessing gaze on hers and kept it there. "Always, I am ashamed to say."

Ashley blinked, not sure if she wanted to hug him or slug him as she stammered, "But you never—"

Cal held up a hand. "Because it would have been wrong to hold you back," he interrupted gruffly.

Now he was sounding like her parents. Aware she wouldn't be able to bear it if she ended up being a failure in his eyes, too, she said, "You want to see me succeed. Just like my parents do."

"Yes," Cal admitted, closing the distance between them and taking her into his arms. Holding her against the warmth of his tall, strong body, he gently stroked her cheek. "But I also want you in my life. I want you here with me...too," he told her softly.

Ashley had no doubt he was speaking from his heart. She shook her head, regretting all the time they had spent apart. "I wish you had told me this," she whispered unhappily.

He tightened his hold on her possessively. "Why?"

"Because," Ashley pushed her hands against his chest in escalating frustration, aware she had already endured more disappointment in one lifetime than she had ever expected to endure, "I've wished we could put us first, too! Damn it, Cal, I missed you so much the entire time I was in Hawaii." And had they just been honest with each other, he would have known it!

He grinned victoriously, looking as if he'd had an enormous weight moved from his shoulders. "And here I thought I was the only one who had to force myself to be positive about the separation."

Joy flowed through her in enervating waves, as she realized they had been on the same page after all! Most of the time, anyway. She wreathed her arms about his neck, hitched in a quick, bolstering breath. "But we don't have to be separated anymore." She studied him hopefully. "Do we?"

He looked down at her as if he loved every inch of her. Misunderstandings and all. "Not if I can help it," he promised in a low, gruff voice.

He lowered his head. The next thing Ashley knew they were kissing. Passionately. Tenderly. Hungrily. She curled her fingers into his hair and surged against him, loving the taste and touch and wonder of him. She could feel his arousal, pressing hard against her, as surely as her own blossoming need. And yet, underneath her love for him was her ever-present fear that letting her guard down all the way was risking his discovery of *her* past mistakes. Errors in judgment that a family-oriented man like Cal might find very hard, if not downright impossible, to forgive. And she couldn't bear it if he looked at her with the same disappointment and disillusion her parents always did.

Trembling, Ashley ended the kiss and pulled away. Their marriage was healing—not dissolving—and she was *not* going to lose Cal, she reassured herself. He was not going to find out about the terrible secret she had kept from the very first days of their marriage; he was not going to discover the lengths she had gone to protect him.

Mistaking the reason for her sudden withdrawal from their

steamy embrace, Cal sighed. Apology radiated in his dark-gray eyes.

He obviously wanted to make love as much as she did.

He chuckled cheerfully and tossed her a playful glance that raised her pulse another notch. "We better think of something else for us to do fast, if we don't want to end up doing what we've always ended up doing."

Making wild, passionate love. "Well." Ashley thought out loud, her confidence building. "We could try to have fun." She grinned impishly as she thought about the possibilities of the Thursday evening ahead, the joy of just having time to spend with him again. "Some *other* way," she added, hoping for a little inspiration. Because heaven knew all she could think about were the broad shoulders straining against his cashmere sweater, and how it felt to be enveloped in their seductive warmth.

Cal seemed to be struggling with the same feelings, even as his eyes lit with mischief. "And I know just the thing."

"HIDE-AND-SEEK!" Ashley regarded Cal in amazement. "You've got to be kidding."

He wasn't.

Ashley threw up her hands. "That's the most ridiculous thing I've ever heard," she declared.

One hand around her waist, he tugged her close and nibbled playfully on her ear. "Afraid you're going to lose?"

"Hardly," Ashley murmured back, trying not to notice how good it felt—how good it always felt—to be in his arms this way.

He lifted his brow. The mischief sparkling in his eyes brought out an answering devilry in her. "Well, you *should* be afraid to lose, sweetheart. You don't know this house half as well as I do."

She tossed her head, already thinking ahead to ways to beat

the pants off him. "Even so," she drawled in the most bored tone she could manage, egging him on in the same way he was deliberately baiting her, "it wouldn't be much of a challenge."

He chuckled in anticipation of the competition. "And you always have to be challenged."

Ha! Ashley slapped her hands on her hips and countered indignantly, "Like you don't!"

"True." Cal pulled the kitchen timer out of a drawer and tossed it to her. "Best two out of three."

Her breath hitched in her chest. "And the prize?" Ashley asked.

Cal shrugged and flashed her an impertinent grin. "Whatever the winner wants."

Ashley knew what she wanted—Cal, and their marriage the way it had been at the very first, before their careers had gotten in the way. "Agreed, as long as it doesn't involve seeing me naked," Ashley cautioned.

He had to think about that. But only for a minute. "All right."

She imagined he was thinking of myriad ways to get around that. "I don't trust that grin."

"As well you shouldn't," he told her significantly, the recklessness in him spurring the wildness in her. "I'll step outside the front door. You've got three minutes to hide. And I've got the same amount of time to find you."

"Okay."

Not surprisingly, he won the first round.

She won the second.

The third time they both ended up in the coat closet tucked under the stairs. In just under three minutes, darn it. Which meant.... "Okay," Ashley said breathlessly, as he shut them in there together. "You win, bucko. So what do you want?"

"This," Cal said.

One long, hot kiss that went on and on, until her lips were parting under the onslaught, and she was meeting him touch for touch, stroke for stroke. Until she was moaning softly in her throat and clinging to him helplessly. Until she knew—as did he—that old hurts were healing and their marriage really was on the road to recovery.

Chapter Nine

Ashley rushed down the back stairs at seven the next morning, clad in her pink and white flannel robe and slippers. "Cal, have you seen my black dress?"

Cal tore his gaze from her cleavage visible in the V of the shawl collar. No doubt about it, Ashley's body was a hell of a lot more voluptuous than it had been five pounds ago. Not that he'd had opportunity to investigate the changes for himself, as she had refused to let him her see her in any form of undress since they'd reunited a week ago.

"Cal!" Ashley said again, even more impatiently this time.

Cal struggled to recall what the question had been. With little result. "Um…"

Ashley came closer, until she was standing right next to him. She smelled of soap and shampoo and the orange blossom perfume she wore. And unless he was wrong, she didn't have much of anything on under that calf-length robe, definitely not a bra.

"It's the kind of stretchy one," Ashley continued jogging his memory deliberately. "I wore it the first night back when we went over to your Mom's to see the family. I can't find it anywhere."

And with good reason, Cal thought, since it was currently

with the dressmaker, who was making the dress Ashley would wear when they renewed their wedding vows. Stalling for time, he gave the scrambled eggs another stir. "Did you check the wash?"

Noting breakfast was almost ready, Ashley went to the fridge and brought out the milk, butter and jam. Her arms full, she shut the door with her hip. Watching her lower half in action made him want to groan. He was still aroused from their extended kissing session the evening before. But a promise was a promise, and he had sworn he would demonstrate to her there was a lot more to their relationship than simply sex.

"I didn't put it in the wash." Ashley popped slices of whole grain bread into the four-slice toaster they'd gotten years ago, as a wedding gift.

Cal shrugged, as he cut a grapefruit in half and put the halves on plates. "Well then it probably wouldn't be there."

Scowling, Ashley sat down at the table while he dished up the eggs and sat down opposite her. "I wanted to wear it today."

"Well…" Cal tried to think of a way to get her off the subject, as he pointed to the small TV mounted under one of the cabinets. It was tuned to a morning news show, and the local weather map was on the screen. "You should probably wear slacks anyway. If the snow that they've predicted hits later this afternoon, you're not going to be want to be caught in a dress, anyway."

Not to be dissuaded, Ashley continued, "And I can't find my favorite black bra and black satin panties either."

Cal had done laundry once since she'd been back. So had she. "Maybe they're with the dress?" he said, struck by how pretty she looked this morning—her golden skin glowing with health, her cheeks flushed a becoming peach.

Ashley added a tiny bit of butter and a generous amount of blackberry jam to her toast. "I can't believe this!"

Neither could Cal. Had he realized she was likely to want her dress and that particular set of undies, he would have picked those items up by now. "They're probably somewhere. You're just not seeing them. Or you put them somewhere and you don't remember," he fibbed.

Leaning back in her chair, Ashley regarded him humorously. "Are you hinting I'm losing my mind?"

"No." But he was going to lose his soon, if he didn't get to make love with her again in the very near future.

Wordlessly, Cal offered her coffee. She declined with a shake of her head and continued to sip her milk.

"I am, however, saying you have had an awful lot on your mind lately, what with helping out Carlotta this week, fielding visits with both our families and trying to figure out where you're going to look for a job."

The laughter left Ashley's china-blue eyes as suddenly as it had appeared. "That at least I know," she told him quietly. "I'm looking for a position right here in central North Carolina and I don't care if it's a high-powered job or something distinctly low-key. I just want to take care of pregnant women and their babies. And that, Cal, is why I wanted my black dress. I wanted to go see the med-center administrator and talk to him about the possibility of me joining the staff at the hospital right here in Holly Springs."

Cal struggled not to let his own selfish needs take control. "That would be terrific," he told her just as seriously. Forcing himself to be as supportive of her professional goals as she deserved, he continued, "But are you sure you don't want to follow up on the lead your mother gave you for an academic posting?"

Years from now, he didn't want her looking back with regret, or blaming him for any dreams not realized. Because that would be just as detrimental to their relationship as his refusing to support her now.

"I'm certain." Ashley leaned across the table to take his hand and squeeze it affectionately. "I may not have had my priorities straight before this, but I do now," she told him, looking deep into his eyes. "And you, Cal, and the—"

"And what?" he said when she stopped in mid-sentence. He studied the stricken expression on her face.

"And our life together," Ashley finished, flushing self-consciously as she squeezed his hand again and smiled, "come first."

ASHLEY COULDN'T BELIEVE she had almost spilled the beans like that. Part of it was due to the intimacy she was feeling with Cal, since their mutual confessions last night. Knowing he had missed her as much as she had missed him had given her hope that, with a little more time and continued effort, they could make their marriage everything they had once wanted it to be.

And to that end, black dress or no, she had things she wanted to accomplish that morning. Starting with a talk with the hospital administrator in charge of physician recruitment.

Unfortunately, the situation wasn't as positive as Ashley had hoped it would be.

"We're all set with the number of OB's we need right now," Frank Hodges told her. "But I'll talk to the board anyway, see if there isn't something we can do, because we'd love to have someone with your background and training on our staff. In the meantime, I'll make some calls for you, find out which hospitals in the area need an obstetrician," he said. "I'll get back to you on that as well."

"Thank you. I'd appreciate it," Ashley said.

"Bummer," Carlotta said, when Ashley filled her in over lunch in Carlotta's private office. "I was hoping they'd have room for you so I could ask you to join my practice."

That would have been easy. Nice, too, because she and Carlotta worked together so well. "Something will come up," Ashley said confidently. She would see to it. Even if the position she ended up with did not please her parents.

"How are you feeling?" Carlotta asked, as the two of them worked on their turkey sandwiches.

"Pretty good, actually."

"How's the morning sickness?"

Ashley made a seesawing motion with her hand. "Comes and goes. Cherry Life Savers seem to help."

Carlotta grinned, commiserating with a shake of her head. "For me it was lemon-flavored water. If I could take a sip or two of that, I was usually okay."

"How are things on the home front?" Ashley asked. The usually immaculately put-together Carlotta had a jelly stain on her slacks, and instead of the navy flats she should have been wearing with her outfit, she had on black. "Any word on when Nanny Beatrice is coming back?"

"Another ten days. Minimum." Carlotta sighed. A troubled look crossed her face. "Mateo and I are trying our best, but according to the kids, we're just not cutting it. It's almost like she's the parent and we're the stand-ins."

"Surely—"

"No. It's true." Carlotta speared a baby spinach leaf and twirled it around and around on her fork. "And it makes sense, if you think about it." She glanced over at Ashley, sadness reflected in her dark eyes. "Beatrice cared for Juan from the time he was born. Of course she was just a sitter then; he stayed with her while I was in undergrad classes. It wasn't until Elizabetta was born that Beatrice actually moved in with us. And she was a member of the family by the time Lorenzo came along. The simple truth is that our medical practices are so demanding the kids have spent more time with Beatrice than they have with either of us."

Ashley could easily imagine the same thing happening to her and Cal. "Do you regret that?"

"I don't know." Carlotta gazed at the picture of her kids on her desk. "I'm beginning to think I have missed out on more than I ever knew."

CARLOTTA'S WORDS stayed with Ashley the rest of the day, as she saw patients at the office, and even when she stopped at the grocery on the way home along with everyone else in town to stock up on essentials before the snowstorm hit.

The only problem was there was no milk on the shelves. None. When she asked one of the teenage stock clerks if they could bring out more from the back, he just laughed. "We haven't had any since noon and we're not going to get any more until after the snowstorm."

Ashley supposed there were other ways to get the calcium requirement the baby needed. "When exactly is the storm supposed to get here?" Ashley asked. "Have you heard?"

He pointed to the storefront windows. "Lady, it's here now."

Ashley looked. Sure enough, there was snow coming down in big, fat wet flakes. She wished she had paid more attention to the weather report that morning, and probably would have, had she not been looking high and low for her black knit dress. "How much is predicted?"

"Radio said a little while ago eight, maybe ten inches."

Yeow. Which meant they could get snowed in out at the farm.

Ashley wheeled her basket down the aisles, putting cottage

cheese, yogurt, evaporated—and powdered—milk into her cart. The bread was all gone, too, so she picked up biscuits from the freezer section, and corn-bread mix, plus several packages of meat, fresh and frozen vegetables, and cereal. The checkout lines were packed, so she ended up standing in line longer than it had taken her to gather her groceries, but finally she was headed out to the lot.

The pavement was slick, so she navigated carefully. As soon as her groceries were in the trunk of the Mustang, Ashley started the car and cleaned the thin layer of snow off the windows. She was shivering by the time she got back into the car. Aware she couldn't get home a moment too soon, Ashley started the drive back to the farm.

The first four blocks went okay. But as she neared the edge of town the roads suddenly got a lot more dicey.

"This isn't the first time I've ever driven in snow," Ashley reminded herself, hands gripping the steering wheel. She had grown up, dealing with winter weather. But she hadn't been pregnant then, Ashley thought worriedly. And she didn't like the way this vintage sports car was handling on the slick city streets.

She was about to turn back, stay in town for the night, or at the very least wait for Cal to drive them home in his SUV, when a teenager came barreling around the corner, going way too fast for either his experience or the weather. Ashley had time to gasp, and steer the wheel to the right, to avoid a head-on collision. And then he was spinning past her, continuing on down the street, completely out of control, while the Mustang jumped the curb and headed straight into someone's front yard.

"ASHLEY? Are you okay?" Mac Hart asked.

Ashley turned to see her brother-in-law coming toward her.

He was wearing his Holly Springs sheriff's uniform. His patrol vehicle was parked at the curb.

"I'm fine." Aware this wasn't the first time Cal's older brother had come to her rescue, Ashley climbed out of the Mustang on shaking legs, aware the snow was coming down even harder now. "I was trying to avoid a collision with another car and ended up jumping the curb." A move that while not exactly laudable had been a lot better than the alternative.

"Yeah. One of the neighbors saw it and called it in. I was in the vicinity, so..."

Ashley drew in a quick, jerky breath, glad Mac had only been a minute or two away when it happened. "That teenager—"

"Just totaled his car. He's about two blocks up. Another officer is assisting him. I don't know how the fool didn't get hurt," Mac lamented with a disgruntled frown. He bent to look into her face. "You sure you're okay?" he asked her quietly.

Ashley had already done a medical assessment, and except for a slightly accelerated pulse, she had come out of the incident unscathed. "Yes. I was only going about fifteen or twenty miles an hour when I hit the grass." She knew she was pale— a look in the rearview mirror had told her that—and shaky. But those were normal reactions to any near accident. "It just scared me to have such a close call." Ashley shuddered, recalling. "I thought he was going to hit me." She'd thought that she would lose her and Cal's baby. She swallowed hard around the growing knot of emotion in her throat. "But he didn't. And except for the bump as I went over the curb I didn't even get knocked around at all." Her safety belt had held her in place. Although now that she thought about it, a shoulder harness would do a much better job of protecting her and the baby...but those hadn't been invented when the '64 Mustang had been made.

Mac gave her a hard, assessing look. "You want me to take you to the hospital?"

Ashley turned her collar up, and moved so her face was no longer directly in the blowing snow, which seemed to be coming down harder and thicker with every second that passed. She saw a few people beginning to gather in yards, a distance away, watching. "No. That would be a fool's errand. I'm serious, Mac. If I thought there was any reason for me to go to the ER, I would." *In a flash.* "But there isn't. It'd be like going to the doctor for a single hiccup." And she wasn't about to do that.

He was still watching her carefully. "If you say so."

"I do."

He clamped an authoritative hand on her shoulder. "I'm taking you home anyway."

Ashley turned and looked at the Mustang. "I can't just leave my car sitting in someone's front yard." She considered herself fortunate she hadn't taken out any of their trees or landscaping. They probably did, too, although they didn't appear to be home....

"I'll get it out for you," Mac continued to propel her in the direction he wanted her to go.

"My groceries—"

"We'll get those," Mac promised her kindly, as gallant as ever. "But first, I'm putting you in the patrol car."

Mac was nothing if not efficient. Fifteen minutes later, Ashley's Mustang was safely parked in a church lot down the street, and they were on the way out to the farm.

"Thanks for doing this," Ashley said, relieved not to be behind the wheel herself at this moment.

"No problem."

"I needed to talk to you anyway."

Mac lifted a brow, but kept his eyes on the road.

Anxiety welled inside Ashley. She turned her eyes to the side of the road. An inch of snow had already fallen, and it was coming down fast. "I never told Cal about what happened that day you took me to the hospital."

Expression grim, Mac adjusted the windshield wipers to a higher speed. He shot her a quick glance. "So he doesn't know you were ever—"

Pregnant, Ashley thought. "No." Another chill went through her. She folded her arms in front of her. "And I don't want him to know."

Mac adjusted the heat, so more of it was flowing directly onto Ashley. "Do you think that's wise?"

Good question, and one she had asked herself maybe half a million times. "I probably should have told him at the time, but you know why I didn't." Because she hadn't known how to tell him he had lost what he had never even known he had. "And now it's too late." Ashley's voice caught, tears pressing behind her eyes. "He'd never understand."

When they stopped at the next stop sign, Mac turned and regarded Ashley with concern. "He has a right to know, Ashley."

As Mac continued driving, guilt flooded her heart that she could ever have done something so short-sighted and foolish in the first place. "I would tell him, Mac, if I thought he could forgive me for keeping something like that from him, but—" Ashley's voice trembled and she had to force herself to go on "—I know now that he wouldn't be able to, and I don't want to risk my marriage for something that can never be changed anyway." Because as much as she wanted to undo the past, she just couldn't.

Mac looked as if he still disagreed with her, but he did not argue the point further.

"What's brought this all up?" he asked compassionately.

Ashley took a deep breath. Although she knew she could confide in Mac and trust him to keep whatever she chose to tell him secret, there was no way she was letting him know what Cal still didn't.

Not this time anyway.

"Cal and I are working on our marriage," she said simply. "I don't want anything to interfere with that." Nothing from the present, and certainly nothing from the past.

"I KNEW IT! YOU'RE NOT FINE!" Cal rushed into the family room, where Ashley was reclining on the sofa before the fire. He had thrown a coat on over his scrubs. His med-center badge was still clipped to his shirt.

Ashley tried not to make too much of the fact he had left the hospital before changing into his street clothes, something he never did. She flushed self-consciously, aware she had been "resting" pretty much ever since she got home. Not because it was medically indicated—but because she wanted their baby to know she would do whatever it took to ensure he or she came into the world, healthy, happy and safe. This time there were going to be no regrets, no "what if's" or "if only's." No looking back and wondering...

She put the decorating magazine she'd been reading before falling asleep on the sofa aside. "I gather from that wild look in your eyes that you heard about my mishap with the Mustang?"

Cal grinned wryly in response to her comically exaggerated description, but the serious light remained in his eyes. He took off his coat and sank down beside her on the sofa, next to her raised knees. "Mac came by the med center and told me in person." Cal paled slightly as he continued relating, "He didn't want me seeing the Mustang parked there when I was driving home, 'cause he'd figured I would wonder why it was there when you weren't and get all worried. And dammit, Ashley—" Cal's brows knit together in aggravation, as he continued scolding her "—why didn't you *call* me and let me know what happened yourself?"

Because if I had talked to you on the phone just then I probably would have burst into tears for no good reason other than I love you and don't want to lose you. And the incident had reminded her that they could lose each other, just that quickly, should luck and wisdom not be on their sides next time.

But she didn't know how to say any of that without sounding…pregnant.

Ashley sighed and ran her hands through her hair. She had left the blinds open, and outside she could see darkness had fallen. The snow was now three or four inches deep and still coming down.

Cal continued to wait for an explanation.

Ashley gestured helplessly. "Because I knew you were in surgery this afternoon and I was fine. So I figured I would tell you when you got home *which I would have* had your big brother not beaten me to it."

He took the blanket off her lap and visually checked her out, his hands moving over her limbs as if he were conducting a medical exam. He seemed barely able to reassure himself. "You're absolutely sure you're fine?" he insisted.

"Yes," Ashley retorted firmly. She batted his hands away. "Now stop playing doctor, Doctor," Ashley teased, capturing his hands in hers. "And take a breath and calm down."

Cal's eyes grew abruptly moist. "I couldn't bear it if anything happened to you," he told her in a low, hoarse voice.

That quickly, Ashley got choked up, too. She went into Cal's arms and hung on tight. "I don't want anything happening to you, either."

He held her to him fiercely and they clung together like that for several minutes. Eventually, she heard Cal's voice muffled against her hair. "You can't scare me like that again. I mean it, Ashley. Anything happens, you let me know. *Right then.*"

Guilt flashed through her, more potent than a tidal wave. Ashley closed her eyes against the pain in her heart. "I promise," she said thickly. "I won't ever ever hold anything back from you again."

The present, the future, she could fix.

It was the past she couldn't control.

"IT'S STILL SNOWING." Cal stared out the kitchen windows in amazement. At 11:00 p.m., there was a good six inches on the ground. The trees were coated in white and moonlight reflected off the snow, giving everything a tranquil wintry glow.

"It's been so long since I've seen snow," Ashley murmured, appreciating the beauty of the big fat white flakes still falling from the sky. She shook her head wistfully. "I wish I could go out in it."

Cal came up behind her and wreathed his arms around her waist. He buried his nose in the hair on the top of her head. Their bodies touched in a warm, electric line. "So what's holding you back?"

"We're not kids."

He guided her around to face him and winked at her playfully. "That's not what you said when we were playing hide-and-seek last night."

Ashley laughed softly. "As I recall, that game had a very sexy ending." She still tingled every time she remembered his hot, passionate kisses.

A speculative gleam came into his eyes as he leaned close. "So could this one."

Ashley flushed at the sensual promise in his low tone.

The Harlequin Reader Service® — Here's how it works:

Accepting your 2 free books and gift places you under no obligation to buy anything. You may keep the books and gift and return the shipping statement marked "cancel." If you do not cancel, about a month later we'll send you 4 additional books and bill you just $4.24 each in the U.S., or $4.99 each in Canada, plus 25¢ shipping & handling per book and applicable taxes if any.* That's the complete price and — compared to cover prices of $4.99 each in the U.S. and $5.99 each in Canada — it's quite a bargain! You may cancel at any time, but if you choose to continue, every month we'll send you 4 more books, which you may either purchase at the discount price or return to us and cancel your subscription.
*Terms and prices subject to change without notice. Sales tax applicable in N.Y. Canadian residents will be charged applicable provincial taxes and GST. Credit or debit balances in a customer's account(s) may be offset by any other outstanding balance owed by or to the customer.

If offer card is missing write to: Harlequin Reader Service, 3010 Walden Ave., P.O. Box 1867, Buffalo NY 14240-1867

NO POSTAGE
NECESSARY
IF MAILED
IN THE
UNITED STATES

GET FREE BOOKS and a FREE GIFT WHEN YOU PLAY THE...

7 Lucky

Just scratch off the silver box with a coin. Then check below to see the gifts you get!

SLOT MACHINE GAME!

YES! I have scratched off the silver box. Please send me the 2 free Harlequin American Romance® books and gift for which I qualify. I understand I am under no obligation to purchase any books, as explained on the back of this card.

354 HDL D36C   **154 HDL D36S**

FIRST NAME

LAST NAME

ADDRESS

APT.#	CITY

STATE/PROV.	ZIP/POSTAL CODE

7	7	7	**Worth TWO FREE BOOKS plus a BONUS Mystery Gift!**
🍒	🍒	🍒	**Worth TWO FREE BOOKS!**
♣	♣	♣	**Worth ONE FREE BOOK!**
🔔	🔔	🍒	**TRY AGAIN!**

www.eHarlequin.com

(H-AR-02/05)

DETACH AND MAIL CARD TODAY!

"Not in the snow," she protested. It was too cold to stand out there, kissing.

But Cal was not to be dissuaded. "It could start there," he told her affably, already off collecting their cold-weather gear. "But it would end up before the fire."

Ashley let him help her on with her winter coat. Still of a mind for the ultimate in comfort, she said, "Or in the bed upstairs."

Cal stopped suddenly and stared at her. "You really want to make love tonight?"

Why were they still holding back? Hadn't they already proven there was a lot of love—and life—left in their marriage?

"Maybe," Ashley allowed cautiously.

He grinned as he helped her on with her boots.

Then again... Ashley bit her lip, unable to decide. She wanted Cal. No question. On the other hand, their no-sex situation definitely had them communicating a lot more, and that had them getting closer than ever. "Or maybe not," Ashley said finally.

Cal shrugged on his own coat, stepped into his boots. "Playing hard to get?"

Maybe. And maybe I'm just scared that one step in the wrong direction would have us feeling distant and alone again. Wanting to keep the light mood, she batted her eyelashes at him flirtatiously. "Is it working?" she asked him dryly.

Cal thrust out his chest. Every muscle in his body looked taut, ready for action. He tilted his head slightly to one side. "You know us competitive types, when it comes to challenges...."

Ashley managed not to smile, but could do nothing about the happiness glittering in her eyes. "Hmmmm."

They stepped outside, still inching on their gloves. "You know what this reminds me of?" Cal asked as he took her hand and they trudged through snow piled on the front porch, down the porch steps and in great drifts on the ground.

Ashley savored the feeling of being there with him. "What?"

"The first year we were dating," Cal said as they walked through the stillness of the cold winter night, their breath forming frosty puffs of air. "When you were a freshman at the university and I was in first year in medical school."

"And sometimes the only time we could make our schedules mesh and see each other was late at night," Ashley finished for him.

Cal nodded, remembering. "And we used to walk around campus. And talk. And go to the library and stay up all night, studying. And then go have breakfast."

I felt so close to you then. Ashley smiled at him affectionately. "Those were fun times," she said quietly.

He considered her for a moment. "We still have fun times ahead."

Looking into his eyes, she believed him.

"In fact," Cal continued playfully, "we could have a fun time now." He ducked down and came up with a handful of snow. A few running steps backwards, and a ball was arcing her way.

It hit her in the shoulder just as Ashley was reaching down to scoop up a palm full of snow herself. By the time she had it patted into an orb, he'd hit her two more times, once in the thigh, the other ball had ghosted across the top of her head. Grimacing, Ashley threw hers and…missed.

Laughing, Cal looked as if he were a superhero operating in fast-forward. He circled around her and hit her four more times, while Ashley stayed her ground, boot-clad feet firmly planted in the snow.

Cal darted back around to face her. He stopped just short of her, rubbed his gloved hand across his jaw. "You know," he drawled thoughtfully, "you'd come out better if you ran a little instead of just standing there, taking all my hits."

"You think I got a raw deal?" Ashley shook herself from head to toe. To little avail, as there was still snow all over her. Ashley knelt and got another handful of snow, then straightened to her full height.

"Didn't you?" he said.

"Well, let's see." Ashley tranquilly continued shaping her weapon. "Which one of us is all out of breath?"

"Clever." He came toward her to take her in his arms. As he reached her, she rubbed her snowball into the back of his neck. He grimaced as the cold wet stuff went down his shirt, and he looked at her as if he had expected her to do something just like that to him before all was said and done. "You know I'm going to have to punish you for that."

"Now, Cal," Ashley said, laughing at the teasing expression on his face. She put her hands up in front of her. "You wouldn't hurt a lady."

"Maybe not with snow," Cal allowed wickedly. "But I'm not promising anything…about…my lips." He caught her around the waist and tugged her close. The next thing she knew her eyes were closing and his mouth was on hers. His lips were cold and the inside of his mouth was hot. Feeling as though she had come home again, as though she had found her heart again at long last, Ashley melted into the kiss, melted into him.

"Okay, you win. I surrender," she whispered finally, winding her arms about his neck and kissing him back with all the pent-up passion she had inside her.

Cal stroked his hands down her back. "We've got all night. Playtime doesn't have to be over…yet." Cal flashed her a mischievous grin as he tugged on a lock of her hair. "You want another chance? I'll let you have a running start."

Ashley shook her head. Serious now, she kissed his jaw, his cheek, his lips. "I'm not ever running from you again."

"ASHLEY, this is ridiculous," Cal murmured from the other side of the locked bedroom door.

"Says the person with the perfect body." She opened the door and motioned him in.

In no hurry—he wanted the night to last forever—Cal followed her inside, drinking in the compelling fragrance of her orange blossom perfume. The master bedroom was softly lit and he took the opportunity to admire the way Ashley filled out her pale-yellow flannel nightshirt. The rounded fullness of her breasts and pouting nipples pressed against the soft cotton, a hint of cleavage visible in the notched collar. His whole body tightened as his gaze dropped lower, and he took in the sexy swell of her hips, the hint of long slender thighs visible beneath the knee-length hem, sexy calves, trim ankles and dainty feet. Honestly, he didn't see what she was so self-conscious about! He smiled in sincere reverence. "You look perfect to me."

Ashley flushed, her gaze drifting over his gray jersey boxers and the arousal clearly visible beneath. "Well, I'm glad you like it." Her glance went to the apex of his thighs before she dashed back to the bed and climbed beneath the covers, which were promptly pulled to her chin.

Abruptly, she looked as nervous as a virgin on her wedding night. "Now turn out the lights," she ordered even more hastily.

As confused as ever, Cal obliged nonetheless and climbed beneath the covers beside her. Maybe this new phobia of hers was something they should talk out, he reasoned. Delaying the moment that he took her in his arms, and losing sight of everything but making her his once again, he reached over and stroked a lock of her dark silky hair. "I don't get it." He let his eyes adjust to the darkness of the bedroom. "You used to really like making love with the lights on."

Ashley sighed and cuddled closer. She turned onto her side, facing him, and ran her palm across the bareness of his chest. "And one day soon I will again."

He felt her hands stroke his shoulders, upper arms, before moving back to the mat of hair on the center of his chest. "Just not right now?"

She leaned down to kiss the U of his collarbone. "I'm feeling a little shy," she continued breathlessly.

Cal could have sworn from the tone of her voice that she was fibbing. He took her hand and pressed it to his lips. Then he kissed the inside of her wrist and forearm. "I was able to help you with that once," he whispered back as her skin heated and she trembled against his lips.

Ashley took his chin in hand and held it still as she brought her mouth to his. She wanted him and let him know it with a sweet, searing kiss. "You don't need to remind me you're the one who helped me lose my virginity."

Deciding she had been in the driver's seat long enough, he turned her onto her back and moved his body over hers. The timing of their encounter and the darkness of the bedroom may have been her call, but in what fashion they actually made love for the first time since she had been back home was going to be his.

"Now that was a fun night." He used his knee to separate hers and slipped between her thighs. Taking both her hands in his, he lifted them up over her head and pinned them there, then moved up, until his arousal fit against her femininity. Her breath caught at the intimate contact. The cotton of their undergarments provided a pleasurable friction.

Still holding her wrists in one hand, he threaded his other hand beneath the nape of her neck, and angling her head beneath his, he kissed the top of her head, her temple, the sensitive place behind her ear. She shifted beneath him restlessly, moaning as he found his way to her other ear.

"Cal."

"Hmm."

"I want you," she whispered as he lifted the soft veil of her hair and kissed his way down the exposed line of her throat to the U of her collarbone.

"I want you, too," he murmured. Bending his head, he took advantage of the languid ribbon of desire threading through her, kissed her full on the mouth, until a hot flush swept through her entire body and her toes curled against the mattress. Then he kissed her again. And again. And again, knowing no matter how long they were together, he would never get enough of her. Never stop desiring her. Cal had been wanting to make love to Ashley for days now. And his desire was a helluva lot more than just a search for physical release. He wanted to kiss her, touch her and possess her, make her see how right they were together. He wanted her to see how much they were meant to be together, not just for now or next week, but forever. And the best way he knew to do that was by letting their emotions run wild in hot, fevered kisses and caresses, marathon lovemaking sessions and nights spent cuddled in each other's arms.

Whether she wanted to admit it or not, Ashley had been his from the moment they had made love for the first time, years ago, and she always would be, just as he was hers, and hers alone.

A lot of things had driven them apart. Things he still didn't understand. But when he held her in his arms like this, when he kissed her and she kissed him back, he wanted Ashley as he had never wanted any woman. More telling was the fact that he needed her just as desperately. And judging by the way she was clinging to him, she needed him, too.

He was already undoing the buttons on her nightshirt. Tendrils of white heat swept through her as his mouth moved sensually on the hollow between her breasts, then returned with devastating softness to her mouth.

"Tell me you're not too shy for…this," he whispered in a low sexy voice that stirred her senses, as he deepened the kiss and slipped his hand inside to cup the soft curve of her breast.

Ashley arched against him, unable to think of a time, since first meeting Cal, when she hadn't wanted him more than life. He was everything to her, so much more than just her husband…so much more than he ever knew. "You know I'm not," she moaned as his fingertips closed over her nipple, massaging it to a point, then he followed it with his mouth. The pleasure was almost unbearable; everything around her went soft and fuzzy except for the gentle caresses of his lips and teeth and tongue. How was it that he always knew just how to kiss her and touch her? she wondered dizzily, as the familiar feeling of tenderness and excitement swept through her. How was it that he could always make her want to give up everything for him? How was it that he could make her feel so damn good, and so damn vulnerable, all at once? All she knew for sure was that he was so strong and wonderful. He tasted—and felt—so good, so undeniably male, so right.

Cal chuckled softly. "How about this?" he murmured in masculine satisfaction, sliding ever downward and tasting the silky stretch of skin across her ribs.

Ashley's desire to keep a self-protective wall between them faded and she made a soft, yielding sound as he dipped his tongue into her navel. Then he was letting go of her hands, divesting her of her nightshirt. Desire trembled inside her, her tummy feeling weightless, soft. Heat swept through her. Her whole body straining against him, she gave an exultant cry as he slid lower yet, ran his palms across her thighs and found her…there.

The swiftness of her pinnacle caught them both by surprise, as did her wantonness and lack of restraint. The next thing she knew he was slipping off his boxers with the same sense of unbridled urgency. Moving over her once again in the moonlit shadows of their bedroom, he parted her thighs and slid in between. He raised her knees, and entered her— slowly, deliberately—watching her face as he did so. Joy swept through her as their bodies became one and the boundaries that still existed between them dissolved. For the first time in what seemed forever, she felt as if they were really husband and wife. Equal partners. Lovers.

Cal brought her even closer, so her breasts were pressed against the unyielding hardness of his chest. Their mouths mated, just as their bodies did, in one hot, incredible, endless kiss that went on and on…until her breaths were as short and shallow as his, and he was obliging her with ever deepening thrusts that she met with a wild abandonment of her own. Until she was experiencing everything it was possible to feel. Loving him without restraint, and still not able to get enough of him…would never be able to get enough of him.

Just when she thought she could stand it no more, he slipped a hand between their bodies. Her hips rose instinctively to meet him as he touched and rubbed and stroked, and loved her with an intensity that took her breath away. And then there was no more thinking, only feeling. Her heart soared and he took full possession of her. She urged him on, her body tightening implacably around his. He thrust forward, surging completely into her, and then all was lost in the intimate physical passion that defined their marriage.

Chapter Ten

The pain came out of nowhere. One minute Ashley was walking down a street in Charlotte, North Carolina, with her brother-in-law, the next she was doubled over in agony.

"Ashley?" Mac wrapped a strong arm about her waist. "What is it?"

Ashley felt the warm liquid running down her legs, even before she saw the drop of blood hit the sidewalk. "Oh, God, no," she cried. "No…" This couldn't be happening. She couldn't be losing Cal's baby!

"Ashley! Come on, Ashley. Wake up, honey."

With difficulty, Ashley opened her eyes. The lights in their bedroom were on. Cal was bending over her, a concerned look on his face. Her face was damp with tears and, to her horror, she heard herself sobbing out loud.

Cal's hands tightened protectively over her shoulders as she struggled to get control of herself. "It was just a dream, honey."

"More like a nightmare." Ashley sat up, wiping the tears from her face.

Cal let her go, albeit reluctantly. "You were calling Mac's name."

A cold chill went through her. "What else did I say?"

"Nothing that made any sense. Just 'No. This can't be happening. God, no.' Things like that." Cal paused. "Were you dreaming about your car going off the road this afternoon?"

Ashley shuddered as another chill swept through her, more devastating than the first. She turned her glance away from Cal's and buried her face in her hands. "I must've been. I— I just know I was really scared something awful was about to happen."

She swallowed hard and threw her legs over the side of the bed. One hand went to her abdomen, testing. To her relief there was no pain. She seemed fine. The baby seemed fine. "I think I need to get up and walk around," she said. "Shake it off. Maybe go down to the kitchen and get some warm milk or something."

"Good idea," Cal said. "I'll join you." He got out of bed and went to the closet to get his flannel robe. He was shrugging it on as Ashley disappeared into the bathroom.

To her relief, there was no blood. Nothing to indicate cause for alarm. Which meant, it had only been a dream. Brought on, no doubt, by what had happened earlier…and her guilt.

Mac had been right about one thing, Ashley thought. Keeping secrets from your spouse was a hell of a way to live.

She was going to have to tell Cal what had happened some day. And she would, just as soon as she felt their marriage was strong enough to handle it.

"I don't know how you're going to feel about this," Cal said. "I know I just bought you that Mustang. But I think we need to trade it in for something with airbags, all-wheel drive and antilock brakes."

Ashley thought about the baby she was carrying, and how devastated she would be if anything happened, especially something that could easily have been prevented by a little common sense on their part. "I think you're right."

"Sentiment is one thing."

"Safety another."

He stirred the milk in the saucepan on the stove. "You want me to put some cocoa in this?"

"Thanks, but the caffeine might keep me awake. If you want some, though—" Ashley knew Cal was no fan of plain warm milk.

"How about a dash of vanilla then and a little bit of sugar?"

"Okay."

He added both to the pan, then poured the steaming milk into two mugs and joined her at the kitchen table. Outside, it was still snowing.

"There's something that's been bothering me. You remember that argument we had right before you accepted the fellowship in Hawaii?"

How could she have forgotten? That had ranked as one of the lowest days of their entire marriage. "The one about me not wanting to have a baby until after I finished my fellowship and settled into a job?"

Cal nodded. "I accused you of reneging on a pretty fundamental part of our marriage."

"It just wasn't the right time."

"I know that now. It was unfair of me even to bring it up. I just want you to know I'm sorry for having said the things I did that day. For the record, I think you'd be a phenomenal mother. But if you decide that isn't what you want, if you can't do it all, I understand—because you are an incredible doctor. And someone with your gift should be practicing medicine."

Ashley's heart began to pound. She regarded him warily. "You're saying it'd be okay if I didn't have a child?"

Cal gestured offhandedly, then stood and went to the cupboards. He rummaged around until he found a box of vanilla shortbread cookies and brought them back to the table. "I'm saying that my rose-colored glasses are off. I've seen other two-physician families trying to juggle everything simultaneously. It's not an easy road." He paused. "So if medicine is all you feel you can realistically handle, then—" he swallowed, making light of the enormous sacrifice Ashley knew he was making "—I'm okay with that, too."

TWO AND A HALF YEARS before, fresh from a devastating loss she wasn't at all sure she would be able to bear, never mind go through again, Ashley would have welcomed such a free pass from her husband.

Now, full of hope and joy and fear once again, Ashley's outlook was much different.

But if the same thing happened that had happened before, if she found out she was flawed in some fundamental way, she was going to need Cal to keep thinking this way.

Her feelings in turmoil, her knees shaking beneath the hem of her flannel night shirt, Ashley stood and went to the kitchen window. She looked outside, at the big white flakes still coming down from the sky. "I can't believe it's still snowing," she murmured.

She heard Cal push back his chair and close the distance between them. Standing behind her, he wrapped his arms around her waist and buried his face in her hair. "I love you," he murmured softly.

Tears filled Ashley's eyes. "I love you, too." She turned so she was facing him. Going up on tiptoe, she pressed her lips to his, the yearning to have nothing standing between them stronger than ever. "So very much…" Then his mouth was on hers in a kiss that was shattering in its possessiveness. He kissed her until desire streamed over her, until she was warm and safe, until she knew as well as he that their making love to each other again was inevitable.

Ashley took Cal's hand in hers. "Upstairs," she murmured.

He looked both disappointed they weren't going to make love then and there—and intrigued to find out what was on her mind.

Bypassing the guest room and the comfort of the master-bedroom, she led the way into the master bath. "The stipulation of only-in-the-dark has been lifted?" Cal asked hopefully.

Her actions a lazy counterpoint to his, Ashley shook her head. "Not…exactly." She led him into the shower/steam room big enough for two, and over to the long marble bench against one wall. Curling a hand around the swell of his bicep, she urged him to sit down in the center of it.

He shifted so he could look up at her, his rock-hard thigh bumping up against her knee. "This is getting interesting," Cal said.

Ashley grinned. She needed something to get her mind off the nightmare she'd had. A little playtime was just the thing. "Stay right there," she teased, aware just how easy it would be to get used to being with Cal like this and making love with him every night, instead of just every few weeks.

"Believe me. I wouldn't think of moving," Cal drawled.

Ashley sent Cal a coy look—glad to surprise him with something he desired for once—went back into the bedroom and returned with two candles. She set them on the long marble counter beside the sinks. Aware Cal was watching every move she made, his glance moving lazily over her newly voluptuous figure, she paused to light the candles and then turned off the overhead lights. The entire bath was ensconced in a mellow romantic glow. "Nice," Cal murmured, his voice moving over her like a soft warm blanket.

Ignoring the jump in her pulse—it wouldn't do to get too excited too soon—Ashley grabbed a couple of bath sheets and stepped into the enclosed glass shower with him. She turned on the handheld showerhead, adjusted the water streaming out of it to a nice, warm temperature, then temporarily shut off the flow and moved toward him. She set the sprayer down on the bench next to him. "This has to come off." She helped him out of his robe. "And this." She knelt to ease his boxers down his legs.

Cal shook his head in amusement. "How about you?" Looking ready to strip her down, too, he plucked at the hem of her nightshirt.

Trying not to thrill at the possessiveness in his low voice, she disengaged his fingers from the soft cotton flannel. "'Fraid not."

"Ah."

"Trust me. In a few minutes you'll forget all about wanting me naked."

"I don't know that I'd bet on that," Cal told her as she ran the sprayer over his body, wetting down his satiny, hard-muscled flesh.

A sexy smile on her face, Ashley lathered up the sponge with his favorite soap. "Just relax."

"I hate to tell you, Ashley," Cal said, looking all the more mesmerized by what she had planned for them, "but when you're soaping me up where you're currently soaping me up, I'm up not going to be relaxing anytime soon."

"You're right." She held the length of the most male part of him in her hand. Her confidence building, Ashley grinned. "You only seem to be getting more excited."

Cal groaned, this time making no effort to contain his pleasure.

Ashley caressed him daringly. "Maybe I can do something to soothe you."

He made a sound that was part chuckle, part groan. Let his head fall back. "Much more of this and I'm going to be way ahead of us both."

Trying not to think about how his lips felt moving over hers, or how much she wished she could race on ahead of what she had planned and kiss him again, Ashley continued her pattern of lazily soaping and rinsing and flirted back instead, "So I'll catch up."

Cal sighed, his expression one of pure ecstasy as she worked her way across his chest. He leaned closer, bringing with him the tantalizing fragrance of soap and damp masculine flesh. "You're right about that."

Being careful not to get too close lest she lose her focus, Ashley had him lean forward, so she could do his back. "Meantime, I'm in the driver's seat right now," she said as she gently washed his broad shoulders and beautiful back. "So to speak."

Cal smiled at her in a way that could have inspired a thousand love songs. "Yes," he said softly, "you certainly are."

Although she could tell that if he had his way it wouldn't be for long.

Her pulse racing, Ashley made her way back to the most intimate part of him again. As she lathered up his inner thighs, she could see him begin to throb in much the same way she had earlier. Pleased to have the same effect on him as he'd had on her, Ashley smiled in a way that raised the stakes another notch "Close your eyes," she instructed softly. *I want to drive you wild.*

He shook his head and replied in a voice that sent shivers of awareness ghosting over her, "I think I'd rather watch."

Ashley felt her nipples tighten. And he hadn't even touched her yet. Except with his eyes. She swallowed around the sudden tightening of her throat. Lower still, there was a sudden equally telling dampness between her thighs. "Okay, then." Ashley backed up subtly, putting a tad more space between them. "Watch. Just let me do…what it is I want to do…"

"All right," he said as the air around them grew hot and steamy, and the air between them reverberated with excitement and escalating desire. "You win," he said gruffly, teasing.

When he could bear her torturous seduction no more, he pulled her against him. Mindful of her determination not to let him figure out what she had yet to tell him, Ashley reached beneath her nightshirt. She drew her panties down and off and then knelt astride him, one knee on the long bench on either side of them.

Achingly aware of every hard, muscular inch of him, Ashley dropped her head, lowered her mouth to his and let him lead her where he wanted her to go. She whimpered as he delayed entering her and kissed her with a passion so hot it sizzled.

One hand on her waist, holding her precisely where he yearned to have her, he used the other to stroke, touch, explore. She trembled and he kissed her again, taking her mouth in a caress that was so intimate it had not an ounce of restraint. Her skin grew hot and damp, and her thighs splayed to better accommodate his searching fingertips. Until her breath caught in her throat. "Cal, I can't…"

"I know," he rasped back, leaving a trail of burning kisses across her neck. He cupped her breasts through the fabric of her nightshirt. "I feel the same…"

And then she was whimpering again—this time in frustration, moving down onto him, taking the hot velvety length of him all the way inside her. His hands caught her hips, dictating the slow, sensual rhythm. Commanding everything she had to give, while at the same time giving back everything she had ever wanted, everything she had dreamed…

Again and again, Ashley tempted and teased him, driving them both mad with desire. Withdrawing nearly all the way, then lowering again, closing tight. Until she was able to hear the soft, whimpering sounds in her throat, and the fiercer sounds in the back of his. Until sensations inside her ran riot, thrilling, enticing.

Her spirits soared as he pressed into her as deeply as he could go, making her his, letting her know he was as wild for her as she was for him.

Needing him the way she had never needed him before, wanting to feel connected to him, not just in body, but heart and soul, Ashley continued to kiss Cal back as thoroughly and passionately as he kissed her. Her heart was beating in urgent rhythm to his, and her love for her husband was pouring through her. They took each other to heights and depths they had yet to discover, until they were both lost in the pleasure and in one another. And this time, when they lost control, and surged heedlessly into ecstasy, something changed.

This time, Ashley knew, there was no turning back or away.

No hiding behind the demands of her chosen career.

Or the expectations of her parents, teachers and colleagues.

She had one future. With Cal. And the baby he still knew nothing about.

"NOT THAT YOU don't already know this, but you and the baby are both fine," Carlotta said the next morning when she and Ashley met at Carlotta's office to compare notes and review patient charts.

Ashley had known that, even before she'd had her friend take a look at her, before they got started on their conferencing. Still a kaleidoscope of emotions twisted through her. She didn't know why she was so nervous about this pregnancy. Was it because of what had happened before? Her guilt over not telling Cal yet? Or just the pregnancy hormones that were making her fiercely protective, and on edge? "That's good to hear," Ashley said finally, as she got off the exam table and adjusted her clothing.

"But," Carlotta continued gently but sternly, as the two women continued on down the hall to Carlotta's private office, "if you were worried you should have gone to the ER yesterday or called me, and I would have come back to the office and examined you."

Ashley knew all that, but it hadn't been necessary. Her mishap with the car had been just that. She'd been more upset about what could have happened, than what actually had.

"So why didn't you at least call me and let me know what had occurred?" Carlotta continued, as she shut the door behind them.

Ashley frowned, knowing she had to be completely honest with someone. She dropped into a seat while Carlotta took the chair behind her desk. "I was with Mac and I didn't want him figuring out I was pregnant," Ashley said.

Carlotta picked up a stack of charts. "Did you think he would tell Cal?"

"No." Ashley turned a ballpoint pen end over end. "Not if I asked him not to do so. Mac can keep a secret." He had certainly done so for her in the past. There had been another reason why she hadn't wanted Mac to find out. Ashley clamped her lips together determinedly. She looked her friend in the eye. "The first man who's going to know about this baby I'm carrying is Cal."

Carlotta's gaze softened compassionately. This, she understood full well. "So tell him," Carlotta advised, one woman to another.

Ashley tensed up again. She got up to pace the small confines of the room and pull two soda cans from the small fridge in the corner. "I can't. Not yet."

"Because of what happened the last time?" Carlotta took a diet cola while Ashley kept the caffeine-free regular soda. Carlotta popped the lid. "Ashley, you know that wasn't your fault!"

Ashley wished she could believe that. She sighed wearily, took a sip of her lemon-and-lime flavored beverage. "I should have taken better care of myself. Realized that twice weekly thirty-six-hour shifts and a pregnancy don't mix."

Carlotta scowled, flat-out disagreeing. "If that baby had been meant to be born, it would have been—no matter what hours you kept or how you rationed your sleep," she lectured. "Your miscarriage was due to the fact that the placenta was abnormal and could not have supported a baby. There's absolutely no indication the same thing will happen this time around. Everything looks normal. And you're only two weeks away from the three-month mark."

"After which time my chances of miscarrying again go down drastically," Ashley recited the information she had been over countless times herself. Information she had no trouble believing when it came to someone else.

"Right."

Struggling with a mixture of fear and relief, she looked Carlotta in the eye. "I'm an obstetrician. I know all this."

"And yet?"

Ashley shook her head, knowing she had to talk to someone. "I'm scared, Carlotta," she said quietly.

Carlotta looked at her with the wisdom of a woman who had been happily married for years. "Cal could be a great help to you right now, Ashley," Carlotta said quietly.

Ashley knew that. And yet…. "I don't want him to have to worry the way I'm worrying. It's bad enough I'm going through it." She felt the tears rise to burn the backs of her eyes. "Besides…" She blinked them back in frustration, hating this sign of weakness in herself. She ought to be gutsier when it came to Cal. Heaven knew she didn't have trouble communicating her needs or answering his in bed. It was out of bed, when they were talking about everything else—their relationship, careers, whether or when to have kids—that she struggled. As did he.

"He still doesn't know about the previous pregnancy?"

Ashley shook her head miserably.

"Oh, honey, and I thought my life was a mess."

Ashley wiped away her tears. "Let's talk about your life. How are you and Mateo and the kids doing without Beatrice?"

It was Carlotta's turn to look conflicted. "Well, the good news is the kids are beginning to accept me as Mommy."

Ashley paused, confused. "You've always been Mommy."

"I thought I was Mommy," Carlotta corrected, ruefully. "I think Beatrice was Mommy." Carlotta paused, looking more torn than ever as she ran a finger around the outside of her soda can. "The truth is, I've been missing in action more than I've been around. I was never there to bathe them and feed them and read them stories at night, at least not in an everyday way. Beatrice did all that. So it makes sense they would look to her for the comfort they need, not me. Since she has been gone and Mateo and I were forced to step in, that's begun to change. We realize what we've been missing, and so do they."

"You're saying what? That being a doctor and a mother don't mix?"

"No." Carlotta relaxed slightly. "I'm just saying I think I've been doing a less stellar job on the mommy front than I thought. I'm glad Beatrice has been with us, and I'm very glad that she is coming back in another eight days to be an invaluable presence in all our lives again."

"But?" Ashley discovered her heart was pounding.

Carlotta shook her head. "I'm beginning to realize that with three kids and a husband and a thriving practice, something's gotta give. I just haven't figured out what yet."

"IF I WERE the jealous type, you'd be in trouble about now," Cal told Mac the next day as the two of them climbed out of Mac's SUV, picked up their shovels and headed for the Mustang. It was just where Mac had left it, surrounded by a foot and a half of drifting snow on all sides.

Mac furrowed his brow as if wondering where this conversation was headed.

"Ashley had a nightmare last night and she called out your name," Cal explained as the two of them trudged through the mostly empty church parking lot near the edge of town.

Mac stuck the blade of his shovel in the snow and purposefully began to clear a path. "If I was in her dream, it probably *was* a nightmare," Mac quipped.

Cal chuckled at the joke, before turning serious once again. "I think her nightmare was provoked by the mishap she had with the Mustang yesterday."

The blades of their shovels scraped steadily against the blacktop beneath. "Yeah, she was pretty shaken up for such a minor event," Mac reflected. "Of course I guess any time you lose control of your vehicle, it's frightening," he said as he threw another load of snow onto the lawn. "Particularly for someone who hasn't driven in the snow for several years."

"Except," Cal theorized slowly, "Ashley is normally such a together woman. I mean, nothing fazes her." He watched as their breaths materialized in the cold winter air. "But this did." More so than he would have expected.

"What are you saying?" Mac asked. He paused to wipe the sweat from his brow.

"I'm not sure." Cal had cleared enough to get the trunk open. He extracted the long-handled ice scraper. "I know it sounds ridiculous, but I keep thinking there is something she isn't telling me."

His face expressionless, Mac continued shoveling while Cal cleared snow off the top of the Mustang. "Have you asked her about it?"

Cal squinted against the glare of the sun bouncing off the snow. Was it his imagination or was his brother now the one acting almost too cool for comfort? "Sort of."

Mac looked at Cal down the bridge of his nose. "What do you mean you 'sort of' asked her?" Mac demanded, whatever else he was thinking hidden behind his aviator-style sunglasses.

Uncomfortable with the close scrutiny, Cal shrugged. "It's not an easy thing to do without coming off like I'm accusing her of something, only I don't know exactly what. I don't think that would be a good way to get our marriage back on track."

Worse than the gnawing suspicion in his gut was the feeling of foolishness accompanying it.

"Speaking of your marriage, how are things going now that Ashley is back on the mainland?"

"Lots better." Cal liked being able to confide in his older brother, knowing that these days anyway, he could trust Mac not to keep him out of the loop on family matters. "Except for her calling-out-your-name-in-her-sleep thing," Cal added wryly.

"Well, there's one way to fix that." Mac flashed a devil-may-care grin.

"Get her to call out mine first?" Cal guessed in a low dead-pan tone.

Mac slapped Cal on the shoulder. "Sounds like you've got your work cut out for you, little brother."

Chapter Eleven

NO DOUBT ABOUT IT, Ashley thought several days later as she looked at herself in the mirror. The pants that had been loose when she had purchased them two and a half weeks earlier were not "roomy" any longer. She could still get the zipper up with nary a struggle but, realistically, she wasn't sure how much longer that was going to last. Or even if, ten days from now, when she hit the three-month mark and could finally tell Cal about the baby, they would still fit.

She had gained only another three pounds, according to the scale, but that combined with the five she had gained in the first two months, seemed to have gone straight to her waist and hips.

"What I ought to do is just go to the maternity store and buy some pants that don't look like maternity slacks," Ashley mumbled to herself as she turned this way and that, examining the new pudginess of her torso.

But, fear that if she did that, one of the women in the family would recognize the trousers as pregnancy clothing kept her from doing it. And anyway, there were only ten more days. After that she would no longer have to protect her husband. She could tell Cal he was about to become a daddy and buy herself some clothing more suited for a mommy-to-be.

"What are you doing? And why are you muttering to yourself?" Cal asked from the open doorway. He, too, was getting ready to go to work. He was freshly shaven and his ash-blond hair was damp and scented with shampoo. Shoeless, his shirt open and un-tucked, he looked so sexy and handsome he took her breath away.

"I'm not doing anything." Ashley swiftly released the hem of her burgundy turtleneck sweater, so it fell back over her hips.

He closed the distance between them in three lazy strides. He lifted his brow. "You were obsessing over your figure again, weren't you?"

Ashley battled a self-conscious flush.

"I wish you'd just relax about it," Cal said, wrapping his arms around her waist. "And let me see you naked again."

Ashley wanted that, too, if only because it would mean she could see him naked. She had always enjoyed the sight of his handsome, well-honed body. Soon, she promised herself, there would be no more secrets between them. No more reason to hold him at arm's length. She turned around, so they were face to face, and tipped her head back. "I've got to start working out first," she stalled.

And she knew what she was going to do, just as soon as she had time—a pregnancy yoga routine.

Tightening his hold on her, he kissed his way down her neck. "You've got everything you need right down the hall."

He had been very generous when it came to outfitting their new home "gym." Deciding it would be best for both of them if he weren't quite so undressed, she began buttoning his shirt, from the hem, up. "I know." As her fingers brushed his fly, she couldn't help but note his arousal.

Soon, it matched her own. It seemed she couldn't be near him like this without feeling that telltale flutter in her middle, and the tightening of her breasts.

"Yet I haven't seen you on the bike or the treadmill," Cal continued, gently stroking his hands through her hair.

The truth was; Ashley was afraid to get on the fitness machines. Afraid that if she stressed her body in the slightest she would lose their baby. And though, as a physician, she knew intellectually this wasn't true, that moderate exercise was good for her, the mother's heart inside her was busy churning out warnings to "be extra, extra careful" night and day.

"Surprise." She pulled away from him and went to the mirror to finish brushing her hair. She shot him a glance in the reflection. "You've got a very lazy wife."

Cal sauntered over to find a tie on the rack that matched his pale-yellow shirt. "If you're trying to be mysterious," he teased her affably, "it's working."

"That's a nice way to spin it," Ashley joked back. "Mysterious, instead of lazy." While he tied his tie, she twisted the length of her hair and secured it in a clip. "And much as I would love to stay here and discuss my sudden reluctance to exercise, I've got to get a move on. I need to be at the hospital to make rounds by seven, and in the office by eight."

"How come you're going in this morning?" Cal asked, swiftly hunting down his socks and shoes. "I thought you were only working afternoons."

"Carlotta called while you were in the shower," Ashley said. "Elizabetta has strep throat and Carlotta wants to stay home with her. So I said I would go in for the whole day."

"You want to go in together then?"

Normally, Ashley would prefer taking separate vehicles— she liked being able to come and go as she pleased, and she knew Cal did, too.

"If not," Cal continued affably, "I could drive the Mustang, if you want to take the SUV."

Ashley shook her head. "No, let's go together." There was

too much snow still on the ground for him to drive the Mustang. Her concern wasn't only for her and the baby. She wanted Cal safe and sound, too. "The roads are still icy in places, where the snow has been melting during the day and then refreezing overnight. I don't want to take a chance on one of us getting in an accident."

"Okay."

"You're not going to say I'm being silly?"

He studied her a long moment, as if trying to figure out the change that had come over her. She knew what he was thinking—she had never used to worry about such things, and in fact, had poked fun of people who were too safety-conscious.

All that had changed when she became pregnant again, however. Now their family couldn't be safe enough...she couldn't be with him enough.

And though he couldn't quite figure it out, he didn't really seem to mind.

Finally, Cal shook his head. A wistful look came into his eyes, the same one he used to get after one of their commuting rendezvous together whenever he had to say goodbye to her. "Not silly. Beautiful." He put his arm around her waist, guiding her close. "And sexy." His voice dropped another gruff notch. "And bound to make us both late if we don't get our coats and get out of here."

"YOU'RE KIDDING ME, right?" Hannah stared at Cal over the hood of the car she was working on. "You can't want me to sell the Mustang for you and Ashley! Now? When you just gave it to her a few weeks ago!"

Cal wasn't surprised by his sister-in-law's response.

Hannah's business, Classic Car Auto Repair, revolved around vintage automobiles. She not only worked on them, she understood the value, and the Mustang Cal had given Ashley was a fine automobile. Hannah knew, because she had not only helped Cal buy the vehicle, she had spent months getting it into top running form and realized full well how sentimental and heartfelt a present it had been.

Cal struggled not to feel remorse at getting rid of the convertible, especially since their reasons for doing so were valid. "It's a great car, and you did a beautiful job restoring it, but we've decided we want something with more state-of-the-art safety features," Cal told Hannah practically. "And we can't really afford to have a twelve-thousand-dollar car we never drive sitting in the barn at the farm, so it's going back on the block."

Understanding lit her eyes. "I'll put the word out. I don't think we'll have any trouble finding a buyer."

Cal nodded, relieved. "Thanks."

Hannah touched Cal's arm. The two of them were more than in-laws, they were good friends and had been even before Hannah had married Cal's sports-announcer brother, Dylan, the previous autumn. "Is everything okay with the two of you? I know how much that Mustang meant in your relationship."

Cal smiled. "It actually was a great gift. Ashley was thrilled when I first gave her the car that we had our very first dates in." And the car, as he had hoped, had marked a turning point in their marriage. So maybe all hadn't been lost, maybe it had served its purpose, and it was time to move on.

Hannah guessed there was more to the story. "But—?"

Cal grimaced. "She lost control of the car in the snow and jumped a curb."

"Dylan and I heard about that—Mac told us. But we understood she wasn't hurt and the car had no damage."

Cal had an idea what Hannah was thinking. They could put

snow tires on the vehicle. Or chains on the tires. Or simply not drive it at all in wet winter weather. It didn't snow in their area of North Carolina more than a couple of times a year, if that. During those times, he and Ashley could share his SUV, as they had been the past few days. "That's right."

"But you're getting another vehicle anyway?"

"Tonight, after work." Cal was hoping he and Ashley could find something she liked right away. "We're headed for a dealership in Raleigh that specializes in vehicles with state-of-the-art safety features. The near miss made us both realize we had to be practical as well as romantic. And since there's no way to install air bags in a vintage car like that...we opted to go with something else for her to drive."

Hannah nodded, understanding completely.

"Is everything else okay with you two?" Hannah asked.

Cal paused, not sure how to answer that. On the one hand, he and Ashley had never been happier. They were both living and working in the same place. After several years of guarded exchanges and cautious politeness, they were opening up to each other again. Laughing. Snuggling. Making love—albeit in the dark. For the first time in several years, he felt hopeful they would have the kind of equitable, satisfying marriage they had both always wanted. And yet, there were times, like this morning, when he had the strong sensation that Ashley was still withholding more than she was telling him, and that there were things about her life she would rather he just not know. And for the life of him, Cal couldn't figure out how to get past that.

"ADMIT IT," Ashley said, later that evening after they had parked their two cars side by side in the garage, and emerged to stand between them. She pointed to the shiny fire-engine-red car she had driven home from the lot, while he followed in his SUV. "This wasn't the vehicle you expected me to pick out for myself this evening."

No kidding, Cal thought, seeing no reason to fib. "I admit I've always seen you as the sports-car type."

"Instead of a station wagon." She turned to survey the buttery-soft cream leather seats and carpeting, seating for five, a generous cargo area, and a luggage rack on top, then turned back to him. Her lips formed a perplexed pout.

"What don't you like about it?"

The fact, Cal thought, that there is still something you're not telling me. But not wanting to start a fight by accusing Ashley of he didn't quite know what, Cal merely smiled. "I think it's a perfect family car," he said.

Ashley tensed at the mention of the *F*-word.

"Not that I'm pushing you to have a child right now," Cal corrected himself hastily. "I know that the time has to be right for both of us, and—"

Ashley pressed a silencing finger to his lips. The haunted look was back in her china-blue eyes. "Let's not talk about this right now, okay?"

"Then what would you like to talk about?" he asked her softly, unable not to note how gorgeous she looked, even after a long day. In the subdued light of the garage, her classically beautiful features were all the more pronounced. Her dark hair had been blow-dried straight and caught in a clip on the back of her head, but wispy tendrils escaped to frame her face and the nape of her neck.

Ashley shrugged. "Well…"

"Yes?" He could practically see her switching gears. Anything, he figured to get them off the subject of family and children. And when—if ever—they were going to have them.

Ashley swallowed, her expression as distracted as it was uneasy. She turned back to the station wagon that was outfitted with every safety feature currently being made, including air bags, steel beams, a car engine that would drop down instead of coming through the passenger compartment on impact and an emergency communication/navigation system.

Ashley turned back to him and sashayed toward him seductively. "It's obvious to me that you don't think this car is sexy enough." She slipped her hands beneath his coat to caress his chest, in much the same way she had in the past when they'd had problems she didn't want to discuss and preferred to sort out—or maybe just forget altogether—in bed.

This had occasionally irritated Cal in the past…although he never passed up a chance to make love with her.

Making love always made them feel closer—even if their problems remained.

Which was maybe where Ashley was headed with this?

The tactic was one she had said she wanted to avoid. And they had. But maybe she was having second thoughts about this all-or-nothing method of dealing with conflict between them.

Maybe she was trying to guide them onto middle ground.

He couldn't say after the years spent living away from her, and the temporary moratorium on their sex life, that he would mind. Especially when it looked as if she were contemplating initiating a little fun.

"But the car could be sexy." Ashley lowered her hands recklessly.

Cal felt the caressing sweep of her hands down the front of his thighs. Damn, if he wasn't already hard as a rock. "If we were to christen it?"

Ashley glanced back at the vehicle they had just purchased. "The front console could be a problem." She paused, bit her lip in a thoughtful way that had him wanting to kiss her and never stop.

"Fortunately," she continued happily, "the passenger seat folds down."

Cal slipped his hands beneath her coat, too. He removed her hands from his body and brought her against him, so her feminine softness curved against his growing arousal. He pressed kisses into her hair, across her forehead, temples. "Sure we won't be too chilly?"

Ashley trembled in his arms and kissed him back—on the lips. "Not if we closed the garage door, got some blankets, and let mutual body heat do the rest."

Cal brought his hands around to cup her buttocks and lift her against him. "Damn if you aren't full of surprises," he murmured, lowering his head once again. They were about to kiss again when they heard the sound of a car moving toward them and found themselves caught in the sweep of yellow headlights.

Too late, Cal realized he should have shut the overhead door as soon as they pulled their vehicles into the garage. Maybe then, they could have pretended not to be home. As it was, they had been caught by the female Hart posse—all three of his sisters-in-law and his sister, Jancy.

There were times when family was not welcome. This was one of them.

Not that he would ever be rude. It wasn't their fault that their timing stunk.

"We hate to interrupt," Emma Donovan Hart said as she stepped out from behind the wheel.

Hannah Reid Hart, Lily Madsen Hart, and Janey Hart Lantz soon joined them. "But we were in the area and thought we'd drop by and say hi."

"We also brought some wedding cake for you to taste," Janey said, cradling several white pastry boxes in her arms. "I've been developing some new recipes and I need some

more opinions on whether or not to offer them at the shop."
Janey paused. Although she knew they had interrupted a romantic moment it did not seem to be deterring her in the
least. "You don't mind giving me some fresh perspective, do
you?"

"Of course not," Ashley said, shooting Cal a curious look
no one else could see. One that said, *What the heck is going
on here?*

He had a pretty good idea.

He just couldn't say.

"And maybe some coffee, too?" Lily said, falling into step
beside Ashley as Ashley closed the overhead door behind
them with a press of a button and led the way into the farmhouse. "If it wouldn't be too much trouble."

"Before we go in, would you mind letting us have a look at
your new car?" Hannah said, waylaying Cal, along with Emma.

"I've been thinking about getting something a little safer,
too," Emma said.

Cal waved Ashley, Janey and Lily on inside.

As soon as the door shut behind them, he turned. "What
the—?"

"The black dress you left with the dressmaker has Lycra
in it," Emma said in exasperation. She opened her oversized
shoulder bag and got out a small Ziploc bag with Ashley's undies and handed it over to Cal along with Ashley's black
dress. "That's what makes the fabric so stretchy." Emma dem-
onstrated before handing the dress over, too.

"So?" Not wanting to get caught with either, Cal opened
the back passenger door of his SUV and tossed the clothing
onto the seat.

"So we can't get a valid measurement off it." Emma threw
up her hands in frustration. "We don't know what her waist
size is!"

"What about the underwear?"

Hannah rolled her eyes. "It was bikini, in case you hadn't noticed. It doesn't go all the way up to her waist."

Cal flushed. He hadn't thought about that. "Oh."

"So, at the moment," Emma continued whispering, "all we've got is her bra size, and given the fact she's gained a little weight recently—"

"In all the right places," Hannah sighed enviously.

"Realistically, her bust measurement could be off, too," Emma finished.

"So what do you want me to do?" Cal asked, embarrassed he had goofed this up to such a degree, when the surprise "wedding vow-renewal-ceremony" was only a week and a half away….

Hannah removed a tape measure from her pants pocket. "We want you to take this tape measure and go upstairs and measure the waist and hips and inseam on a pair of pants that you know fits and give it to us. And while you're at it, get us her shoe size, too."

"She only has two pair of pants that she has been wearing since she got back. One of 'em is on her right now. The other is hanging in her closet. But I'm not sure I know exactly how to measure…"

"Can you get me up there without her seeing me then?" Emma asked.

Nodding, he looked at Hannah. "But you have to stay downstairs with Lily and Janey and make sure she doesn't come upstairs."

Hannah smiled, confident as ever. "No problem."

"So why were they really here?" Ashley asked Cal an hour later.

"What do you mean?" Cal asked, ducking his head as he

rinsed the coffee cups and plates in the sink. He had never been any good at subterfuge. The fact the fibs were necessary to pull off the surprise anniversary celebration he was planning at the Wedding Inn wasn't making it any easier. He didn't want any secrets between them.

Ashley positioned herself between Cal and the front of the dishwasher. She folded her arms in front of her. "I mean, it's obvious they all wanted to talk to you. And I'd like to know what about. Did the men in the family send them over here?"

Cal frowned and wrapped his arms around her waist. It was time this conversation took another tack. "Why would they do that?" he asked, gently rubbing his hands up and down her spine.

Ashley narrowed her eyes at him as she splayed her hands across his chest. She tilted her head up to better search his face. "You said a few weeks ago the whole family was concerned about us. So was tonight more of the same?"

Cal did not like the feisty look in Ashley's blue eyes. That look always guaranteed trouble. And they'd had enough trouble up to now. "No."

She assessed him obstinately. "Then why did they all show up here and why did Lily and Janey and Hannah do their best to keep me occupied in the kitchen while you-all stayed out in the garage and then went up to the exercise room with Emma?"

"Hey." Cal aimed a thumb at his chest. "I know for a fact that Janey honestly wanted your opinion on those cake samples she brought over."

"And Lily?"

Cal could feel her body melting against his even as her will remained as difficult as ever.

"Why was Lily suddenly so interested in my opinion of various flowers she was thinking of doing for Polly Pruett's wedding?"

Cal shrugged and tried not to think about how much he enjoyed feeling the soft, feminine warmth of her body pressed up against him this way. He smiled, hoping to tease her out of her suspicious mood. "Because she thinks you have good taste?"

Ashley frowned.

"And anyway," Cal continued, kissing the top of her head, "what does it matter why they were here as long as they're gone now and we're once again alone, ready to christen the car we just bought?"

Ashley broke free of his light, protective grasp and whirled away from him. "You're changing the subject," she declared heatedly.

"You bet I am." Cal grabbed her arm and whirled her right back. "I'm tired of talking about my family," he told her. Smiling, he stroked the pad of his thumb across the silken invitation of her lower lip. "When all I want is you."

Her lips parted under the pressure of his touch. He had her backed against the counter, and she leaned back, bracing her hands on either side of her, and putting as much space as possible between the two of them. Which wasn't much, Cal noted. Maybe an inch.

"I'm not going to forget this," she warned.

Deciding they had done far too much talking for one night, he threaded both his hands through her hair. "Then I guess I'll just have to convince you."

The clip was in the way of his fingers. He took it out, and let her hair fall down around her shoulders, like tangled ribbons of dark brown silk.

Ashley caught her breath as he moved his hands through the soft thickness of her hair. "Cal—" It was part admonition, part plea. He chose to obey the latter. Engulfing her with the heat and strength of his body, he lowered his head and delivered a breath-stealing kiss. She moaned, soft and low in her throat. His body responded, heating and surging to life. And he kissed her again, deliberately shattering what little caution she had left. Her lips parted beneath the pressure of his, and he enjoyed the sweet, hot taste of her. He groaned as their tongues twined urgently, and his body took on an urgent pulsing all its own, until there was no doubting how much they wanted and needed each other.

Ashley sighed, trembling and cuddling against him, when they finally broke the kiss. "You are so bad for me sometimes."

He kissed her again, letting her take him where she wanted to go this time, not stopping until the last of the distrust between them had dissolved. "I take it you mean bad in a good way," he teased, as he rubbed his fingers across the tips of her breasts, then slipped his fingers beneath the hem of her sweater and bra, to caress the pearling tips even more intimately.

She shuddered as he traced the weight and shape. "Bad in every way," she teased right back.

"I want to make love to you," he kissed his way down the nape of her neck, pushing the rolled collar of her turtleneck aside.

"I want that, too."

"We could stay in front of the fire."

Ashley shook her head, stubborn as ever. Her hand dropped to his arousal. She enfolded him in her palm with the same tender care he was cupping her breasts. "I want to go back to our original plan and christen the car." He grinned as she used her other hand to unbutton his shirt, and continued her role as aggressor. "You have to start thinking of that station wagon as sexy."

He reached around behind her to unfasten her bra, and fill

his hands with her silky warm flesh. "Making love with you in it will do that all right," he promised.

Ashley stepped back, away from him. Knowing, as did he, that if they didn't stop now, they'd never make it out of the kitchen. "You get the blankets and maybe a pillow or two. I'll open up the back and put down the rear seat." She started for the door to the garage.

Cal watched the gentle sway of her hips, and wondered if she knew just how enticing she was, or how much he had enjoyed taming her and making her his. "Just don't start without me," he teased.

Ashley turned and shot him a sultry look that upped his pulse another notch. "Don't you wish."

He grinned.

"Meet you in five," she dictated cheerfully.

"Or sooner," Cal said, his spirits lifting the way they always did when he was about to make love to his wife. Only, when he gathered up the items she had asked for and met her in the garage, Ashley wasn't standing in front of her new car, but rather his SUV. And she looked anything but pleased as she held up her sexy lace undies and black dress and drawled, "I can't wait to hear the explanation for this."

Chapter Twelve

"I just bet you can't," Cal said, walking past her and over to the new station wagon. He opened up the back and the sides, and began the process of putting the seats down.

"You knew I was looking for this dress," Ashley stormed, waving it around like a red flag in front of a bull.

"Uh-huh." Cal leaned into the car and spread the quilts out, making a soft cozy bed for them.

"And the undies I usually wear with them," she continued heatedly.

His ash-blond brows drew together as he looked over at her in mock seriousness. "Right."

Ashley stomped over to him, her flat soles connecting loudly on the cement floor. She clasped the missing items in her hands. "So where were they?"

"I could tell you," he said, mischief glimmering in his eyes. He leaned toward her, his voice low and sexy. "But I'm not going to."

Ashley stiffened, aggravated at the way he'd had her searching high and low for her clothing when he had obviously known right where it was all along! "And you expect me to accept that?"

"I don't see that you have any choice," he said good-naturedly. "Unless you want to hire a private detective." He squinted at her thoughtfully and screwed up the corners of his lips in comical fashion. "Or perhaps grill your clothes on where they've been."

"Har de har har." She watched him plump the pillows, remove his tie, and begin to unbutton his shirt. "And that's it? That's all you're going to tell me?" she demanded in exasperation.

He inclined his head to one side and thought about it some more. "Yep." Somehow, he managed to pry the clothing from her hands and put it back in his SUV. "Now, are we going to have to do this in the dark again or shall there be light?"

A look of distinctly male satisfaction on his face, he took her resisting body in his arms. Ashley stiffened, trying hard not to notice how warm and strong and solid he felt. She tossed her head imperiously. "Who says we're doing it at all?"

Cal chuckled and shifted her closer still. Giving her no chance to argue more, he lowered his head and claimed her mouth with his. Ashley tasted the masculine force that was Cal, felt his mastery in the plundering sweep of his tongue. She still didn't want to give in to him, but his will was stronger than hers. She clutched at his shoulders as he moved his hips against hers and delivered a deep, demanding kiss. With a low moan of surrender, Ashley tilted her head to give him deeper access. His tongue mated with hers, and he delivered another steamy kiss that left her limp with longing and faint with acquiescence and wondering at the magical power he seemed to hold over her heart. They had been a couple for nearly ten years now, married for almost three, and yet every time he took her in his arms, every time he kissed her, her heart pounded and a shiver of unbearable excitement went through her.

"With the lights or without?" he murmured.

"Without."

He helped her into the back of the car, then went back to shut off the overhead light in the garage and returned to her side. He climbed in after her, shutting the tailgate. There was just enough moonlight coming in from the decorative half-moon windows across the top of the garage door to let them make out each other's shapes. The mood went from slightly cantankerous to highly charged in an instant. The back of the wagon had been a little drafty as she first climbed in. When he joined her, it soon became hot and close. Ashley's heart pounded with anticipation, as they turned onto their sides and tried and failed for several moments to get comfortable.

Ashley began to laugh at the ridiculousness of the situation. And once started, she couldn't seem to stop. He wanted to claim her, and she wanted him to claim her, and at the rate they were going, it was never going to happen; they were never even going to come close to making love in here and christening their new car. They weren't going to be able to lie down, even if they did it at an angle. They were both too tall and the bed of the wagon wasn't long enough, even with the two rear seats folded flat.

"This is absurd," Ashley decided, still laughing. She was ready to call it a wash and head upstairs.

Cal caught her around the waist and brought her back to him before she could beat a hasty retreat. "Not so fast," he told her. Laughter edging his low voice, too, his hands slipped beneath the hem of her sweater, to tenderly caress the bare skin of her ribs. "We haven't tried everything yet."

She sucked in her breath as he reached around behind her to unclasp her bra. Her skin tingled and heated. "Well, almost—"

Cal shifted onto his back, so he was lying flat against the

blanket, and guided her on top of him. "You know what they say," he whispered huskily.

"What?"

"Where there's a will, there's a way."

Ashley was about to counter that they'd never get comfortable enough, when his hands claimed her breasts, working the tips into tight, aching buds of arousal.

Suddenly, the situation was seeming much more workable.

Getting the idea of how he wanted this to work, she shifted her body until she was over him, straddling his torso, and then she framed his head with both her hands. His knees were raised, his feet flat on the cargo bed. The back of her hips brushed up against the wall of his rock-hard thighs. Nice, except their heads bumped against the back of the driver's seat. Cal cursed and Ashley began to giggle uncontrollably. "Still no good."

"Patience, Ash."

"Cal—"

He brought her head down to his for a slow, leisurely kiss, coaxing response after response from her. "I'm not giving up. Not yet."

When he put it that way...

She went up on her knees to give Cal room to maneuver as he reached around behind him and grabbed the pillows. He stacked them one on top of the other and pushed them up against the driver's seat, then sat up partway, his long legs stretched out flat in front of him.

Maybe this would work. Ashley thought as he continued to kiss and caress her. She was certainly getting excited. Now if they could just figure out a way to enable him to enter her, make their bodies one.

"Unzip me," he ordered hoarsely.

He caught her hand and guided it to him.

She did as he bid. He was hard and hot and so damn large in her hand.

"Now bring my pants down, just enough. Yeah. That's it," he said as she did his bidding. "And yours should go entirely."

A shudder went through her. She wasn't sure she could wait for the time that would take. "Cal—"

"I want you naked, Ashley," he ordered gruffly. "At least from the waist down."

What did it matter? Ashley wondered as her body throbbed and burned with wanting him. He couldn't see her in this shadowy light. Not enough to be able to figure out what was happening with her body, anyway. Wanting to please him as much as she wanted him to pleasure her, Ashley slipped over onto her side. Her fingers trembled as she complied with his wishes. When she would have moved over him once again, he caught her against him and held her so she was still curled up on her side, her head tilted just to the left of his.

He found her mouth at the same time as his hand found her dewy softness. He kissed her and caressed her until the world faded away.

She climaxed with surprising speed. And then he lifted her on top of him once again, caught her waist in his hands, and entered her with one long, slow, incredibly sensual stroke. Ashley felt the heat. Passion. Need. All combined to fuel the fires burning within them, and soaring, they found the release they had been craving.

"You're sore, aren't you?" Cal said the next morning as Ashley struggled to get out of bed.

She nodded ruefully. "Not only where you might expect." Given the heat and ardor with which they'd made love the previous night, she had expected—and was definitely experiencing—the residual tingling in the most feminine part of her that came with being well-loved. "But I'm feeling the effects of our rendezvous last night everywhere else, too," Ashley lamented as she stretched her arms languidly over her head in an effort to work the kinks out. "Arms, legs, heck—" she chuckled and shook her head "—even my derriere hurts!" Which was what they got for never having—um—"exercised" quite that way before.

"Well, if it will make you feel any better, I'm a little stiff this morning, too," Cal said. He swaggered toward her, looking buff and fit, clad in nothing but his boxers. Muscles flexing, he helped her to her feet. "But we can feel good about one thing." He favored her with a sexy smile that did funny things to her insides.

"And what would that be?" Ashley luxuriated in the feeling of his arms around her.

He looked at her gently, protectively. "Our new station wagon not only got christened, it has been established as one very sexy vehicle."

Ashley laughed at the mischievous twinkle in his eyes. "Just tell me we don't have to do it again." She ran her hand across the manly stubble on his jaw.

He caught her thumb between his teeth and caressed it softly with his tongue. "We don't have to do it again. The SUV on the other hand…"

Ashley groaned in mock reluctance. She clapped both hands over her ears as if to shut out what he was saying.

He pried her hands from her head and held them in his as he continued, all confident male "…has a larger cargo hold. Or we could try the front seats."

Ashley groaned louder. What had she started? "How about the bed?" she teased back.

He turned and cast a look behind him. "You mean this old thing with the comfy mattress and plenty of room and nice soft flannel sheets?"

Ashley looked at the king-sized haven with the sleigh bed frame. "Mmm-hmm." She ran her hand over the velvety mat of ash-blond hair on his chest, appreciating the satiny-smooth skin and rippling muscles beneath.

"Well, it sounds nice. But what sounds even nicer, once you get over your newfound shyness, is the master bath." He kissed the nape of her neck, the sensitive area behind her ear. "The master bath is perfect for showering together."

Ashley'd had much the same thought. She curled a hand around the swell of his bicep. "Give me another ten days or so and I promise," she said softly. "We'll explore the master bath."

He teased in a soft low voice that sent thrills coursing over her body, "I'm going to hold you to that, you know."

Ashley loved the playful curl of his mouth, the seductive glint in his eyes. "I know." She rose on tiptoe to give him a sweet kiss to seal the deal.

Cal sighed his regret as the sultry caress came to a halt. "Unfortunately for both of us, I have to get ready for work. Otherwise, I'd be content to hang out here with you all day."

Ashley would've liked to stay and make love with Cal all day long, too. A fact that both pleased and bothered her. She was glad she and Cal were feeling so close, and worried that they were once again letting their desire for each other take precedence over all else. Because if they hadn't made love last night, in the garage and then later, in their bedroom, she was pretty sure she would have found out where her dress and un-dies had been. Not that this was important. She was sure there was a good explanation for it since Cal was not the type to hide her clothes from her for no good reason.

Although what that reason could have been...

Was he attempting to buy her a new dress?

Had he taken the garments for sizing?

That at least made sense.

Aware he was watching her, and that if he didn't hurry, he would be late for morning rounds at the hospital, she said, "You hit the shower. I'll make breakfast today."

"See you downstairs in ten." He stripped down to his shorts, tossed them in the hamper, and naked, strode for the bath. Ashley grinned at his retreating backside. There wasn't an inch of him that wasn't beautiful, from the width of his powerful shoulders, muscular back and handsome buttocks, to his long, sturdy legs. She had missed seeing him buck-naked, climbing out of her bed. Missed making love with him and being held in his arms all night long. She didn't ever want to go back to the way it had been, prior to her homecoming.

And now that they were close to sharing everything—including the heartbreaking secrets that she had shouldered alone for the past two and a half years, as well as the happier secret she was dealing with now—they wouldn't have to.

All she had to do was work up the nerve to tell Cal the truth. About everything.

"So what is it, Dr. Hart?" Polly Pruett asked anxiously as she scratched at the red bumps appearing on her abdomen.

Ashley explained as she finished examining her patient, "It's called a PUPPP rash. Pruritic urticarial papules and plaques of pregnancy. It sometimes appears during pregnancy and then goes away after you deliver your baby. We can give you some topical medicine to put on it and an antihistamine to stop the itching."

Polly frowned. "Will that make the rash go away entirely?"

"Probably not," Ashley told her sympathetically. "But

the meds will make you more comfortable, and the rash is usually limited to the body—it doesn't appear on the face. What I am more concerned about here, Polly, is the fact you've begun to dilate."

Polly looked over at her fiancé. Peter Sheridan was standing against the wall, holding the pregnancy manual Polly carried with her everywhere. "How much?"

Ashley made a notation on Polly's chart. "Two centimeters."

Polly bit her lip. "I could be that way for a couple of weeks, couldn't I?"

"Yes," Ashley told Polly and Peter gently, "but other signs point to you going into labor some time in the next seven days or so."

Polly sat up as quickly as she could on the exam table. She fumbled with the sheet across her waist as she wailed, "But I'm supposed to be married in three days!"

Opposite her, Peter frowned. He looked as unhappy as his fiancée.

Ashley patted Polly's shoulder. "Which is why you might want to think about moving the ceremony up a bit," Ashley suggested.

"I can't do that!" Polly looked as if she might burst into tears. "We have two hundred people coming, and a lot of them from out of town! We have to wait until the weekend."

Peter moved away from the wall. "Polly—"

"Don't even say it." Polly glared at her fiancé, stubborn as ever. "I am having this wedding according to plan."

Peter swallowed and looked at Ashley for help. She wasn't sure what she could do. Polly and Peter's baby was going to be born when he was ready, whether Polly or Peter or the two hundred guests they had invited to their wedding liked it or not. Finally, Ashley said, "My husband and I are both planning to be at the Wedding Inn during the ceremony, so if there are any problems, Cal—who is a doctor, too—will be right there."

Peter breathed a big sigh of relief. Healthy color came back into his face. "Thanks, Dr. Hart," he told Ashley soberly.

"Don't mention it," Ashley said. She turned back to Polly. "In the meantime, I want you to be sure and rest as much possible…"

While Polly got dressed and went out to make her next appointment, Ashley retired to the private office and sank down behind Carlotta's desk. She returned several calls, then smiled as Carlotta breezed in.

"Good news," Carlotta said cheerfully, setting down a stack of medical insurance paperwork she had taken home with her to complete. "Beatrice is back!"

That was good news, Ashley thought, fully aware how much Carlotta's family had yearned to have their nanny with them again. But upon closer inspection, Ashley noted, Carlotta didn't look as if the news were all that good. "So everything is back to normal?" Ashley asked, trying hard not to think about what this might mean to her.

Carlotta nodded, still looking a tad distracted. She ran a hand through her hair. "I know I've imposed enough as it is, but I was wondering if you would consider continuing to help me out through the end of the week, so I could go home at two or so every afternoon and be there when the kids get home from school. It would also give Beatrice a chance to settle back in."

"No problem," Ashley said, glad to continue to be of help. And not just because she owed Carlotta, but because she enjoyed working in the small private practice with her old friend.

But she also knew, as she packed up and left the office for the day, that she hadn't done nearly enough looking for a permanent position for herself.

She could not delay any longer.

She went to the medical center, and caught the hospital administrator as he was getting ready to leave for the day. "Ashley!" Frank Hodges said. "I was going to call you."

"Perhaps we could talk now, then," Ashley said with a brisk, professional smile. Whatever it was, she wanted to get it over with.

He ushered her in and closed the door behind them. He waited until both were seated before he continued reluctantly, "I talked to the board of directors. We're all in agreement we can't take another obstetrician on staff right now—the medical center doesn't have the labor and delivery rooms to support such a move. We could use another gynecologist, though. So if you were willing to give up delivering babies and limit your practice until one of the obstetricians on staff leaves or retires, then we would be able to offer you a spot."

This, she hadn't expected.

Frank rummaged through the scraps of notepaper on his desk. "I've also done some checking with other hospitals in the area. Most are fully staffed with Ob/Gyns at the moment, but Carolina Regional Medical Center has an opening. And they would very much like to talk to you if you're interested in working there." He handed her the name and phone number of the person to call.

Ashley studied the paper, grateful for the lead. And yet... "That's a good hour's drive from here."

Frank nodded soberly. "Right."

Doing her best to contain her disappointment, Ashley got to her feet. "I'm really going to have to think about it. And talk to Cal."

"I suspected that would be the case." Frank stood, shook her hand. "If I can be of further assistance, Ashley," he finished kindly, "please let me know."

ASHLEY KNEW there was something wrong the moment she walked in the door. She could tell by the glum, tense expression on Cal's face. She put her things down slowly, shrugged out of her coat. "What's going on?" she asked Cal.

He pointed to the answering machine on the kitchen counter. "There's a message for you."

Okay. Ashley went over to the telephone and pressed Play.

An unfamiliar woman's voice filled the room. "Hello, Ashley. This is Shelley Denova, from Physician Search. We received your résumé and I'm happy to report Yale would very much like to interview you…"

"You told me you weren't applying for that job," Cal said. Once again, he seemed to be watching and weighing everything she did.

"I'm not, and I didn't." Ashley was already picking up the phone. She dialed by memory. Waited several rings.

Her mother's voice came on the line. "Margaret Porter."

Temper soaring, Ashley said in a clipped, brittle tone, "Hello, Mother."

"Ashley!" Margaret sounded delighted to hear from her. *Too bad the feeling wasn't mutual,* Ashley thought.

"I have a bone to pick with you," Ashley said.

Margaret paused. When she spoke again, she sounded confused, "And what might that be?"

Ashley drummed her fingers on the tabletop next to her. "I had a call from Shelley Denova at Physician Search."

"Good news, I hope?" Margaret chirped cheerfully.

Ashley gritted her teeth. She looked over at Cal, ignoring the censuring light in his gray eyes. "I never sent her my résumé."

Another pause, shorter this time. "I had my secretary draw one up and send it over."

Ashley felt the beginnings of a tension headache. She rubbed at her temples. "Why?" she demanded, aware she was very close to losing it with both her mother and her husband. With Margaret, because she had interfered in Ashley's life one time too many. And with Cal, because he had thought the worst of her, when all she had wanted was for him to believe in her, believe in them....

"Because the position was going to be filled before you ever got around to it, that's why!" Margaret scolded tersely. "Honestly, Ashley, what has gotten into you, anyway? You never used to be so lax."

Ashley's temples throbbed. She sat down and dropped her head into her hands. "Listen to me, Mother. I am not applying for that job. And I am not calling Shelley Denova back." She spoke slowly, carefully enunciating every word.

Margaret harrumphed. "It would be very rude if you didn't. You can't afford to burn bridges."

There was only one Ashley wanted to burn at the moment. "Then you better do something about that, hadn't you?" Ashley hung up the phone.

"Whoa," Cal said, looking impressed.

"You have no idea." Ashley was shaking, she was so angry.

He came toward her, hands out. "I'm sorry I jumped to conclusions."

Ashley swept her hands through her hair, encountered a clip, and then just took her hair down. She realized she had a choice here, stay angry with Cal and vent her feelings on him, too. Or let it go. Move on. She found she wanted to do the latter. "It's all right," she told him wearily, forgiveness pouring through her. She shook her head, took a deep bolstering breath. "If the situation had been reversed, and I had come home and heard a message like that on the machine, I am sure I would have wondered what in the heck was going on, too." She tightened her lips together ruefully. As long as they were on the subject, she figured she might as well tell him the rest of it. "Not that I'm exactly flooded with offers right now, in any case."

Cal blinked. "What do you mean?"

He stepped behind her to massage the tense muscles of her shoulders. His fingers were like magic, bringing warmth and welcome relief.

Ashley swallowed, wishing she had better info to relate. "I talked to the hospital administrator in Holly Springs today." Briefly, Ashley explained the situation.

Cal got another chair from the kitchen table and moved it, so they were sitting knee to knee. "Are you going to apply for the job at Carolina Regional?" He looked into her eyes.

Ashley shrugged, her feelings all over the map. Restless, she stood and began to pace the confines of the kitchen, talking anxiously all the while. "If I were to get a job as an Ob/Gyn there, I would have to live within fifteen or twenty minutes of the hospital." She paused to regard Cal practically. "At least during the nights that I was on call. And since you have to do the same here, it would mean we would be apart again, at least four days a week, maybe more."

Cal looked about as enthused as she felt about that prospect. Which, oddly enough, made Ashley feel better.

She didn't want him pushing her away again, telling her they had to toughen up and make these sacrifices for their careers, and put their relationship, their marriage, second at every turn.

"Anyway," Ashley continued softly, beginning to pace again, "I was thinking on the drive home. Maybe the thing to do is take the Gyn position at Holly Springs now, and just wait for an Ob/Gyn slot to open up. It wouldn't be all that long. And we wouldn't have to move or be apart." She paused, searching his face, aware her heart was racing as she tried—without much success—to decipher his non-reaction. "What do you think?"

"I think I'd be happy," Cal said carefully after a moment, looking as if he too were afraid to put his heart all the way out there, lest it get stomped on. He stood and walked to her side. "But," he asked gruffly, "what about you, Ash? What about your needs, wants, desires?"

Ashley swallowed hard and went into his arms. "All I need is you, Cal." She buried her face in his shoulder and hugged him fiercely. But even as she spoke the words, she wasn't quite sure she believed it.

Chapter Thirteen

"We know you want this to be a big surprise for Ashley, but we're all really nervous about just presenting Ashley with a gown she has never tried on," Janey told Cal during the impromptu family conference at the Wedding Inn.

Emma agreed. "I plan a lot of weddings, Cal. The most important thing to most brides—even those like Ashley who are simply going to be renewing their vows—is their dress. And since you want Ashley to have a new gown, I really think we need her input on which one she wears."

"How are you going to do that without ruining the surprise?" Cal asked.

His mother patted him on the arm. "We've got an excellent plan," Helen reassured him with a smile. "All you have to do is make sure that Ashley arrives at the Wedding Inn on Saturday morning, along with the rest of the Hart women."

"They want me to model wedding dresses for a photographer?" Ashley asked Cal later that evening, as the two of them prepared dinner together.

She had been doing yoga when he came home and was still clad in a leotard, tights, socks, and an oversized T-shirt that kept slipping off one shoulder.

Cal nodded, glad the event he was pitching to Ashley was

also completely on the level. He didn't think he could lie to her. Even for a good cause. "A lot of the brides who come to the Wedding Inn—especially the older ones—don't want to try on dozens and dozens of dresses. But it's hard to tell on the hanger what a dress is going to look like on an actual model. So my mother and Emma had this idea that you and Lily and Janey and Hannah could all try on half a dozen dresses on Saturday. Mom has arranged to have a seamstress there to pin the gowns so they will look as though they are perfectly fitted, and a photographer will take pictures of all angles of the dresses. Mom and Emma will compile the photos in an album and then when prospective brides come in— especially busy career women like yourselves—and want to cut to the chase they can flip through the books and pick out the ones they want to try on."

To Cal's relief, Ashley looked amenable to the idea. "They ought to do the same for tuxes." She brought out the makings for a salad while he grilled turkey cutlets on the stove.

Cal flushed, beginning to feel a little guilty at the depth of the deception, despite the necessity of the subterfuge. "They are. My brothers and I have all been roped into doing the same thing on the same day." He went to the fridge to get out the Asian cooking sauce. "So, will you participate?" He poured a little sauce on each cutlet, straight from the bottle, then spread it to the edges with a basting brush. "It will mean a lot to my family if you do."

Ashley had a tendency to feel overwhelmed when surrounded by too many Harts at once. But this sounded like fun. Except for one thing. She hesitated, aware she was going to have to be very careful not to let on to the other women what was going on with her. "Ah…they know I'm just getting back in shape after a period of not working out at all?" she said, thinking of her thickening waist and swelling centerfold breasts.

Cal flashed her an exasperated look. "That's the whole point, Ashley. All of you are gorgeous and accomplished grown women, not anorexic teenagers made up to look like adults."

Well, put that way... "Okay, then," Ashley said, going over to kiss Cal on the cheek. When he took her in his arms, she made it a full kiss on the lips, tender and sweet. She was trembling when they drew apart. She rubbed her thumb across his cheek and looked into his eyes. "I'll be happy to help out." She was pleased to have been asked.

"So WHAT do you think, Ashley?" Helen inquired Saturday morning as she presented Ashley with a huge rack of dresses that several bridal shops had brought over. "If you were getting married today—maybe for the second time—what kind of gown would you choose?"

"Hmm. As much as I liked the scoop-necked gown with the white tulle skirt I wore the first time around, I think if I were getting married now—especially for the second time— I would choose something a lot less Cinderella-ish. I like this one." Ashley pointed to a satin A-line gown, with long sleeves and a fitted alençon lace bodice. "And this one." Ashley fingered a high-necked white lace gown with a straight skirt. "And especially this one." Ashley selected a white silk off-the-shoulder gown with a fitted bodice, basque waist and chapel train. "It's really elegant."

"And it's the type of style that makes your waist look so tiny," the seamstress said.

"Then that's the one for me," Ashley joked, blushing a little as she thought about her ever-expanding waistline. Another week from now, when everyone knew she was pregnant— especially Cal—it wouldn't be so embarrassing, but right now Ashley knew it just looked as though she was not being very disciplined in her diet and exercise. Which, of course, was all the more reason for notice or comment since Ashley was one of the most disciplined people around.

"Let's try the one you like the most on first," Helen said.

The bodice originally had a lot of give, but when the seamstress had put the pins in, it looked absolutely perfect. As Ashley looked at herself in the three-way mirror, she remembered what it had felt like to be a bride. How full of hope—and happiness—she had been that day. How little she'd known about the heartache and the difficult decisions that lay ahead...

"What are you thinking?" Lily teased, standing still while the photographer snapped photos of her in an ivory tulle dress with a halter bodice.

Ashley forced herself to concentrate on the problems of the past and think about the promise of the future. Her pregnancy was proceeding well. Physically, she felt better every day. Emotionally, more relieved. And as for her relationship with Cal, it seemed at long last to be on the right path again. She could feel the two of them getting closer with every day that passed. And she knew now that it was much more than great sex holding the two of them together. They still had some things to work out, but she was beginning to feel confident that they could deal with anything that came their way now, instead of letting problems drive them apart, as they had in the past.

Janey moved to the mirror, too, studying Ashley's reflection. "Yes. Do tell what you're thinking about that is making you look so happy and content."

Ashley smiled. "How happy I am, actually." *How hopeful about the future.* "I know I've been married almost three years now but I still feel like a new bride in a lot of respects."

"Ahhh," everyone said in unison.

"Maybe it's that extended honeymoon you and Cal have

been on lately," Hannah teased as she stood still, so the seam-stress could pin the sleeves of the gown she had on.

"I've got to say I've never seen Cal looking happier," Janey added.

"Or more in love," Helen Hart said with a smile.

"So how did it go?" Cal asked when he and Ashley met up for lunch in town, close to the tuxedo shop where the Hart men had been trying on tuxes and getting photographed.

"Great, actually," Ashley reported cheerfully as Cal held the door to the sandwich shop and followed her in. "We had a lot of fun."

They threaded their way to a corner booth. "I'm glad," Cal said, looking pleased. He plucked two plastic-coated menus from behind the salt shakers, gave her one, and kept the other for himself.

"For the first time…" Ashley started awkwardly, not sure how to say the rest without offending.

Cal reached across the table and took her hand in his. He searched her face. "What?"

Shrugging, Ashley cleared her throat. Aware she might sound foolish, she pushed on nevertheless. "I really felt a part of your family this morning, Cal. Like I belonged there with the other Hart women. I don't know." She tightened her fingers in his and looked into his eyes. "It was just so easy today to feel as if I fit in."

"What's this?" Ashley asked when Cal walked into their bedroom carrying a box with a big red ribbon on it.

Unlike Ashley, who was still clad in a tightly belted robe that covered her from throat to ankle, Cal was already partly dressed for the evening ahead in pin-striped gray suit pants and a silver-gray dress shirt that brought out the color of his eyes. He hadn't buttoned the top two buttons of his shirt yet, and the sophisticated red-and-gray-patterned silk tie he planned to wear was draped around his collar.

"Open it and see," Cal advised in a sexy voice that sent thrills coursing over her.

Ashley looked up into his face. He had shaved before his shower, and the sea-and-sun scent of his cologne clung to his handsome jaw. Her fingers trembled slightly as she untied the ribbon on the box. "You have to stop giving me presents," she chided. It made her feel guilty to be lauded this way, when she felt she had done nothing to deserve it.

Cal grinned. "You want me to stop? You're going to have to stop giving me reasons to give you presents," he told her lazily.

Ashley sauntered closer. She loved it when they flirted like this. She put the present on the dresser next to him. "What did I do to deserve this?" Ashley asked softly, for a moment feeling as if she could drown in the depths of his gaze.

Hooking an arm about her waist, Cal pulled her against him and looked down at her tenderly. "That's easy," he told her huskily in reply, curving an arm about her shoulders and bringing her closer still, so she was intimately situated in the hard cradle of his thighs. "You love me—the way I love you."

His softly murmured confession was like a balm to her soul. Ashley's heart fluttered in her chest as she felt his arousal pressing against her, and then his lips were on hers once again, fusing in passion and heat, want and need. He swept the insides of her mouth, languidly at first, then with growing passion until she was lost in the touch and taste and feel of him, lost in the ragged intake of his breath and her own low, shuddering moan. Her arms wreathed his neck, and her body surged into the strong, protective shelter of his. The kiss deepened even more and Ashley sighed. Contentment swept through her entire being. "If we keep this up, we are never going to make it to Polly Pruett's wedding," she scolded ruefully, wishing they could just skip the wedding and stay home—together—in bed. But they couldn't. Not when she had a pregnant patient counting on her.

Cal dropped another kiss on the slope of Ashley's neck, then drew away. "Then we better open that box…hadn't we?"

Brimming with curiosity, Ashley picked the present up again and worked off the lid. Inside, in tissue paper, was a red jersey dress. It had long fitted sleeves, a ballet neck and tea-length circle skirt. "It's the closest one I could find to the black dress that you've been wearing so much."

And it looked comfortable as could be, Ashley thought, longing for the day when she would not have to hide her expanding waistline. "Ah, yes, the one you borrowed without explanation," she said with a smile.

Straightening, Cal began tying his necktie. "I figured if I was going to get you any clothing, I better have some help. Taking something you already loved along with me to the dress shop, seemed like a good idea."

So she had been right about why he had surreptitiously absconded with her clothing. Why then, Ashley wondered, did she still feel as if he weren't quite confiding everything? Pushing her unease away—she was probably projecting her own guilt here—Ashley kept up her half of the teasing. She looked down her nose at him in mock indignation. "Cal. Tell me you didn't show the saleswoman my undies."

Cal grinned, mischief curling the corners of his lips. "Wasn't necessary. But, had she needed more specific measurements, I would have been prepared."

Ashley shook her head, relaxing at their easy banter. "You're a little crazy sometimes."

"Determined." Cal reached behind the knot of his tie to fasten the top two buttons of his shirt. "And yes, I am, when it comes to seeing you have absolutely everything you need."

Ashley watched him draw the knot up to his throat. "You keep this up and you are really going to spoil me," she scolded him affectionately as she straightened the knot, and smoothed the collar on either side of it.

He winked at her. "That's the plan, all right."

Ashley knew if she succumbed to that look, they definitely wouldn't make it to the nuptials. She stepped back a pace, holding the red dress like a stop sign in front of her. "Hang on, while I go put this on."

"You could stay here and do it," Cal suggested hopefully.

Ashley did her best to ignore his devil-may-care attitude and the spike in her pulse. "Yet another attempt to see me naked—or almost?" she taunted.

"Hope springs eternal." He raised his eyebrows in a familiar and charming expression, then looked downward. "As do other things."

Ashley's gaze followed his, as he knew it would. Simultaneously amused and aroused, she flushed at the proof of his desire for her. *Hold that thought for later,* she mused wryly to herself. But in the interest of getting out of there at all that evening, managed only a "Very funny. I'll be right back."

Cal chuckled as she disappeared into the guest bedroom— where all her clothes were located—and locked the door behind her. "You have to get over this newfound shyness of yours sometime," he called after her.

And she would, Ashley thought, as soon as she hit the three-month mark at the end of the following week.

Then, she could—and would—tell Cal everything, Ashley thought, pulling the dress over her head and studying the way she looked in the mirror. And she wouldn't have these damn secrets still wedging distance between them.

She walked out, loving the way the stretchy knit dress fit.

She looked voluptuous, in that fifties-movie star way. "It feels wonderful, Cal."

He eyed her appreciatively. "It looks stunning, too," he told her gruffly. He paused to help her with the clasp of her necklace. "As do you." He shifted her hair aside and kissed the exposed slope of her throat, just behind her ear.

A shiver of desire swept through her.

Cal sighed, regretful. "I suppose we better head to Polly Pruett's wedding."

Because if the two of them stayed there much longer, Ashley knew they were definitely going to make love. She leaned up on tiptoe and kissed him. "Hold that thought for later," she murmured against his lips.

Cal hugged her back. "Will do."

"ARE YOU FEELING all right, Polly?" Ashley asked.

Her patient had been rubbing her lower back off and on the entire time she had been in the bridal suite getting ready.

Polly's brows knit together. "I must've slept funny last night because my back has been aching ever since I got up."

Ashley watched as the hairdresser and Polly's mother worked to get the veil attached to the tiara already through Polly's upswept hair. "Any other complaints?"

Polly's eyes sparkled with a mixture of excitement and happiness. She shook her head in exasperation as she adjusted the pearls around her throat. "Relax, Dr. Hart. I'm not in labor."

Are you sure about that? Ashley wondered. But not wanting to upset the bride, Ashley merely confirmed, for her own peace of mind, in yet another way, "Then you've had no contractions today at all?"

"Not a one," Polly reported as she moved away from the mirror in a swirl of satin and lace. "Nor has my water broken. Trust me. I am getting through this ceremony and the reception and after that…any time the baby wants to come out and join the world is just fine and dandy with me."

Ashley had to admit Polly's color did look good. "If you're feeling okay, then, I'm going to go out and have a seat with my husband." Ashley leaned forward to give her a hug for luck.

"Sounds good." Polly hugged her back warmly. Then she caught Ashley's hand, squeezed. "And thanks, Dr. Hart, for being here tonight."

Ashley smiled. "No problem."

"How is she?" Cal asked as Ashley slid into the row and sat down beside him. The soothing music from the string quartet and the soft lighting combined to make a very romantic atmosphere.

Ashley turned her head to the candelabras being lit, on either side of the white latticework wedding arbor, where the couple's vows would be said. Ashley took a deep breath, not sure why she was so nervous, except for the fact that her gut was telling her everything was not as tranquil as it seemed. "She says she's fine."

Cal's brows knit together. "You don't believe her."

"I don't know." Ashley paused and bit her lip. She dropped her voice a confiding notch. She didn't want anyone else to overhear. "Polly could be in the early stages of labor." Ashley shook her head, shrugged. "Then again," Ashley murmured quietly in Cal's ear, "the backache Polly's had all day could be nothing more than the result of all the extra baby weight she is carrying right now." Polly was lugging around an extra thirty pounds—most of which was concentrated in her abdomen. That had to take a toll.

"Well, we're here, no matter what," Cal soothed as he took

Ashley's hand in his, "and the hospital is only a fifteen-minute ambulance ride away."

"True."

Cal gave her palm a comforting squeeze. "So just relax and enjoy the event," he advised, leaning over to kiss Ashley's brow lightly.

Ashley knew Cal was right, so she did as he advised—until the bride actually made her entrance on her father's arm. "She's perspiring," Ashley noted to Cal, as Polly lumbered down the aisle as gracefully as an eight-and-a-half month pregnant woman could.

"I've got to admit," Cal whispered back over the music of the string quartet, "it's not looking good."

And it looked worse shortly after Polly's father kissed her cheek and gave her away.

Whatever the minister said was drowned out by Polly's loud gasp and the horrified look on her face.

"What?" Peter Sheridan demanded as parents on either side of the aisle jumped up out of their seats.

"I think—oh my gosh, my water just broke!" Polly wailed.

Everyone looked back at Ashley, who was sitting several rows back on the aisle. Aware Polly's labor was indeed happening, just as Ashley had suspected, Ashley stood and made her way to Polly's side.

"And now I think I feel the baby coming!" Polly screamed.

Okay, that did it. Ashley took Polly's arm. Peter Sheridan took the other. "We've got to get Polly where she can lie down as quickly as possible," Ashley told Peter.

"I can't walk!" Polly cried, gripping her fiancé's hand, hard. "Oh, my…I— Oh, Dr. Hart, it hurts. It hurts so badly!"

Ashley and Cal, who was suddenly right there to assist, helped Polly down to the floor. "Clear the room. Now!" Ashley ordered.

"Oh, dear God—the baby's coming!" Polly cried hysterically as guests stampeded for the exit.

"Call an ambulance, and keep everyone else—except my mother—out of here," Cal told the minister, who quickly rushed to comply.

Ashley had never been more glad to have Cal at her side. She needed his strength and calm in an emergency, now more than ever. "What do you need?" Cal asked Ashley.

Ashley was fighting her way through Polly's sodden organza petticoats. "I've got to see what's going on."

"Scissors?" Cal guessed.

"And sterile cloths," Ashley ordered, distracted. "Whatever you can find to wrap the baby in."

"Is the ambulance going to get here in time?" Polly whimpered, crying in earnest now, while Peter Sheridan crouched beside her, patting her hand helplessly.

Please God, don't let *him* faint, Ashley thought, looking at the groom's increasingly pale color. "Hang in there now, Dad," Ashley told Peter firmly. She looked at him, willing him some of her calm and strength. "We need you to be strong here." She spoke as if underscoring every word.

Peter swallowed hard and nodded in compliance as Ashley finally ripped through the last of the petticoats. Ashley got a look at what was going on. Polly was right, Ashley noted grimly. Ashley could definitely see the baby crowning.

"Do we have time to get to the hospital?" Peter asked as Polly continued whimpering and crying out in pain.

"I don't think so," Ashley said, quickly assessing the best way to proceed. "This little guy seems to be in a hurry."

Polly screamed in terror as another contraction gripped her.

Ashley grabbed Polly's hands and squeezed as Cal rushed back in with a pair of scissors. It wasn't going to be easy, but they had to keep things under control. "Polly. Calm down. Breathe. Just like you learned in Lamaze class. That's it…that's wonderful…no…don't push, honey…not yet… we've got to get you cut out of this dress."

Cal was already cutting through the layers of expensive fabric as swiftly and efficiently as if he—rather than the nurses—did this every day.

"Okay, now. We're ready." The voluminous skirts and petticoats cleared away, Ashley placed a several-inch-thick bed of table linens beneath Polly's hips. "You can push, Polly. Yes, that's it, that's good."

Polly moaned and bore down. Once, twice, three times, until the baby's head popped out. Quickly, Ashley cleared the baby's nose and mouth of mucus.

"One more push, honey—a big one. Yes, yes, keep going…"

Polly complied as Peter cheered her on and their baby slid out the rest of the way. He was a perfect little boy who—going by the scowl on his little face—was none too pleased by the traumatic turn of events. Dark hair, handsome features, about eight pounds. Ashley cradled him, one hand beneath his head, the other under his hips, and picked the new little Pruett-Sheridan collaboration up for his two stunned and elated parents to see. He began fighting almost immediately—little arms and legs flailing—and let out a loud, lusty cry just as the ambulance crew came rushing in.

"WELL, THAT WAS ONE WEDDING we won't soon forget," Cal lamented, several hours after he and Ashley had left the Holly Springs medical center where mother and baby were resting comfortably.

"Nor will anyone else in attendance. But all's well that ends well," Ashley said as she sipped her hot cider. They were home again, relaxing before the fire.

"At least they were able to get married once they were at the hospital and all the post-delivery stuff was done," Cal said.

Ashley grinned at her husband wryly, happy their own wedding hadn't been that eventful. "Again, not exactly how Peter and Polly planned it."

"But, look at it this way." He toasted her wordlessly. "They'll have a birthday to celebrate along with their anniversary every year."

"True." Ashley stirred her cinnamon stick around in her drink.

Silence fell between them.

Ashley snuggled into the cushions and stared into the licking flames, feeling remarkably content.

"You were incredible tonight, you know," Cal said.

She felt the weight of his head come to rest against hers. Ashley looked down at his hard-muscled thigh, pressed next to hers. She curled her foot and dug her toes into the rug. "You've seen me deliver a baby before."

"But not in those circumstances." Cal lifted his head and she looked over at him. Respect glimmered in his gray eyes. His gaze drifted over her lazily, before returning to her eyes. Then he said what she least expected. "It's going to kill you not to be able to deliver babies while you wait for a slot to open up at the medical center, isn't it?"

Ashley cleared her throat and turned her gaze back to the fire. How did he know what she had been silently lamenting, ever since delivering Polly and Peter's baby? "I'll probably be able to take a call now and then for some of the other Obs in town." She put the best spin on it she could.

And he still wasn't buying it. "That's not the same as seeing your own patients through conception and delivery and postpartum, or delivering a couple of babies a week," Cal disagreed.

No, it wasn't. But maybe the loss of that particular thrill was just the price she was going to have to pay to get everything else she wanted in this life. "I'll get by, Cal," she told him stoically.

Cal frowned. "You just went through four years of college, four years of med school, and three-and-a-half years of fellowship training in maternal-fetal medicine. You shouldn't have to just get by, Ashley. You should be able to be doing exactly what you want at this point in your life."

Or so she had thought. But Ashley had learned the hard way that work satisfaction alone was not enough to make her happy. Not nearly. "I am doing exactly what I want to be doing, Cal." She put her cider aside and slid over onto his lap, so she was seated sideways, her arms wrapped around his neck. She looked deep into his eyes. "And that is be here with you."

Cal threaded his fingers through her hair. "And I'm glad you are," he murmured, wrapping his other arm around her waist, before moving it up and down her spine, "but I also want you to be happy."

Ashley swallowed as she felt the familiar pressure to be everything she could be professionally once again. Not from her parents this time, as was usually the case, but from Cal. She gritted her teeth as she struggled to contain her emotions and attempted to slide off his lap. "We went down this road once before, remember?" she told him tensely. "I ended up in Hawaii, three thousand miles from you."

Cal caught her before she could completely escape and held her in place. His body was as tense as hers. "There has to be a way for you to practice obstetrics now without shortchanging our marriage," Cal repeated stubbornly.

"If there is," Ashley said, suddenly weary to her soul once again, "I have no clue at all what it is."

Chapter Fourteen

"Let's just drop it," Ashley said as she pried his hands from around her waist and slid off his lap. She bristled as she got to her feet and moved to the fireplace.

Cal remained slouched on the sofa, arms stretched straight out on the cushions on either side of him. "Ignoring our problems won't make them go away."

Ashley flushed beneath his close scrutiny and ran her hand along the roughhewn wood of the mahogany mantel. "Taking my career goals down a notch does not qualify as a problem, Cal." She forced herself to turn and face him once again. There was understanding in his eyes and a strength of purpose that had developed during the two-and-a-half years they had been apart. He wasn't going to let her run this time. Or evade.

Cal countered calmly, "I might agree with you if we hadn't already been down this road."

He was talking about that first summer they were married, the summer she had lost their baby, Ashley recalled miserably.

He stood and came toward her. "But we *have* been, Ashley. You tried to forget what you wanted to do professionally when your fellowship program abruptly lost its funding and got cancelled that spring." His calm steady voice penetrated her defenses, like a battering ram against a barricaded door.

"You said, 'No problem, Cal. I'll just forget the lofty goals and go into a regular residency program where I don't have to write a thesis and get the equivalent of a master's degree in medicine.'"

Ashley released a shaky breath—she had said just that.

They stood near enough that she could see the lines of strain on his face and the old hurt in his eyes. And along with that, the determination that their future—and the future of their marriage—would be better.

"So you applied to the other programs in the area and got accepted and were all set to stay here with me." Cal paused, swallowed hard. "And then the fellowship offer came through from Hawaii, out of the blue. Remember?"

Ashley nodded. She hadn't expected it. "The fellowship program director here had called around until he found a place that would take me," she recollected. It hadn't been easy. Most fellowship programs had only two or three slots per specialty and carried long waiting lists of students, wanting admission. Trying to find a place for a student suddenly displaced mid-stream had been a nightmare.

"And you decided to take that instead," Cal reminded her, his expression hard, unflagging.

Yes, she had. But not for the reasons Cal thought, Ashley knew. Stricken with secret grief and guilt over the loss of their baby, Ashley had wanted only to get away from everything familiar—including Cal—to forget the loss that haunted her.

Cal shook his head, looking equally remorseful as he continued with self-effacing honesty, "Of course, the fact you were so eager to leave was all my fault." He ran both his hands through his hair and left them laced together at the back of his neck. "I shouldn't have been pressuring you to take the unexpected time-out of your education to get pregnant and have a baby. I should have accepted at that point that your medical training had to come first."

Ashley struggled to contain her soaring emotions. She shook her head grimly, not about to let him put this on himself. "You weren't to blame, Cal. We had talked about me having kids during my fellowship before we got married." And agreed they both wanted them, sooner rather than later, just like their friends Carlotta and Mateo Ramirez. Ashley felt her whole body tense. "I just didn't realize how taxing it was going to be on my body working those thirty-six-hour shifts that first year."

"Then you found out how physically and emotionally grueling first-year fellowship is, and you no longer thought it best we try and get pregnant then after all," Cal said.

Because she had miscarried and was afraid to try to carry a baby again, at least during her training years, for fear the same thing would happen. Or worse, she'd find out there was something wrong with her that would keep her from ever carrying his child.

Had their argument only ended there, with her unilateral decision, perhaps it would have been easier to recover. But it hadn't. Cal had told her what was on his mind and in his heart, and the memory of that still stung her unbearably. "And you," Ashley recalled, with no small degree of pain as she looked Cal straight in the eye, "said if we weren't going to have kids then what had been the point of us getting married in the first place."

Cal grimaced at the memory of that awful time. He came toward her, arms outstretched. "I didn't mean it. You know that."

Ashley knew there was a grain of truth to everything that was ever said. She held up a palm to keep him from encompassing her in a hug. She didn't want him to touch her now. "You were right to be angry with me for my reversal in positions, Cal."

Cal dropped his hands, stepped back. "I was selfish."

"The point is," Ashley continued carefully, making certain to broadcast her own culpability in their marital problems, "you never misrepresented your desire to have a large family similar to the one you grew up in." He at least had remained steadfast from the day they had said their vows. Ashley angled a thumb at her sternum. "I was the one who briefly changed my mind."

"You don't feel that way anymore?" Cal questioned, his expression strained as he leaned a shoulder against the mantel, too.

Ashley nodded as feelings of loss and longing, hope and joy, filled her heart. "I want to have a baby with you," she said cautiously.

"I want that, too."

He started toward her. Again, Ashley backed away.

She saw the confusion in his eyes as she continued to keep her distance. "But what would happen if I were infertile or had some problem that wouldn't allow me to carry a baby to term?"

He shrugged his broad shoulders and retorted matter-of-factly, "Then we'd adopt."

"And you'd be okay with that?" Ashley pressed on. She bit her lip nervously. "You wouldn't feel cheated?"

A pulse throbbing in his throat, he continued to probe her face. "Where is this coming from?"

Anxiety swept through her in near-debilitating waves. *Tell him*, Ashley thought. *Tell him now.* But when she opened her mouth, the words wouldn't come. She was too afraid Cal would get that disappointed look in his eyes, the same one her parents had whenever she didn't quite measure up. And she didn't think she could bear it. "I—I don't know," Ashley said finally. And to his considerable frustration, she left it at that.

CAL WASN'T SURE when he had been so discouraged. All he knew was that Ashley was shutting him out again. And she shouldn't be. The two of them should be closer than ever after delivering Polly Pruett and Peter Sheridan's baby together tonight. And for a short time they had been. Until talk of children had come up and Ashley had closed down once again.

"I'm really tired." Ashley stepped past him and moved around the sofa, toward the adjacent kitchen.

Abruptly, she looked as battle-weary as he felt, Cal thought. And not just in her pretty face. Fatigue was in the set of her shoulders and the weary strides of her long legs. But it was no wonder after the day his wife'd had—spending the morning at the Wedding Inn trying on wedding dresses and being photographed, plus that evening's wedding and the unexpected emergency delivery. Ashley *should* be exhausted.

She sent him an apologetic sideways glance. "I know we had talked about making love earlier, but…would you mind if I just got a glass of milk and went on up to bed?"

Cal was already turning off the lights. "I'll go with you. I'm beat, too."

When they got to their bedroom, Ashley disappeared into the hall bath to put her pajamas on and get ready for bed. By the time she emerged, face scrubbed and teeth brushed, he was waiting for her in the master bedroom.

But instead of cuddling up to him, as she had been doing the previous nights, she turned onto her side, away from him, and went to sleep. Just the way she had done the first summer of their marriage, when she had first started putting up walls between them and put him—and their marriage—low on the list of priorities of her life.

But Cal knew that time had been different from now. He had been behaving selfishly, devoting himself to his own career, to the point that he neglected her and their marriage terribly. He had not been doing that since Ashley had come back to North Carolina. He had, in fact, been doing everything he could to make her understand just how much he wanted to get their marriage on the right path again and make her happy.

Her moodiness tonight—brought on by the resumption of their discussion about career and family—had merely resurrected old wounds. It was not a predictor of the future, Cal tried to reassure himself.

ASHLEY ROSE EARLY. Not wanting to pick up where they had left off the night before, she showered and dressed while Cal was still sleeping. Then she went over to the hospital to check on Polly, Peter and their baby. To her satisfaction, all three were glowing with health and happiness. "So I guess I should call you Mr. and Mrs. Sheridan now?" Ashley teased, admiring the matching wedding rings on the happy couple's left hands.

"Or Mom and Dad." Peter winked as he cradled his sleeping newborn son in his arms.

Ashley paused to admire their newborn, then speaking quietly so as not to disturb the slumbering infant, told them both, "Dr. Ramirez is going to be taking over your care now. I just stopped by to offer congratulations."

"You mean you're not going to be part of her practice anymore?" Polly's face fell.

Ashley shook her head. "My helping out was just a temporary thing." They had explained that to all of Carlotta's patients, when she started.

"But I liked having both of you there!" Polly protested. "It was nice, knowing one of you was always available in case there was a problem or something."

"Where are you going to practice medicine?" Peter asked.

"I haven't decided yet," Ashley said. Cal had been right. She would miss delivering babies. But she would miss him more if she had to go elsewhere to do it.

"We're all hoping she stays at the Holly Springs medical center, but that has yet to be worked out," Carlotta said, walking into the room, chart in hand. She looked at Ashley and the Sheridans. "I guess I missed a very exciting delivery last night," Carlotta said.

"And then some," Peter agreed.

"Have you examined Polly?" Carlotta asked Ashley.

"No. I'm just here on a social call," Ashley said. She started to step out of the room.

"Meet you in the staff lounge?" Carlotta said.

Ashley nodded. She was still down there when Carlotta joined her a few minutes later. "Polly looks great," Carlotta said. "I think we'll be able to send her and the baby both home from the hospital tomorrow."

"Good."

"About your job options…" Carlotta said.

"I've been wanting to talk to you," Ashley said. She had been thinking about it off-and-on since their last conversation on the subject and come up with a few ideas that might—if Carlotta were amenable—offer Ashley the best of both worlds, personal and professional.

"Let's go over to my office then," Carlotta suggested pleasantly, "where we can talk privately."

The two women walked out of the hospital and into the three-story building next door, where many of the doctors' offices were housed.

"I meant what I said about hoping you stay," Carlotta told her soberly as soon as the two women were settled.

Ashley knew Carlotta did. "And I think," Ashley said slowly, hoping her idea might seem as good to Carlotta as it did to Ashley, "I may have figured out a way for that to happen."

CAL SMELLED SOMETHING delicious cooking the minute he walked in the door Sunday evening. He had spent the day doing two back-to-back emergency surgeries. The one time he had been able to get away to call Ashley for a minute, she hadn't been home.

She breezed toward him, the angst and fatigue of the evening before forgotten. "You look happy."

Cal took in the loose cloud of dark hair. She was wearing her black slacks and one of his dress shirts—a medium-blue button-down that fell to her thighs and disguised the new voluptuousness of her figure. Excitement sparkled in her blue eyes. "That's because we're celebrating."

He lifted a brow as she wrapped her arms around his neck and kissed him soundly. "I think I've worked out my job situation," Ashley told him, drawing back. "But I wanted to talk to you first before I agreed to anything."

Cal inhaled the orange blossom fragrance of her perfume, felt the softness of her lower body pressed against his. "But you want to agree?" Cal guessed, stroking a hand through her hair. He had a sinking feeling she was going to be commuting to a job again.

Oblivious to his worries, Ashley nodded. She stepped back so they could talk more seriously. "Carlotta and I talked about the fact that we both want to practice obstetrics and gynecology here in Holly Springs, but we also want more satisfying personal lives. So I'm going to join her practice and we're both going to continue to work part-time, just the way we have been. For now, she will work weekday mornings and I'll work weekday afternoons, and we'll alternate our call nights. The money won't be as good—I'll only be making half of what I would be making if I were to work full-time—but I can stay here with you. And then one day, if another full-time staff Ob/Gyn position opens up at the medical center, well, I'll have the option to increase my patient load—within our joint practice—and my income."

"The hospital administration?"

Ashley gave the spaghetti Bolognese sauce simmering gently on the stove another stir. "Carlotta and I talked to Frank Hodges this afternoon and pitched him our idea. I'm happy to report he's one-hundred-percent behind our proposal. They've been losing too many female physicians who can't handle sixty- to eighty-hour work weeks and a family." Ashley paused. "I wasn't sure how you'd feel about it."

Cal blinked. "Are you kidding? I love the idea. As long as you're okay just working part-time." He knew what a go-getter Ashley was. She had always liked to be busy one hundred percent of the time.

For a moment, the veil was back over Ashley's emotions. He felt the familiar distance between them and had the sensation she was withholding every bit as much as she was telling him.

He wanted to talk further, see if he couldn't discover whatever it was that was bothering her, but she was giving him that smile and turning off the burners on the stove. Going up on tiptoe, she fastened her lips to his. As their kiss turned hot, passion took over. And as he swept her up into his arms and carried her up to bed, he figured whatever it was just below the surface could wait. He wanted—needed—to feel close to Ashley. If this was the only way she could let him do that, then so be it.

"WELL?" Ashley said the following Friday afternoon, after Carlotta had finished examining her. Another excruciatingly slow week of not being able to tell Cal about the pregnancy had passed. "How am I?"

Carlotta wrote a couple of notes on Ashley's chart. "Weight and blood pressure are fine, the size of the uterus and the height of the fundus are exactly where they should be. Congratulations, kid. You've made it to the beginning of the second trimester." Her smile fading, Carlotta paused. "It must be killing you not to tell Cal."

Ashley nodded, reflecting on the sacrifice she had made in order to protect her husband. "It has been." She adjusted her clothing and hopped down from the table. "But all that is changing this evening."

The two women walked through the deserted office to the private office they were now sharing. "He's going to be upset about your previous miscarriage."

"I know." Finished for the day, Ashley gathered up her things.

"But you *are* going to tell him," Carlotta said, as she did the same.

"Eventually." Ashley shrugged on her winter coat and looped her carryall over her shoulder. "I'm not sure if it will be tonight."

Carlotta gave her a scolding look. "Ashley!"

Ashley held her ground. "If I tell him tonight it will dull the good news."

Carlotta rummaged for her keys then turned off the lights. "The longer you wait, the harder it is going to be."

"I know that." The two locked up and walked out to the parking lot.

Carlotta paused next to Ashley's new station wagon.

"Maybe you should tell him about the miscarriage first, and then the pregnancy."

Ashley turned her collar up against the chill February air. "I've been considering that." She turned her gaze to the bleak gray sky.

"But?" Carlotta prodded, when Ashley didn't go on.

Ashley lifted her hands helplessly. "If I tell Cal what happened before, he's going to be worried the way I have been all along. That means he's going to have to grieve the loss of the baby we lost. And although I think he should do that sometime," Ashley set her jaw stubbornly, as the familiar feelings of grief and guilt welled up inside her, "I'm not certain Cal has to do the two things simultaneously."

CAL STOPPED by the Wedding Inn that evening, en route home from the hospital, to make sure everything was on track for the following evening. To his relief, he found everything was all set. He was on his way back out to his car, when he encountered Mac on his way in.

"Yes," Mac said, before Cal could get a word in edgewise. "I have picked up my tuxedo. And so have all your other brothers. So you can stop worrying. The repeat of your wedding to Ashley is going to go without a hitch."

"I'm counting on it," Cal said.

Mac gave Cal a look that reminded Cal no matter how old the two of them got, Mac was still his big brother, and as such, intended to look out for Cal and the rest of the Hart family. "As long as we've got a moment, how are things going between you and Ashley these days?" Mac asked.

Cal wasn't sure how to answer that. He leaned against the wrought-iron railing that edged the semi-circular steps leading up to the portal of the Wedding Inn. "You heard she accepted a part-time position at the medical center, and is now a partner in a shared Ob/Gyn practice with Carlotta Ramirez."

Mac nodded. He pushed the Stetson that was part of his sheriff's uniform away from his brow. "How's it working out?"

"So far so good," Cal said cautiously.

"And the marriage?"

"Is better than it ever has been."

"And yet…" Mac prodded.

Cal shrugged. Knowing he had to confide in somebody, and that he could trust his older brother to keep a confidence as no one else could, Cal said finally, "She's just so moody these days. One minute she's laughing, the next she's crying. Sometimes I feel closer to her than I've ever felt in my life and then she shuts down, and I feel like she's got secrets and feelings I'll never be let in on, no matter how long I'm with her."

Mac's brow furrowed. "What kind of secrets?" Mac said, pulling his hat down across his brow.

Cal looked at him in frustration. "That's just it. I don't know," he confessed quietly. "And it really bugs me. I'm starting to think I'm a little paranoid. And that's not a good feeling to have where your wife is concerned. Not that you'd know—" Cal couldn't resist ribbing Mac a little "—since you've never been hitched." Except for his engagement, years before, Mac had never even come close to settling down with any one woman. And now, at age thirty-five, Mac was the only one of Helen Hart's brood who was still single.

"Why would I want to do a fool thing like that when I've got my hands full looking after all of you?" Mac jousted right back.

"You're not responsible for anything that goes right or wrong in our lives," Cal said.

Briefly, something akin to guilt flickered in Mac's eyes. And then to Cal's consternation, Mac shut down as surely and completely as Ashley had been doing lately. "Now you're doing it, too," Cal pointed out sagely.

Mac frowned. The barriers went even higher. "What?"

"Cutting me out. Looking guilty."

Mac reached over and brushed a knuckle across Cal's head, the way he had when they were kids. Shaking his head, Mac pushed past and continued up the steps to the Wedding Inn. "You've got too much time on your hands," Mac threw the admonishing words over his shoulder. "Go home to your wife."

Exactly what Cal planned to do. "Remember. It's a Valentine's dinner for the family tomorrow night," Cal shouted up to Mac. "And that's all Ashley knows until she gets here."

Mac waved his acknowledgment and went on into the inn.

The question was, what kind of mood was his wife going to be in? Cal wondered as he drove on out to the farm.

Good, as it turned out. *Exceptionally* good, judging from the dinner cooking on the stove and the red silk robe she was wearing. A table had been set up before the fireplace. It was set with their wedding silver and china. Cal watched Ashley light the candles on the table. Damn, she was beautiful, and unless he was mistaken, she was completely naked under that frilly confection. "Valentine's Day is Sunday," he said, aware Ashley hadn't cooked this many times for him in one week since before they were married.

Ashley turned toward him, her hair falling softly across her shoulders as she moved. "We're celebrating early." She glided toward him in a drift of perfume.

Cal's throat felt parched. As Ashley drew ever closer, his lower half pulsed to life. "So I see."

As Ashley neared him, he noticed the imprint of her nipples pressing against the silk of the robe he ached to untie.

"Because we have something very special to celebrate," Ashley went up on tiptoe and whispered in his ear.

Cal wrapped his arms about her waist, as hers moved to wreathe his neck, and the soft fullness of her breasts pressed against his chest. "We do?"

"Yes." Smiling, Ashley cuddled all the closer. She loosened the knot of his tie, and began to work it free. "You see, there's a reason I've been gaining weight. And feeling peculiar. And craving French fries dipped in chili in the middle of the night."

His heart racing, Cal struggled to take it all in.

And then Ashley was saying the words he had dreamed of hearing for years.

"By August, there were will no longer be two of us, Cal. There will be three."

Chapter Fifteen

Cal's feelings soared as the impact of what Ashley had just told him sunk in. He wrapped her in a hug, then drew back to look into her face. Tears of happiness glittered in her eyes and fell down her face. But beneath the joy was something else…something uncertain…and full of conflict. Not sure where that emotion was coming from, Cal stepped back slightly to better survey her upturned face. Suddenly, his heart was beating as hard and erratically as hers. "You're sure?"

Ashley swallowed hard and forced another smile. "I've had blood tests, the complete obstetrics work-up."

Cal ran a hand down her arm. No doubt about it—she was trembling. And not in a good way. He tried to reassure her with a steadying touch. "And everything's okay?"

Ashley nodded. "Absolutely."

Then what was behind her sudden shift in mood, from all-out happiness to edgy apprehension? Cal wondered. Was there some medical reason for her uneasiness that she had yet to disclose? And was she trying, even as they stood there, to work up the courage to do so?

"Everything is on track for an August delivery by the stork," Ashley joked.

Cal struggled to search out the possible cause for her anxiety. "August," he repeated, focusing on the facts she had told him thus far. He stopped as her words sank in. "That means you're—?"

"At the very beginning of my second trimester, yes," she confirmed, abruptly looking as if she were hiding something from him again, and worse, feared his reaction to it.

Silence fell between them. The air was thick with tension. Ashley gulped and went back to the table. She lifted a glass of ice water and took a sip. Cal noticed there was a bead of perspiration just above her brow. She really was nervous about this. And not, he thought, because she had feared he wouldn't be happy about the news. No, she had to know that as much as he loved her, he would be over the moon...

He swallowed around the tightness in his throat and stepped nearer. "How long have you known?"

Ashley pulled out a chair at the table, sat down. Looking as if she wanted nothing more than to retreat at that point, she avoided his probing gaze. Probably, Cal thought, because she didn't want him to see the guilt simmering there.

"About three weeks," she said in a low, deferential tone.

Cal shoved a hand through his hair. "And you didn't tell me?"

Ashley blinked rapidly and recovered her composure. In a voice thick with emotion, she revealed, "I wanted to make sure everything was okay. And, well," she lifted her hand helplessly and drew in another unsteady breath, "things were pretty rocky between us back then. I didn't want us staying together only because of the baby."

Did she really think that little of him? Of them? "You should have told me, Ashley." Cal was angry and hurt at having been left out like that. Worse, he felt like a fool. Now, he knew why she hadn't wanted him to see her naked. Why she had resisted buying more than just a few items of new clothing that fit her better. Why she resisted the heavy-duty exercising that would have helped her get her figure back under normal conditions—because it would have endangered the life of their fetus. And most of all, he knew why she had been so upset when she had briefly lost control of the Mustang he had given her, why she hadn't wanted to drive it again in the ice and snow and why she had agreed to something with every safety option possible....

Abruptly, Ashley looked as unsettled as he felt at the news of her pregnancy and the fact she had chosen not to tell him till now. "I'll never keep anything like that from you again," Ashley promised him sincerely. She looked at him, love—and hope—shining in her eyes.

Cal had a choice. Stay angry and force them both to deal with his feelings, here and now, and ruin what should be one of the happiest nights of his life—or dig deep and find that compassion inside himself his mother had once found severely lacking, and accept Ashley's mistake for what it was and let it go. Although it went against his gut impulse to have this out, here and now—no matter how unpleasant the confrontation—he decided to let it go.

He took Ashley in his arms and kissed her again, pouring all his love for her, all the hopes and dreams he had for her and the baby into the emotion-filled embrace. She was trembling when he lifted his head. They both were.

"So you're happy about this baby?" Ashley whispered, looking more vulnerable and more in love with him than he had ever seen her.

Cal had wanted a family with her forever. And now she was here with him again, and it was really happening. He wasn't going to spoil that. "Happier than I've ever been in my life," he said huskily, curving his hand around her belly and the baby growing inside. And he meant that with all his heart and soul.

ASHLEY AND CAL stayed up late, celebrating, intending to sleep late the next morning since neither of them were on emergency call that weekend. It wasn't to be. At eight-thirty, they heard the doorbell ringing. And ringing. And ringing. Cal groaned and lifted his head from the pillow. His wife was cuddled up beside him, in all her naked pregnant glory. "Are you expecting anyone?" He sure hoped not. He wanted nothing more than to be able to spend the morning noting all the miraculous changes going on in her body right now, and making love to her again and again. But as the doorbell rang yet again, he realized that wouldn't happen until he got rid of whoever was intruding on their Saturday morning.

"I don't know who it could be," Ashley murmured. "Although I can tell you one thing, they're at the top of my *persona non grata* list right now."

Cal agreed. Who came over this time on a Saturday morning without calling first?

"I'll see who it is." Cal tugged on his slacks, grabbed his shirt, and headed downstairs. "And get rid of them. Pronto."

Ashley lay back down. She thought about the night before, and how nervous she had been delivering the news to Cal. With good reason, as it turned out. He had been hurt at first to realize she had kept her pregnancy from him for even a few weeks. She couldn't imagine how he would have reacted if he had known she'd not told him about the earlier pregnancy or subsequent miscarriage in the two-and-a-half years since.

He would have really been furious.

So she had chickened out again.

And though she knew she still had to find a way to tell him—some way, some time—in the near future, it wasn't going to be today. Or tomorrow, which was Valentine's Day and their third wedding anniversary. She wanted to know their marriage was on very solid ground before she risked seeing that disappointment in his eyes.

Downstairs, the front door opened, then closed. Ashley heard Cal welcoming their guests, then more voices. She sat up with a start, jumped out of bed, dressed and joined Cal as quickly as she could. And not a moment too soon, she noted, seeing the uncomfortable look on his face as he puttered about their kitchen, pouring juice, and taking a coffeecake from the freezer and putting it into the oven to warm.

Ashley stood in the portal wishing she'd had time to do more than put on her black slacks and a red sweater and brush her hair. "Mom. Dad."

Both Harold and Margaret stood and gave her cursory hugs. "We're sorry about the early hour, but this was the only time we could get our schedules together to visit with you," Margaret said.

As usual, both dressed in business attire. Not that either were the type to ever putter around in jeans or sweats....

"We were just telling Cal that we can't stay and have dinner with you this evening." Harold's words seemed rife with hidden meaning as he glanced at Cal.

"That's okay." Ashley smothered a yawn with the back of her hand. "We've got a Hart family thing over at the Wedding Inn to go to this evening anyway. But it's good you're here." Ashley moved to her husband's side. Needing his steadying presence more than ever, she wrapped her arm about his waist and leaned into him affectionately. "Cal and I have some news. We're expecting a baby. Come August, you will be grandparents."

For a second, neither Harold nor Margaret could speak. Then, as Ashley had hoped, her parents both offered her their congratulations and engulfed her and Cal in awkward hugs.

"Well, that's wonderful news, and all the more reason for

you to get your career situation straightened out," Margaret said as the four of them sat down together in the family room.

His expression neutral, Cal walked over to start a pot of decaf in the adjacent kitchen. Ashley knew he was giving her room to deal with her parents as she saw fit, without inserting himself into the situation. "I told you—I'm going to be working part-time for the next few years," Ashley explained patiently.

Margaret and Harold exchanged concerned looks. "Ashley, we know you want to be a good mother and you will be, but you can't shortchange the rest of your life," Margaret said.

"You'll never be happy just working part-time," Harold predicted.

Margaret leaned forward urgently. "Furthermore, they haven't filled the position at Yale—"

"No," Ashley said. "I'm not applying and I don't want to hear any more about it."

Margaret frowned. "But—"

Cal walked back in, ready to help her out, if need be.

Ashley held up a hand, letting Cal know with a glance she could handle this. "You have to stop pushing me," she told both her parents.

"But we want you to be happy!" Margaret insisted.

Ashley nodded, affirming she wanted the same thing. "And I will be. But only," she stipulated bluntly, "if I am living my life my way."

Harold regarded Ashley sternly. "We're trying to help you, Ashley."

Ashley knew that, just as she knew her parents loved her, in their own way. Even if they didn't quite know what to do with her. "If you really want to help me," she told them gently, "then let me be me."

"ARE YOU OKAY?" Cal asked, after Margaret and Harold had left. She certainly looked as if she were doing fine, Cal noted. Although maybe that wasn't a surprise, given the fact that for the first time Ashley had really stood up to Margaret and Harold. She had taken charge of her own life, worried less about what others wanted from her than what she wanted for herself and the two—no make that three now—of them.

Ashley nodded, relief flowing from her in waves. She wrapped her arms around Cal's waist and rested her head against his shoulder. "Promise me that we will never do that to our children," she said quietly.

Cal hugged her close and kissed the top of her head. "I promise."

A contented silence fell between them. Cal stroked his hands through her hair. "They love you."

"That's the sad part." Ashley drew back to look into his face. She splayed her hands across his chest. "I know that. Just as I know I will never live up to this perfect image they have of me. But it's not my problem. It's theirs."

Cal regarded her with a mixture of respect and relief. "So you can deal?"

"With you by my side? I can tackle everything." Ashley smiled.

"NERVOUS?" Cal asked Ashley as he parked in front of the Wedding Inn, and the two of them got out of their new station wagon.

"Not at all." Ashley tucked her hand in Cal's as they ascended the steps of the palatial, three-story white-brick Wedding Inn. In fact, she was looking forward to this evening with the Harts. Cal wanted to announce the impending birth of their baby to everyone in his family at once. They had decided the Valentine's dinner Helen was giving for the family that evening was the perfect opportunity. "I know your family is going to be happy for us," Ashley continued.

"I think so, too," Cal murmured. Looking every bit as contented and optimistic about their future as she felt, he drew Ashley toward him for a steamy kiss beneath the pillared portico.

No sooner had their lips touched than twelve-year-old Christopher came barreling out the grand entrance, and nearly knocked them down. "Hey! You're not supposed to be kissing yet!" he scolded them cheerfully, then stuck his head back in the front door. "Gramma—they're out here! Kissing!"

"Already?" Janey teased as Cal and Ashley came into the grand hall. Cal's sister looked as though she knew something Ashley didn't. As did Christopher and Helen....

Ashley turned to Cal. "What are they talking about?" she asked.

Cal merely grinned in masculine satisfaction and gave her hand a squeeze. "Let's get everybody together and tell them our news first," Cal said.

"I'll get 'em all down here in no time flat!" Christopher raced through the hall.

Five minutes later all of Cal's family were gathered around him and Ashley. Whatever the secret was, Ashley noted, they all appeared to be in on it, too.

"You wanted to talk to us?" Fletcher drawled.

"Ashley and I have an announcement to make," Cal said in a voice husky with emotion. He brought Ashley in close to his side and held her there tenderly. "We're expanding our family. Ashley is pregnant. The baby should be here in early August."

That quickly, every woman in the family gasped in surprise and teared up. The men, looking no less moved, offered hearty handshakes and congratulations. Christopher turned to his mother, perplexed. "Is this why—?"

Janey clamped a hand over Christopher's mouth before he could finish his sentence. "Not yet," Janey warned.

"Someone care to fill me in?" Ashley prompted dryly. It seemed she was the only one in the room who didn't have a clue what was going on.

Cal turned to Ashley. "You remember when I said I was going to have to get you another present for Valentine's Day?"

Ashley nodded, recalling very well the evening he had gifted her with the Mustang convertible. That evening—and the romantic intention behind it—had marked a turning point in their relationship. "But we already got a station wagon," she protested.

"This is a lot better than a station wagon," a starry-eyed Lily declared.

Again, everyone nodded.

"We're saying our wedding vows again tonight," Cal told her in a voice filled with love. "In honor of our third wedding anniversary."

"I CAN'T BELIEVE you all did all this," Ashley said in stunned amazement as the women accompanied her up the sweeping staircase to the bridal dressing suite on the second floor.

Cal and his brothers were headed toward the groom's suite on the other side of the inn.

"Cal's had us busy for weeks!" Janey said, chuckling. "Why do you think I came over asking you to taste cake?"

"And I had you trying on wedding gowns?" Helen added.

"And I had you looking at flower arrangements," Lily said.

Emma nodded. "We thought—correctly, it turned out— your tastes might have changed in the three years since your last wedding, or you just might be in the mood for something different." She took the off-the-shoulder white silk gown with the fitted bodice, basque waist and full gathered skirt off the padded hanger. "We even had this altered for you."

Oh, no… Ashley thought. But unwilling to state they shouldn't have done that when everyone had clearly been trying so hard to please her, she simply smiled. "When is this all supposed to take place?"

"Half an hour. So we have plenty of time to get you ready. Don't worry."

Ashley delayed getting into her dress as long as she could, letting the stylist Emma had hired fuss with her hair and touch up her makeup, but finally, there was no getting around it; she had to get into the gown.

As she feared, the gown was a lot tighter than it had been when she had tried it on a week before, particularly in the area of her rib cage and breasts. She had to suck her midriff in mightily so it would zip. But as long as she stayed that way— barely breathing—it was a perfect fit.

"You look gorgeous," Emma said.

Janey nodded. "Now for the veil."

More fussing, and flowers were brought in. Then Mateo and Carlotta and a few other close friends of her and Cal arrived.

Before long, the harpist was starting. The women were ducking out, to join the others in the upstairs reception hall that had been readied for the ceremony itself.

"You okay?" Lily asked, as she knelt and arranged the chapel train on Ashley's dress.

Except I can't breathe. Ashley nodded, too embarrassed to tell anyone she really shouldn't be wearing that dress…

Lily dashed on ahead, slipping into the room where the ceremony was to be held.

Ashley followed, alone, her bouquet clasped in front of her, for her grand entrance. The pressure on her waist and rib cage and the light-headed feeling got more intense with every step she took.

Don't be silly. You can do this. It's only a few more minutes…and then the ceremony will be done…

Determined not to do anything so foolish as pass out halfway to Cal, Ashley drew a deep, quelling breath, and commanded her knees to stop shaking so. Unfortunately, as her lungs filled, Ashley felt her dress begin to rip along her left side seam. Horrified she was about to put on a show for the entire Hart family, the likes of which they had never seen, Ashley gasped at the soft sound of rending fabric and bent over from the waist, both her hands going to her waist.

Once again, it was the exact wrong thing to do.

The additional pressure of binding fabric against her breasts and ribs pushed the air she had just gulped in right back out again. Ashley heard voices coming at her, as if from a great distance away. A rising murmur of familial concern. The next thing Ashley knew, the whole room was swimming, her limbs went limp, and her nose was buried in her bouquet.

FOR CAL, it was like watching an accident in slow motion.

He'd known something was wrong the moment Ashley stepped into the room. Her cheeks were too pink at first, then too pale, her steps uncertain, wavering. The way she was swaying back and forth, like a sailor on a pitching deck, he would've thought she'd been drinking. Except he knew she hadn't. And wouldn't so long as she was carrying their baby.

But it wasn't until she moaned and bent over from the waist suddenly, clutching her left side, and Mac muttered beside him, "Oh my God! Not again!" that Cal lurched into action.

He dashed down the aisle, toward Ashley, catching her in

his arms just as she dropped into a dead faint. Wondering all the while what the hell his brother had meant when he'd said, "Not again!"

Carlotta pushed her way through the family gathered around as Cal gently laid Ashley down on the satin runner in the center of the room. Shades of Polly Pruett's untimely birth flashed through Cal's mind. Except it was way too early for their baby to be born...

"Everyone clear the room," Carlotta ordered, taking charge as Ashley's Ob/Gyn.

Mac was already herding them out, shutting the door.

Ashley moaned and her eyes fluttered open.

"Ashley," Carlotta demanded. "Are you in pain?"

"What?" Ashley struggled to come to all the way. "In pain? Oh God," she prayed out loud. "Not again!"

What did she mean? Cal wondered. Not again!

What the hell did Mac know that he didn't?

"Are you hurting anywhere?" Carlotta persisted, as she looked into Ashley's eyes and checked her pulse.

"No," Ashley shook her head, clearly sure about that much anyway. Ashley blinked again. "What happened?"

"That's what we're trying to find out," Cal told his wife gently.

Ashley put a trembling hand to her temple as she struggled to recall the moment immediately before her collapse. "I don't know. I felt dizzy and then everything sort of went black."

Carlotta palpated Ashley's middle, checking to make sure there was no tenderness. When she found none, Carlotta looked over at Cal. "I think she just fainted," Carlotta told Cal.

Helen knocked and popped her head in. "Cal? I've got some smelling salts if you need them."

Cal went over to get them.

"Is she going to be okay?" Helen asked.

Cal nodded.

Their marriage was another matter.

CAL LEFT ASHLEY with Carlotta and went to find Mac. "Can I talk to you alone for a minute?"

They stepped into the groom's dressing room and shut the door behind them. "What did you mean when you said, 'Not again'?" Cal demanded. "Have you seen Ashley faint before?"

For once in his life, Mac was at a complete loss for words. "She's okay, isn't she?" Mac asked eventually.

"What would make you think she wouldn't be?" Cal retorted. And why was his law-and-order older brother looking so guilty? "There's something you aren't telling me, isn't there?"

Mac's jaw tightened. He looked away. Didn't answer. "You should probably talk to Ashley about this," Mac advised.

Cal intended to do just that. He strode back down the hall to the suite where he and Ashley were to renew their vows. He knocked and walked in. Ashley was sitting in one of the chairs, Carlotta next to her, and sipping orange juice. They were talking in low, subdued tones. Tellingly, their conversation stopped abruptly when Cal walked in. They smiled— maybe too brightly and officiously. Both looked as if they were hiding something, just as Mac had. *So now there were three people who knew what he didn't.* His temper rising, Cal looked at Carlotta. "If you don't mind, I'd like a word alone with my wife," he said mildly.

Carlotta patted Ashley's hand—as if in silent support—and stood.

"The ceremony is going to have to be delayed. I've got a problem with the dress." Flushing, Ashley held the glass of juice away from her and showed Cal the left side seam. It was shredded from her breast to waist.

"It's probably best we wait, anyway." Cal looked at Carlotta. "Would you please tell everyone and also make sure that we're not disturbed?"

"No problem." With another telling look at Ashley, Carlotta breezed out.

"Do you still feel light-headed?" Cal pulled up the chair beside her and turned it so they could sit, knee to knee, facing each other.

"No. The smelling salts took care of that." She studied him as closely as he was regarding her.

Cal looked at her mouth—it was damp and soft. He wanted to drag her into his arms and kiss her again, reason be damned. He wanted to take her home and make wild passionate love to her again, and then, when they'd exhausted themselves and run the gamut of their feelings for each other, deal with this mess.

He also knew that it was that same head-in-the-sand, hear-no-evil, see-no-evil reaction that had gotten them to this point.

They had been running from certain truths for years.

They could not continue to do so.

Like it or not they had to deal with each other and these secrets, whatever they might be.

"You look upset," Ashley said.

The understatement of the century if there ever was one. "Shouldn't I be?" Cal replied cordially.

Looking as if she wanted to retreat, she took another long drink and turned her glance to the flower arbor where Cal and the minister had both been standing a few short minutes ago. Ashley swallowed hard. "Because I fainted?"

Cal regarded her warily, his heart working like a trip hammer in his chest. "Because Mac and Carlotta both know something that I don't." He paused, fury rising, as he waited for her to return her glance to his. "Were you ever going to tell me about what happened before?"

Abruptly, she looked exhausted and close to tears. "You know about the miscarriage," she guessed sadly.

Which meant, Cal thought, there had been another baby. One he knew nothing about—until this evening, anyway. His muscles were tight with suppressed anger and resentment. Hurt colored his low tone as he replied, even more softly, "I do now."

Ashley drained her glass, put it aside. Cal noted her hand was shaking.

"Then—?"

Briefly he explained what Mac had said and when. And how he'd refused to answer Cal's questions about his comment.

Ashley released a frustrated breath. The color in her cheeks turned from a pale pink to a dusky rose as she declared miserably, "I never should have put him in that position."

His mood grim, Cal stared at the woman he had been married to for three years. "No argument there," he said sarcastically.

Ashley's lower lip thrust toward him contentiously.

Giving her no chance to defend herself, he stood and moved a slight distance away from her. "And how is it that my brother knows you had a miscarriage and I don't?" he demanded, bracing his legs a little further apart and folding his arms across his chest.

Ashley stood and gripped the back of the chair tightly with one hand. "Because Mac was with me when it happened."

Jealousy ripped through his gut. "Which was?" Cal commanded.

Ashley drew in a quavering breath. "The summer I left for Hawaii. I had planned to tell you I was pregnant when you finished taking your board exams that July, but I miscarried before that."

Pain glimmered in her eyes. She gulped and drew in a second, steadying breath. She was holding on to the chair so tightly her knuckles were white, but to her credit, she did not lower her gaze. "Mac and I were having lunch that day and after we left the restaurant, I got hit with what felt like the worst menstrual cramps I could ever imagine. I doubled over and nearly passed out."

Just as she had a short while before, Cal thought, as she'd come down the aisle toward him.

Which explained his brother's reaction.

"Mac took me to the emergency room. I made him promise not to tell anyone. I said I would tell you."

"Except," Cal pointed out bitterly, aware he had never been as angry with her as he was at that second, "you never did."

"Because," Ashley explained, her voice rising emotionally, "the time was never right."

"Oh, I think you could have found the time, if you had wanted to."

She grimaced; she'd deserved that. "You're probably right."

"So why didn't you?" Cal's exasperation mounted until he felt as if he were going to explode.

Ashley threw up her hands and began to pace, ripped gown and all. "Because I didn't want you to hurt the way I was hurting, Cal."

Except he had hurt, Cal recalled miserably. More than he ever would have had she only possessed the courage to tell him what he'd had every right to know. Then and now. He studied her silently, then summed it all up in a low, disparaging voice meant to inflict as much hurt in her as she already had in him. "So, instead you just let me think your unhappiness that summer was about losing your fellowship and deciding to take on a less prestigious residency, and about my desire to use your unexpected sabbatical to have a baby, when you—all of a sudden—weren't quite ready?" What a mess. He scoffed at her in contempt as he concluded his recitation of the chain of events that had nearly destroyed their marriage. "And then, just to make sure we were both as absolutely miserable as we could be, you decided to pursue a fellowship after all and headed for Hawaii?"

Now, she was angry. "You told me to go!" she reminded him.

Cal couldn't believe she was defending her actions. He glared at her, not sure if he wanted to kiss her or shake some sense into her. "I was trying to be supportive!" He had wanted her to be happy. And he'd thought—falsely, he now realized—that her being in the fellowship program had been key.

"And I was trying to spare you!"

"All right," Cal said with as much indifference as he could feign. He hated the mixture of self-doubt and regret her actions had engendered in him. "Let's say I buy all that." But he wasn't sure he did. To him, it sounded like feeble excuses. "Why haven't you told me about the baby you lost during all this time?"

"Because things were already strained enough between us without adding that to the list," she whispered softly.

"So in other words, you were never going to tell me," Cal concluded roughly.

Ashley shook her head disparagingly. "I guess I sort of thought that ship had passed. That if I did tell you, and you found out how long I had kept it from you, you wouldn't be able to forgive me."

Cal couldn't deny he was really angry and hurt, anymore than he could deny they still had a wedding to go through this evening, and a whole family still on the other side of the closed double doors, waiting. He turned away from her wearily, "I'll go get the women and see what can be done about your dress."

"Wait a minute." Ashley rushed after him and grabbed his arm. "You're not really planning to continue with the ceremony this evening…are you?"

Cal turned and regarded Ashley stoically, his sense of duty kicking in. "My family is all here," he reminded her with a weariness that came from his soul. "The room is ready. The dinner, the cake…"

She cut him off with an arch look, stomping closer. "And you and I are in the middle of the biggest fight we've ever had in our life!"

"What does that have to do with renewing our wedding vows?" Cal asked.

What did it have to do with their wedding vows? Ashley wondered silently, upset. Just damn near everything!

She looked at her husband, the sadness welling up inside her almost more than she could bear.

She had never wanted either of them to feel the way they did right now. She had never wanted to be in a position where she had to worry constantly she would make a misstep or not live up to his considerable expectations, and feel his crushing disappointment in her. She wanted to be free to be who she was, to know she could make mistakes and still be wanted and loved. She wanted to know that forgiveness was always an option, that their love and their marriage and damn it— the family they were now creating—were strong enough to weather any difficulty thrown their way.

But Cal obviously didn't feel the same way. "Look," he

said, coming toward her, the aggravation he felt still plain on his face. "You know I'm disappointed in you. And—for the record, Ashley," he continued sternly, "I have every right to be. But that doesn't change what has to be done."

Ashley stiffened. She held her head high as she forced herself to admit, "You're correct about that, all right."

"Where are you going?" When she didn't answer and just kept walking, he moved to block her way. "You can't run out on us again."

He was talking as if she had a choice. Tears gathered in her eyes. "I can't stay and spend the rest of my life having you look at me like that, either," Ashley told him sorrowfully. Her voice caught; it took everything she had to force herself to go on. "I'm not going to be the thing you most regret, Cal." She paused, shook her head. "I spent my entire life never living up to the expectations of my parents and feeling bad about myself. I can't be with someone who can't accept anything less than perfection! Because I have news for you, Cal," she whispered softly, looking deep into his eyes. "I am not perfect and never will be—and neither will our child!"

"Ashley," Cal warned, looking all the more betrayed, "if you walk out on me again, it's over."

"Don't you get it, Cal?" Ashley said evenly. She swallowed hard around the gathering knot of emotion in her throat. "It's already over. It has been for years."

Chapter Sixteen

"So this is it, hmm?" Helen Hart asked Ashley the next morning, shortly after arriving at the farm.

Ashley ushered Helen past the two suitcases, packed and ready to go, in the foyer. Fighting the wave of sadness moving through her, she shrugged her shoulders listlessly, then turned to face her mother-in-law. "It has to be. Cal isn't going to forgive me." Ashley paused, the ache rising in her throat. She blinked back tears. "I guess I knew it all along, which is why I couldn't bring myself to tell him," she confessed in a low, defeated voice.

Helen wrapped a comforting arm around Ashley's shoulders, in that instant giving Ashley all the understanding and compassion Ashley had wanted from Cal. "You were protecting yourself," Helen soothed.

"And Cal." Ashley hugged Helen back, then led the way back to the family room, where they could sit down. "Unfortunately," Ashley reached for a tissue as the tears began to flow, "all I ended up doing was driving him away."

Helen waited for Ashley to wipe her eyes. "Losing a baby is one of the hardest things a woman goes through, I know." Helen caught Ashley's look. "I was pregnant seven times. Six of those times I delivered healthy babies, but once, between

Mac's birth and Cal's," Helen's voice caught, "I wasn't as lucky."

Ashley regarded Helen steadily. "Cal never said anything about that to me."

Helen's eyes filled with suppressed sorrow. "He doesn't know, nor do any of his siblings."

And yet, Ashley thought, you're telling me. "Why haven't you told them?" She twisted the damp tissue in her hands.

Helen lifted her palms in a helpless manner. "Because it hurt too much to talk about, even to Cal's father."

"But he knew that you lost a child?" Ashley ascertained quickly.

"Oh, yes." Helen nodded sagely. "He was there when it happened and he took me to the hospital for the care I needed. But I wouldn't discuss what had happened with him after I was released. I knew he was grieving as much as I was, but I was barely hanging on as it was. I just didn't think I could cope with his sadness, too."

Ashley understood that. She hadn't wanted to deal with anyone else's pity for what she had been through, not her Ob/Gyn's at the time, nor Mac's. And especially not Cal's.

"So I pretended everything was fine, when it clearly wasn't—"

Ashley knew what that was like, too.

"—and six months later, I was pregnant again and we were full of hope and nine months after that we were lucky enough to have Cal. And then of course four more children after that."

"And everything worked out all right in the end." Ashley took comfort in knowing Helen had gone on to have a large, healthy brood, despite her miscarriage.

"To a degree," Helen stipulated cautiously. "I still have my fair share of regrets about how much time Cal's father and I wasted. My husband was the love of my life and I was the love of his, but we squandered too much time quarreling over petty things because we thought we had all the time in the world to set things to right. But we didn't. My point is this, Ashley." Helen gave Ashley a long sober look. "None of us can ever know what the future holds for us. All any of us have is the here and now."

Helen was making it sound easy when it wasn't. "Marriage is tough," Ashley said.

"You're right about that," Helen agreed readily enough. "But that should not prevent you from looking at the big picture and thinking about what really matters."

Ashley knew what really mattered to her—Cal and this baby they were going to have. But that didn't mean she wasn't afraid to fail again. She was.

"A lot has happened," Ashley told Helen wearily, aware even as she spoke that she was getting the unconditional love and understanding from Helen that she had always wanted from her own parents. Cal's mother knew that Ashley was flawed, that she made mistakes, but Helen didn't care. Helen loved her and wanted her to remain part of the family, anyway, Ashley realized, her spirits lifting.

"And a lot is going to happen in the future, too," Helen concurred sagely. "Some of which you'll be prepared for, some of which you won't."

Ashley guessed what Helen was going to say. "But it will be easier for us if we're together."

Helen nodded. She reached over and patted Ashley's hand. "It's not too late. There's still time for you and Cal to get your priorities straight and make your marriage as strong as it should've been all along."

CAL WAS STILL STRETCHED OUT on Mac's living-room sofa when Janey, Lily, Emma and Hannah marched in. All four wives were followed by their husbands and Mac. It looked like an intervention, and then some. The only family missing—save his mother, wife and unborn child—were his nephew Christopher, and Lily and Fletcher's yellow Labrador retriever, Spartacus. And he figured the latter two had been barred on grounds they were too young to hear any of what was about to be said.

Cal used his forearm to shield his eyes from the mid-morning sun. "Go. Away."

"We warned you if you didn't get this right we were bringing the Hart women in," Mac said.

Cal muttered a string of swear words not meant for delicate ears. "I don't need your advice. Any of it," Cal said. Furious, he sat up and swung his legs over the edge of the brown leather sofa.

"We beg to differ," Janey stated coolly. She folded her arms in front of her, still looking as if she wanted to wring his neck.

"Where the devil did you get off walking out on Ashley last night?" Fletcher demanded, slapping his cowboy hat against his thigh.

"You should have stayed and married her!" Lily agreed.

"I'm already married to her," Cal snapped.

"From the gist of your behavior toward her, your vows need some refreshing," Dylan scolded.

"If you will recall, that was the original intention," Cal volleyed right back.

Joe shrugged. "The road to hell is paved with good intentions."

Cal glared at the entire group. "Hell is about where I am right now, all right," he muttered, raking his hands through his hair.

Hannah smiled at him sympathetically. "Tell her you're sorry," she advised.

Cal blinked. "Me?"

"Yes, you!" Dylan replied.

Cal aimed a thumb at the center of his chest. "I'm not the one who kept a secret for nearly three years!"

"Right," Janey acknowledged sarcastically. "You're the husband she didn't feel secure enough to confide in."

Cal slouched back on the sofa. "Hit me where it counts, why don't you?"

"She loves you," Lily said.

"Yeah, well, she has a funny way of showing it." Cal thrust his jaw out pugnaciously. "The minute the going gets a little tough, she gets going."

The women exchanged deeply frustrated looks. "She's not leaving town," Emma said finally.

Yeah? That was news to him. "She went home to pack," Cal bit out. "And she said she would be out of the farmhouse completely by later today. What do you call that?"

Loud feminine sighs echoed all around. They were followed by a few choice, muttered words from the Hart men. "Ashley felt you should live at the farmhouse because you put the work into it," Lily explained. "She is planning to move in with us, since Fletcher and I have the house with the most room."

"I wouldn't advise letting that happen," Fletcher said, giving Cal a warning look.

It seemed as if everyone in the family had turned against him, Cal thought. Which was ludicrous, since he wasn't the one at fault here! He stood, bristling with anger. "I've given that woman everything I could possibly give her. I was even willing to support her taking a job away from me again if that's what it took to allow her to fulfill her dream of delivering babies."

Janey interjected gently, "No one is disputing you're the master of the grand, romantic gesture. Telling your wife to take a two-and-a-half-year fellowship three thousand miles away. Locating and giving her the '64 Mustang you two had your very first date in. Making plans to renew your wedding vows on your third anniversary. Those are all wonderful actions, Cal. But relationships aren't made in isolated, dramatic moments—they're built in the small everyday things. Just being there for her, day in and day out, with a heart full of love and unconditional acceptance would have been enough to make her happy."

"Would it?" Cal wasn't sure. Maybe he had never been what Ashley needed.

"Yes, if you had given her what she most wanted," Emma said softly.

Cal sank down on the sofa once again and buried his face in his hands. "And what is that?" he demanded in frustration.

Janey's husband, Thad, explained in simple coach-like fashion, "The permission to be human, to make mistakes."

"To know," Lily added, "no matter what, that you'll be there for her."

"Her soft place to fall," Emma added gently.

Cal scowled and peered up at them through his spread fingers. "This is beginning to sound like an episode of Dr. Phil."

Hannah grinned, all tomboy mischief. "Would you *like* to be on his TV show?" she asked.

Cal swore like a longshoreman, knowing if anyone could arrange it, Hannah, the inveterate dealmaker, could. "No," he said stonily.

Mac stepped forward, the male patriarch of the Hart family once again. "Then we suggest you take a hard look at yourself and do whatever it is you need to do to set things to rights with Ashley," Mac advised.

CAL SPENT THE REST of the morning defending his actions to himself. But by the time he had gone for a run, come back, had breakfast, showered and shaved, he could no longer deny the truth.

And neither, he decided, could Ashley.

So, swallowing his pride, he slapped on some cologne, and headed back out to the farmhouse he had purchased with such high hopes.

And found, to his stunned amazement, that it looked like a convention of Harts, too. Each and every sibling had a car parked in his drive. His mother's car was parked next to Ashley's new station wagon.

Grimacing, Cal slammed out of his SUV and stalked up to the porch. Damn it all, wasn't it enough his entire family except his mother had read him the riot act? Did they have to barge in and inflict their views on Ashley, too?

Temper flaring, he let himself inside and found to his stunned amazement that the two large empty rooms at the front of the house had been transformed. White folding chairs were arranged in a semi-circle around a trellis decorated with red roses, perfect for Valentine's Day. On the other side of the foyer a buffet reception was being set up by his four sisters-in-law. They were dressed as they had been the evening before, in their Valentine's Day finery. "About time you got here," Janey drawled.

His mother came through the hall, carrying several bottles of fine champagne and another of sparkling cider. "If you're looking for who I think, she's upstairs," Helen said.

Mac strode through the hall. He glanced at his watch, reporting, "The musicians will be here shortly."

Dylan followed. "Ditto the minister."

Cal thought about commenting, then decided enough time had been wasted, enough mistakes made. It was time to set things right, permanently this time. He took the stairs two at a time and continued on down the hall into the master bedroom. Ashley was seated on the bed, wearing the dress she'd had on the evening before, when she'd fainted. It had been expertly repaired and appeared to give her plenty of breathing room this time. If possible, she looked even more gorgeous than she had the evening before. She was sipping a small glass of orange juice as he walked in. She raised it in silent toast. "Just in case."

"Not planning on fainting on me again this afternoon?" Cal asked.

"I am about to marry someone." She drained her glass and set it aside.

"And that someone better be me," he told her gruffly.

"Is that a proposal?" Her voice suddenly sounded as rusty as his.

He nodded. "If you'll still have me."

"Oh, I'll have you all right." Ashley drew him down to sit beside her on the bed.

They sat there quietly, hands linked as surely as their hearts.

"I'm so sorry," they said abruptly in unison.

More silence. And a few tears this time, too.

"I should have told you," Ashley whispered.

Cal tightened his grip on her hand, knowing he never wanted to let her go. "I should have understood why you didn't," he countered thickly.

More tears, his and hers. "I was scared I'd lose you," Ashley confided. Turning, she went all the way into his arms.

Cal lifted her over onto his lap and wrapped his arms around her. "Believe me, I know a little bit about that."

Ashley rested her head on his shoulder, her low voice muffled against his jacket as she clung to him tightly. "I don't want to lose you, Cal."

He tucked a hand beneath her chin and lifted her face to his. "I don't want to lose you, either."

Ashley smiled and kissed his lips. "Then what do you say we go downstairs and make it official…" she whispered tenderly "…the second time around?"

"TO LOVE AND TO CHERISH…in joy and in sorrow…from this day forward…"

"And now that Ashley and Cal have reconfirmed their original wedding vows, Ashley and Cal have something to promise each other," the minister said.

Ashley took Cal's hand in hers. "I, Ashley, promise to tell you everything, the good, the bad, the exciting and the mundane. I pledge to have faith in you and faith in us. The only steadfast rule being that we love and understand each other more with each and every day."

Knowing those vows would be easy to keep now that they finally knew what was important in this life, Cal lifted their clasped hands and kissed the back of Ashley's wrist. He looked deep into her eyes and spoke with all the love in his heart. "I, Cal, commit myself to you and to this marriage with all my heart and soul. I promise always to remember that it's not whether we make mistakes, but *when* we make them, that we forgive each other, learn and grow from them, that is important…because loving each other and standing by each other in good times and tough times…is what marriage is all about."

The minister beamed. "Cal and Ashley. Having affirmed your love for the second time, I now pronounce you husband and wife. Cal, you may kiss your bride."

And Cal obliged.

* * * * *

*Turn the page to read excerpts from next month's
Harlequin American Romance selections.
You'll find a range of stories and styles.
In March, we're offering books from some of
your favorite authors—Judy Christenberry, Leah Vale
and Linda Randall Wisdom—
and from newcomer Lisa McAllister,
a delightful new addition to our lineup.*

The Marine by Leah Vale
(Harlequin American Romance #1057)

This is the third title in Leah Vale's miniseries THE LOST
MILLIONAIRES. In these books, four men—the secret offspring of millionaire Joseph McCoy's son, Marcus—are con-
tacted by the family's lawyers. Marcus is dead—and his sons
are now millionaires.... You'll enjoy this fast-paced, humorous and yet emotional story! And watch for the fourth book,
The Rich Boy in May.

> Dear Major Branigan,
> It is our duty at this time to inform you of the death of
> Marcus McCoy due to an unfortunate, unforeseen en-
> counter with a grizzly bear while fly-fishing in Alaska
> on June 8 of this year, and per the stipulations set
> forth in his last well and testament, to make formal his
> acknowledgment of one USMC Major Rick Thomas
> Branigan, age 33, 7259 Villa Crest Drive, #12, Ocean-
> edge, California, as being his son and heir to an equal
> portion of his estate.
> It is the wish of Joseph McCoy, father to Marcus

McCoy, grandfather to Rick Branigan, and founder of McCoy Enterprises, that you immediately assume your rightful place in the family home and business with all due haste and utmost discretion to preserve the family's privacy.

Regards,

David Weidman, Esq.

Weidman, Biddermier, Stark

"My life just keeps getting better and better," Major Rick Branigan grumbled at the letter he held in one hand....

Rachel's Cowboy by Judy Christenberry
(Harlequin American Romance #1058)

Rachel's Cowboy is the next installment in Judy Christenberry's popular new series CHILDREN OF TEXAS. You'll
find Judy's trademark warmth here, and her strong sense of
family and community—not to mention her love for Texas,
her home state!

A Soldier's Return, the next CHILDREN OF TEXAS
story, appears in July 2005.

For the first time in her life Rachel Barlow had time on her hands.

After working nonstop for the past six months, she stood
in Vivian and Will Greenfield's spacious home feeling at
loose ends, trying to rest. She didn't know how. Her constant
worries and her hectic schedule had caused her to lose weight.
Still, she couldn't stop fretting about her future.

Thanks to her adoptive mother, who'd stolen all Rachel's
savings and even borrowed money in her name, she'd been
forced to take on one modeling assignment after another,
with the hope of repaying the debt and building a nest egg.
But she was about to crack.

Her two sisters—Vanessa Shaw, Vivian's adopted daughter, and Rebecca Jacobs, who was Rachel's twin—were concerned about her. They'd persuaded her to move into Vivian's home, where she could be taken care of.

She looked around the lavish Highland Park home that after six months she still wasn't used to. It was strange not only living in such luxury, but also having a loving family.

When the doorbell chimed, she called out, "I'll get it." Knowing the housekeeper would be in the kitchen, she figured she'd save Betty the trip.

She swung open the door and stared at the one man she'd never wanted to see again.

J. D. Stanley.

Frozen with horror, she said nothing.

Neither did he.

Then, when he took a step toward her, cowboy hat in hand, she asked, "What are *you* doing here?"

At the same time he demanded, "What are *you* doing here?"

Neither of them answered.

Single Kid Seeks Dad by Linda Randall Wisdom
(Harlequin American Romance #1059)

Clever, fast paced and charming, this is a story about match-
makers—with a difference. Take one young boy with a single mother and one older man with a single son and see what
kind of plan they come up with!

A delightful story that's guaranteed to make you smile.

The small, dimly lit room was a dark contrast to the bright
lights and merriment going on in the nearby reception hall.
It was the perfect meeting place for the two conspirators who
faced each other.

"I have to say, young man, that your note was intriguing.
Are you now going to reveal why we're having this meeting
in private?" The older man settled back in a chair and studied the boy facing him. He was impressed that even with the
stern eye he kept on him, the kid didn't waver.

"It's very simple." The boy kept his voice low. "I have a
single mom. You have a single son. We both want to see them
married off. There's no reason we can't work together to accomplish our objectives."

The man chuckled. "I suppose you have a plan?"

"Yes, I do. We're already ahead, because your son's hot for my mom."

The older man shook his head. "I've also heard that she's told him she isn't interested."

The boy shrugged off his statement. "Yeah, but that can change. I did some research on your son, and what I've learned tells me he's perfect for my mom. All she needs is some time to really get to know him."

The man chuckled. "How do you expect to bring them together?"

Nick Donner smiled. "I worked up what I feel is a fool-proof plan." He then proceeded to explain the idea.

The older man's skepticism soon turned to interest as he listened to Nick. "I'll admit that I'm impressed. Do you honestly think something that wild could work?"

"There is absolutely no reason it won't, as long as you're willing to do your part," Nick said with unshakable confidence.

An hour later their plan was mutually agreed on with a handshake. The two participants slipped out of the room separately and returned to the reception hall just in time to watch Nora Summers Walker and her new husband, Mark Walker, cut the wedding cake.

For the balance of the evening the young man and his older partner didn't do anything to betray that they had come up with a plan that if successfully carried out meant another wedding would occur in the near future. That of Lucy Donner and Judge Kincaid's son, Logan.

Baby Season by Lisa McAllister
(Harlequin American Romance #1060)

Welcome to Halden, North Dakota! This small prairie town has always been home to midwife Genevie Halvorson. Veterinarian Josh McBride and his son, Tyler, are new here—and despite his differences with Gen, Josh soon finds himself falling for her.

You'll be enchanted by Lisa McAllister's characters. And you'll enjoy visiting Halden and its nearby ranches. This is American country life at its best!

"Dr. Connolly said you're a midwife. What's a midwife?" Tyler asked from the back seat.

Josh answered before Gen had a chance to reply. "It's a person who helps ladies have their babies."

"Do you do anything else besides help ladies have babies?" Tyler directed this question at Gen.

"Well, helping deliver babies keeps me pretty busy," she replied, "but I'm also an herbalist."

"Oh, that explains it," Josh murmured as Tyler asked, "What's a herbalist?"

"Explains what?" Gen turned to Josh, puzzled. To Tyler she said, "An herbalist is someone who uses plants to make medicines for people and animals." She looked back at Josh, waiting for an answer.

"Are you into all that New Age-y junk or just giving people false hope when there's nothing that can be done?"

Where had that come from? Gen wondered. She bristled at the implication that she was some sort of charlatan. "It's hardly New Age, Dr. McBride. Midwives and herbalists have been around a lot longer than doctors and veterinarians."

"So have witch doctors," he said coolly.

Gen had encountered such bias before. This was the first time, though, that she'd felt compelled to defend herself. What was it about him that made her want to change his mind?

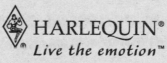

If you enjoyed what you just read,
then we've got an offer you can't resist!

Take 2 bestselling love stories FREE!

Plus get a FREE surprise gift!

Clip this page and mail it to Harlequin Reader Service®

IN U.S.A.	**IN CANADA**
3010 Walden Ave.	P.O. Box 609
P.O. Box 1867	Fort Erie, Ontario
Buffalo, N.Y. 14240-1867	L2A 5X3

YES! Please send me 2 free Harlequin American Romance® novels and my free surprise gift. After receiving them, if I don't wish to receive anymore, I can return the shipping statement marked cancel. If I don't cancel, I will receive 4 brand-new novels every month, before they're available in stores! In the U.S.A., bill me at the bargain price of $4.24 plus 25¢ shipping & handling per book and applicable sales tax, if any*. In Canada, bill me at the bargain price of $4.99 plus 25¢ shipping & handling per book and applicable taxes**. That's the complete price and a savings of at least 10% off the cover prices—what a great deal! I understand that accepting the 2 free books and gift places me under no obligation ever to buy any books. I can always return a shipment and cancel at any time. Even if I never buy another book from Harlequin, the 2 free books and gift are mine to keep forever.

154 HDN DZ7S
354 HDN DZ7T

Name	(PLEASE PRINT)	
Address	Apt.#	
City	State/Prov.	Zip/Postal Code

Not valid to current Harlequin American Romance® subscribers.

Want to try two free books from another series?
Call 1-800-873-8635 or visit www.morefreebooks.com.

 * Terms and prices subject to change without notice. Sales tax applicable in N.Y.
** Canadian residents will be charged applicable provincial taxes and GST.
   All orders subject to approval. Offer limited to one per household.
 ® are registered trademarks owned and used by the trademark owner and or its licensee.

AMER04R   ©2004 Harlequin Enterprises Limited

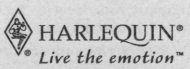

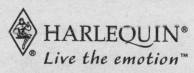

Curl up and have a

Heart to Heart

with

Harlequin Romance®

Just like having a heart-to-heart
with your best friend, these stories
will take you from laughter to tears
and back again. So heartwarming
and emotional you'll want to
have some tissues handy!

Next month Harlequin is thrilled to bring you
Natasha Oakley's first book for Harlequin Romance:

For Our Children's Sake (#3838),
on sale March 2005

Then watch out for....

A Family For Keeps (#3843),
by Lucy Gordon, on sale May 2005

Available wherever Harlequin books are sold.

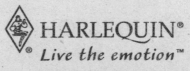

HARLEQUIN®
Live the emotion™

www.eHarlequin.com

HRHTH